Morph

The Resurrection of Angels

Walter Anthony Dinteman

Nancy! Enjoy!
-Walter
8/19/18

Morph: The Resurrection of Angels

ISBN: 150754040X

Chapter 1 The Discovery

Professor Arthur J. Barringer lay on his back staring up at the crackled ceiling of the stark white room. His bleary eyes darted from the brass ceiling light fixture to the corners of the room as he looked for a pattern or, rather, a picture like those imaginary creatures everyone sees in clouds. Yes, there was a face. But it was not human. A demonic visage frowned down at him.

"Get thee behind me, Satan!" Art chuckled.

Art had been fighting demons all his life. His mother, Lillian, passed away in childbirth, leaving his father, James, to rear him, first by having nannies to care for him; then sending him off to a Southern military school when he was eight. "Harbridge Academy is the best of the best." James Barringer said looking down upon the eight-year-old Arthur. "You will enjoy the company of three hundred other boys and in ten years, you will emerge as a man; a son any father would be proud of."

Art could recall only a half dozen times that his father actually came to the school to visit him. Those visits of a half day or less were mainly to settle accounts with the school. The holidays and summers were mostly spent on relative's farms or city apartments of distant uncles, aunts and cousins. The virtual abandonment by his motherand his father's absence manifested in Art an aloof and rather detached adult.

Today it might be said that he also suffered from Post-Traumatic Stress Disorder due to his experience on the battlefields of France in World War I. Since he had been in military school, he was readily accepted as a volunteer in the British Army and was immediately made a lieutenant. When the USA entered the war, Art joined the American Expeditionary Force and was promoted to Major.

Professor Barringer was an academic elitist, a "firm but fair" teacher and a relentless researcher. Students who did not know him well called him "Over-Barringer." behind his back. Now he lay in a bed in a third floor walk-up pension in the city of Amiens, France. Tanned and fit, Art was the picture of the explorer-scientist with his half shaven beard and gold wire-rimmed glasses.

It was unusually warm that August in 1948. A slight cooling breeze from the open window caressed the grey hair on his chest. Lying beside Art was his lover, Myra Rosenblum, a brilliant twenty-three year old blue-eyed brunette, with whom he was having a sustained and passionate love affair for the past two years. She was sleeping on her stomach and looked every bit as beautiful as a Rodin nymph. The curve of her back and bare buttocks seemed sculpted of marble in the faint light of the lavender dawn.

Normally, Art might have awakened her with a nudge and a kiss and, to answer "the call of Eros," as he would say. But sex was far from Art's mind that morning. In fact, Art had been unable to have sex any time in the past week. He had hardly even a thought of sex since the discovery that he and Myra had made at the old bombed out railway station a few days before. In all of his twenty-year career in archeology, new finds had been exhilarating experiences; the resulting highs would have made his ego omnipotent in his profession as well as in bed.

Art and Myra had a kind of "Bogey and Bacall" relationship—scandalous due to their age difference, but a genuine love affair nonetheless. Art had the fame and the academic standing; Myra was young, precocious, beautiful, and very ambitious. Art was a kind and generous man beneath his exterior aloofness. He had helped many a financially struggling student with money left from the estate of his deceased father who had hanged himself in early days of the Crash of 1929. Myra Rosenblum was one of his scholarship students.

She, too, had a tough time in her early life. She was the daughter of middle-class Jews who escaped the rise of the Nazis in Germany in 1935. Her mother, Ruth, and ten-year-old Myra stayed in New York while her father, Levi, went back to Germany to take care of his considerable business interests. Levi Rosenblum thought he would be all right for the month he planned to be in Germany since he had two partners who were both Roman Catholics. Myra and Ruth never saw Levi again. After the war, Myra learned that her father had been beaten to death by some Brown Shirt Nazi thugs when he was involved in a traffic accident in Berlin.

Myra had vivid dreams all her life. In dreams she combined things she's seen in films and her imagination and filled in blanks where reality stopped short. Many of her dreams were happy, even humorous, but she had nightmares as well. She often dreamt of her father's last trip to Berlin:

Papa was wearing his bowler hat as if to disguise himself as a British salesman trying to close a deal with the Third Reich This was the recurring nightmare that Myra endured for many years:

Now Papa is driving a black Mercedes coupe. At an intersection, a truckload of drunken Brown Shirts rounds a corner at high speed and crashes into Levi's car. One of the uniformed men riding in the back of the open truck is hurled into the street. Perhaps his drunkenness saved his life since he was able to rise, daub some blood from his forehead, and join the others in accosting Levi Rosenblum who emerged shaken, but otherwise unharmed from his vehicle.

"You have damaged our truck with your careless driving!" screamed the first Brown Shirt shouting an accusation.

"Good fellow, it was you who disregarded a stop sign and ran into my car." Levi replied in English with his cultivated Oxford accent.

"So, Englishman, you can be in Germany with a fine car and think you own our streets?"

"I am very sorry for this unfortunate accident. Since no one was badly hurt, let's just say, "no fault" and be on our way." Replied Levi, this time in German.

"Oh, now he is German?" a second Brown Shirt spoke up.

"Perhaps he is a spy?" a third Brown Shirt chimed in.

"Let us see your papers," the Brown Shirt leader demanded.

Reluctantly, Levi produced his passport. It had a large yellow Star of David stamped across the first page.

"Hah, a Jew! I knew it! So what is Levi David Rosenblum doing driving around Berlin? And in such a fine car.? Is this Jew trying to kill Germans?"

"I am here on business. My associates Wilhelm Lechner and Friederich von Sondheim can attest to that. Here's their telephone number. Call them." The dignified but outraged Levi replied. "And, young man, I might add that I was awarded an Iron Cross for my service at Verdun. I am a decorated German war veteran."

"No Jews fought for Germany! If you were in the Great War it was as a Bolshevik spy! Willy and Helmut, show this lying Jew what we think of him."

The two thugs punched and kicked Levi to the ground. The others joined in the stomping. One grabbed a tire iron from the truck and beat him until his lifeless body was a bloody mass upon the street.

Myra recounted the dream to Art. "You know, Myra I am very sorry about your father. Ironically, I may have been shooting at him thirty years ago. What an awful war!"

"All wars are awful, Art. And sides change all the time. It's all an international conspiracy to make money for merchants of death and destruction."

"Yes, I read a review of a great book just published on that very idea. It's called *1984*"

"Who wrote it?

"A guy named Orwell, George Orwell, I think."

Subconsciously, perhaps, Art and Myra connected on the plane of their traumatic childhoods. In some ways the common experience of abandonment and a passion for progressive world-changing politics were the bonding elements in their relationship.

They fell in love shortly after Myra appeared in one of Art's graduate seminars. She always sat in the front row and never failed to ask the best questions. She was the one who guessed that Piltdown man most likely had an ape's jaw. Art was impressed that his student's intuition matched his own suspicions.

When Myra arose from the bed in the Amiens flat she found Art at the corner of the room as usual, making coffee. The single gas burner was boiling a blue and white saucepan of water while Art was grinding coffee beans for the French press. A small radio was playing Edith Piaf's *La Vie en Rose*. Since Art insisted on using an old hand grinder which gave Myra time to dress, go down to the bakery across Rue Ste. Germaine and fetch two fresh chocolate croissants. When she returned the coffee was still steeping.

"Art, you hardly slept a wink last night. Our angel should at least have the courtesy to allow you sleep occasionally," Myra joked. "And where is that distant call of Eros? You always seem ready for that call however faint. Wait, I hear him now! A tiny voice saying, 'please fuck me'!"

"Damn it, Myra! You have been laughing and giggling about our mysterious angel-man for the better part of a week. And those wings you made for yourself from bed sheets? Please, Myra, this is serious! We may have here the most earth shattering archeological find in history and you can't stop laughing!" Arthur said, clearly irritated.

"Calm down, Art! Appreciate that I'm happy. You, on the other hand, have been acting like a miserable old fart for the better part of a week. You have become a new species that I have recently discovered: *Fartus Anciens* I'll call you!"

Art responded, "Haha. Well, truth is I am pretty depressed. Here's me, Dr. Arthur Barringer, PhD etc., the 'Great Skeptic,' trying to disprove the existence of a certain Missing Link but what now? Now we have found something even more astounding and preposterous: an *angel*, for God's sake! Imagine the ridicule of my colleagues! And the Press? 'Hey, Perfessor Barringer! Seen any more angels lately?'"

By the 1940's Arthur J. Barringer was regarded as one of the greatest archeologists of the twentieth century. Art's wife, Helen, a Red Cross volunteer had died in the London Blitz of 1940. Her tragic death made Arthur even more focused on his work. Art had studied at Yale, received his undergraduate degree *cum laude* and went on for advanced degrees at Oxford. Now he held posts as Professor of Archeology and Paleoanthropology at Harvard and Research Professor at Oxford. Dr. Barringer had proven that the peoples of North America had migrated from Asia via a land bridge that existed before the last Ice Age. Of course, his "proof" was the preponderance of circumstantial evidence ranging from arrowheads, spear points, pottery shards, and cutting tools found in likeness to those of Siberia and Mexico as well as the very obvious fact that American aborigines do look rather Mongolian.

Professor Barringer had also been one of the leading opponents of the so-called "Piltdown Man" discovery of 1912. He and several colleagues would be hailed when they finally proved that Piltdown was a hoax in 1953. Not only was the discoverer, Charles Dawson, a fraud, but so were a dozen reputable scholars from the British Museum and elsewhere. Their careers were destroyed though hubris and wishful thinking that they had found the long-sought "missing link" of human evolution. So great were the reputations of Professor Arthur Woodward, Chief Archeologist at the British Museum, and others in support of Piltdown's bone evidence that it took Barringer and his colleagues more than forty years to prove the lower jaw of Piltdown was nothing more than an orangutan mandible. Thus was the reason for Art's great trepidation lest his reputation be sullied. Professor Barringer was in turmoil. Instead of digging fox holes and trenches, now the old soldier was digging for a different reason. But the confidence and bearing he normally carried seemed drained away since the very strange discovery.

Just a week ago, Arthur and Myra were excited to be uncovering a promising barrow. The particular barrow was not raised to the size of a small mound, but had collapsed due to the marsh that covered it when a nearby stream had changed course. The barrow was sealed with mud and then covered over by the 19th Century railway station now in ruins.

The anticipation of finding something significant made both of them a bit giddy. As they were uncovering a layer about a foot deep, Myra slipped in the mud and fell face first. She was unharmed, but was fairly covered in marsh slime and black mud.

Art laughed, "Myra, you could pass for the tar baby in *Song of the South*" Art then taunted her by singing *Zippity Do Dah*. Before he got to the line 'there's a bluebird on my shoulder' Myra was pelting him with mudballs. Art returned fire and before long they were both covered in mud head-to-toe. The couple presented quite a spectacle for the locals as they walked hand-in-hand the mile back to their flat.

In the apartment, Myra ran a large tub full of warm water, took off her muddy fatigues and got in. Art was right behind her in the tub. He used a sponge on her back and then, with his hands, made sure her breasts were very clean. "Hey, I didn't have any mud down there!" said Myra giggling as Art also made sure there was no mud between her legs.

"My turn." Art said as he changed places with Myra.

Myra took a bottle of shampoo for her hair and Art's as well and for all other parts of Art's body "that might have any trace whatsoever of that nasty mud." Myra said with a straight face.

After the bath, the couple drained out the muddy bathwater and filled the tub again with warm water and their soiled clothing. Myra used a clean toilet plunger and shampoo to clean their clothes. After rinsing and wringing the pants and shirts out she hung them from a curtain rod. Then she joined Art in bed for some delightful love-making.

Next day they were back at the dig. Art had a feeling that what they were uncovering was something very special. He had spent most of several days with Amiens bureaucrats, such as they were in the midst of the chaos of reconstruction. He wanted to make sure he had access to the site and to keep the press from nosing around. Art managed to get some Marshall Plan funding for work around the railway station through a congressman he knew in Massachusetts.

Myra enlisted the help of a dozen unemployed French soldiers in doing the heavy digging. She was also clever to make sure the whole crew was enjoying the French national holidays when she and Art removed the last layers of from the burial site.

On the third day they reached the lid of a sarcophagus encrusted with semi-precious gemstones. Using their small trowels they were able to find and remove the hardened mud seal around the lid. Normally Art would have been more careful using heavy tools on an artifact, but he decided to open the lid with chisels, a hammer, and a crowbar.

“Golly, Professor, aren’t you being a bit hasty here?” Myra chided him.

“Yes I am, but now that the sarcophagus is uncovered, I can’t just leave it while we get more people involved. And how long would that gem covered lid last, or what else we may find here, in an urban area such as this?”

“OK, Professor, you wrote a textbook entitled *Archeological Methodology*, so I guess you are entitled to revise it.”

Using wedges and a block-and-tackle, Myra and Art were able to slide the lid off and onto the side of the crypt.

13

"Would you look at this?" Art exclaimed as he gazed upon the mummified remains of what appeared to be a noble chieftain.

Burial barrows of nobles, kings and queens, are fairly common in Northern Europe. Finding one, hitherto unknown, was not a unique discovery in-and-of-itself. But what the professor found was indeed remarkable. In addition to the usual artifacts found in barrows: pottery, fur robes, trappings of a revered chieftain, were the remains of a man of unusual size. He was about six-foot-five.

"He's really big, Art!" Myra replied. She was aware that height of the man was interesting because the previous record size of any Neolithic person was about a foot shorter. That, however, was not what astonished Professor Barringer and Myra Rosenblum the most. What raised the graying hair on the professor's neck were the bones of the upper torso of this kingly body and the golden mummified leather skin that covered them. The shoulders, and rib cage, were enormous.

Then what made him fall to his knees in wide-eyed disbelief was a pair of auburn wings, feathers nearly perfectly preserved, lying ceremoniously next to the body.

"Are those eagle wings?" Myra wondered.

"If they are they must be from a raptor. I am not an expert in ornithology, but the wingspan, must be around 11 feet, surely that's unlike anything I've ever heard of. And look at this: the bottoms of wings are placed near each shoulder and the wing tips stretched down to the feet."

At first he thought they were the wings of some, possibly extinct, gigantic bird. While he'd never seen anything like that in a grave like that before, the placement of wings would be consistent with the kind of high praise symbolized by such a gesture.

"Let's turn him over," Myra suggested.

They removed the wings from the crypt and laid them on a canvas tarp. Then they very carefully rolled the golden mummy on its left side. Even the bones of hunchbacked people and other deformities he'd seen in x-rays or in some long ago anatomy class, bore no resemblance to what he was seeing on that sunny afternoon in August 1948. The scapulae were fantastically large and protruded from otherwise unbroken skin.

Art then said to Myra in a Socratic tone she'd heard many times in his classroom, "Now, Miss Rosenblum what do see in the upper portion of this specimen's back?

"Well, Professor Barringer, I see a pair of rather oversized scapulae. They have rough cut edges as if something had been chopped off of them."

"Really? What could have been removed from his scapulae? There should be no more bone protruding from a human shoulder blade."

"I beg to differ with you, Professor. This specimen had something removed."

"And what in the name of Darwin was removed, Miss Rosenblum?"

"Well, Sir, having looked closely at the scapulae and the bottom edges of the wings; I would say that the wings were attached to the shoulder blades until they were forcibly removed."

"Impossible!" replied Professor Barringer in a mocking voice.

On close inspection, however, it appeared to Arthur Barringer that Myra was right: the wings had been detached from the oversized shoulder blades. The base of each wing matched the point of separation on each scapula.

Myra took dozens of photographs of the body, the wings, and close-ups of the outsized shoulders and shoulder blades with her Leica camera. It was the same camera that Art Barringer had used to capture dozens of nude photographs of her. The contrast between the macabre features and wizened body in the crypt and the surpassing beauty of the face and body of young naked woman was astonishing. When Art and Myra later developed the film in the makeshift darkroom set up in their bathroom in the flat, Arthur joked, "Golly Myra, I didn't realize how truly beautiful you are until now."

"Oh, Art, could that be Eros calling?" Myra said with a wide grin.

With the Piltdown controversy raging in archeological circles and the public at large, there was no way that Distinguished Professor Barringer was going to announce that he and his assistant had discovered an angel. Art and Myra made a pact that they would say nothing about this until they themselves tried every way they could to try to debunk their own discovery, secretly, and in their own lab at Oxford University.

The first problem for Art and Myra was how to get "Amiens Man" to Oxford.

Chapter 2A Heist at the Louvre

During the chaos of the early days of the Berlin Airlift, Art and Myra took their small Peugeot van and drove to Paris. Art was at the wheel wearing his professorial herring-bone jacket, white shirt, and paisley tie. Myra rode next to him wearing unaccustomed amounts of rouge and lipstick and in her tightest fitting flannel skirt and red cashmere sweater. Behind them, in an unremarkable wooden box, were the modern remains of one of the million people who died in and about Amiens in the last two World Wars. Art was smiling for the first time in a week.

"I feel like a spy or international art thief," he said.

"Yep, all we lack are the walkie-talkies and guns. And you would be Art the Art Thief!" Myra laughed.

"OK, let's review Plan A" Art began, "I will drive to the service entrance of the Louvre. Since I know interim director Anton Kyrczak, I will ask to speak with him. Meanwhile, you, dressed like a prostitute you imagine you could be, will distract the security guard for twenty minutes."

"Kyrczak? Doesn't sound very French?" puzzled Myra.

"No. He is a Polish refugee. Former curator of the Warsaw Museum. The ex-Director, Philippe d' Montpelier is now in prison for collaborating with the Germans. Kyrczak is a paleontologist I met in Prague between the Wars. He was brought in as *Directuer pro Temps* until they can find a world-class art historian with the administrative skills of Kyrczak."

"Uh, and what was Plan B?"

"There is no Plan B."

Art met with Kyrczak to continue the ruse. "Anton, how are you doing? You have a monumental task here I'm sure."

"Yes, Arthur, it will be years before all art is restored to museum; some may never be found."

"Well, good luck with that. I'm here to pick up those samples of bones from your vast collection of undocumented Neolithic mummies we discussed."

"But of course, Professor Barringer. Just as we discussed by phone last week. Yes, yes. I will get you some assistance."

"I want to take the bones to my lab at Oxford."

"That is good. It vill be years before we do anything with those specimens!"

"And, no assistance will be needed. My own assistant is fully capable of handling bones."

Art and Myra had access to the lower sub-basement of the great museum. While Myra chatted up a security guard, Art wheeled the dolly with the coffin past them and into the bowels of the Louvre.

There they surreptitiously substituted a modern corpse for a forgotten peat bog man. If it hadn't been for the general distraction of the entire staff of the Louvre in recovering art stolen by the Nazis, this theft in broad daylight could not have happened.

On the way back to Amiens Professor Barringer had a lot on his mind including his many reasons to be concerned about his academic standing.

"So whacha doin' next, Master Body Snatcher?" Myra said with an impish grin.

"Well, the Louvre Man gets to meet our Amiens Angel. Tonight of course."

Art wheeled the small van right up to the edge of the dig. By moonlight they unloaded their equipment. With Myra pulling on block and tackle, Art swung the Amiens Angel up and out of the excavation.

Next they used the pulleys to replace the lid on the sarcophagus.

He and Myra were both in high spirits from the heist at the Louvre. They popped the cork on a bottle of Dom Perignon, toasted to 'Archeolarceny', and then made sweaty love in the white room. In the background, Edith Piaf's version of *Les Marseilles* was playing on the radio.

As Myra said, looking up at the crackled ceiling after sex, "Whew! Art, I think you heard that Eros call loud and clear!"

Their next adventure was in getting the Amiens Angel out of Amiens and into their lab at Oxford. They took both the corpse of the Louvre Peat Bog man and their find, packed in ice and heavy insulation, in their Peugeot to Deauville and by ferry to Bournemouth, England and thence to Oxford.

At Oxford there was the general hubbub anytime a major find was brought in for study. This time the ruse was that the bog man was from Amiens. They also "had bones lent to Oxford by the Louvre that they wanted to test for comparison to bog men from Wales and other parts of the UK."

No one but Myra and Art knew that the freezer in the lab actually had two bodies. Like the magician's game "Where's the pea under the walnut shell?" Art and Myra moved bodies around several times. Nobody else knew what if anything was in the refrigerated box number 029.

Professor Barringer phoned Anton Kyrczak to inform him that the crypt in Amiens should be secured and told him the Louvre as welcome to claim the all the artifacts.

Chapter 3 Were Angels Real?

Two years passed as Myra made many studies of Amiens Man and read every book she could find on the history, mystery, and mythology of angels. Arthur pursued his nemesis: Piltdown Man. All the while, Art hesitated to make any announcement about their fantastic discovery. As he reminded Myra many times, "We have to be absolutely sure that what we think we found is true and backed up entirely by science."

After all, his reputation and that of science itself was in jeopardy: The Cold War was raging and it seemed everyone was seeing flying saucers from Russia or outer space; "crazy theories" were at once being condemned by science and popularized by the media.

When Immanuel Velikovsky published his best-selling *Worlds in Collision* in 1950 it raised a storm of controversy. Since Velikovsky was from Belarus in the USSR, his work was seen by some hysterical folk and political right-wingers as a "Communist conspiracy" to somehow compromise science. Even though most of Velikovsky's theories, such as Venus having been a comet expelled from Jupiter, were subsequently proven false, the fact was that in 1950, like the Church of Galileo's time, the scientific establishment attempted to censor Velikovsky who became a Heretic of Science. In fact the academic community of scientists succeeded in mounting a boycott of MacMillan textbooks just because the publisher had dared to put *World's in Collision* on its scientific books list. The single best-selling book of 1950 was sold off at the peak of its success to a small fiction publisher for a bargain price.

Art chided Myra for reading *Worlds in Collision* as "pseudo-scientific bullshit."

But Myra argued, "Maybe his physics is wrong, but you can't deny that there is an enormous amount of very interesting scholarly research in Velikovsky's work. His theory about Venus being a comet was derived from the fact that nearly every ancient people have the planet Venus with a tail. And that's the only planet depicted as such. So there!"

Art had a worried look "Well, you are right about that. You know I should contact Velikovsky himself. I did just read that none other than Albert Einstein defended him. Not that he endorsed his theories, but that he simply encouraged his original thinking and said that Velikovsky had raised some interesting questions. After all, science is not about answers, but about questions."

After several phone conversations, with Immanuel Velikovsky Professor Barringer took the long flight from London to New York and the train to Princeton University. He met Velikovsky in his office at Princeton, just down the hall from Einstein's. This had to be a secret meeting, because Barringer feared the taint of any association with the "writer of fictionalized science."

"Immanuel, call me Art," The two shook hands.

"Good to see you in person, Art!" They made small talk, "How vas your flight?" etc. Then Velikovsky confessed he feared being subpoenaed by the Un-American Activities Committee. Some in Congress, including Senator Joe McCarthy, were sure that the Russian was a Communist or "Pinko Scientist."

"I must be cautious. I lived under Stalin; avoided Nazis; and now I fear Americans!"

"That's preposterous! I am an American citizen, but happy to be living in the UK. They don't have an Un-English Committee! I came here today because you have a unique methodology that I am interested in pursuing in the fields of archeology and paleoanthropology."

"Sank you for coming, Professor, I admire your verk. Vat questions you haff me for today? Sorry for Eenglish . Getting better but thanks be to Gott for American eedeetor on my book. I speak seven and read twelve other languages, but Eenglish ees my veakest!"

Art began his interview, "Immanuel, you cite many myths arising from prehistory to modern times to support your theories, am I correct?"

"Yes, ees true. And from thees facts, namely abundances of seemilar descreeptions of planet Venus having tail, I conclude it vud be fact Venus vas vonce comet. You could say I seemply applied Occam's Razor to phenomenon."

Art nodded, "I see, the Razor implies that given a set of assumptions regarding behavior of matter, that the least number of assumptions should be applied at getting to the truth. So you say, the simplest explanation of the 'Venus with tail' myths is that all those ancient people were observing the *reality* of Venus as a comet. A simple observable fact?"

"Absolutely!" Velikovsky smiled.

"Well then, I have a question for you: All of the civilized societies as well as many of the uncivilized ones that I have studied have mythologies involving angels. These angels are always depicted as flying messengers of the gods or higher spirits. So, I am wondering, if it might be possible, that angels really did exist?" Asked Professor Barringer, getting right to the point.

Velikovsky, grinning, replied, "Very eenteresting question, Professor Barringer. Det's very eenteresting question indeed!"

When Art returned to Oxford, Myra was waiting for him at the station. He was tired from the trip from the USA and hardly prepared for a blitz of information from his lover. After a hug and a kiss, Myra was bursting to get him updated on several fronts.

"Art, we've got to do something about our Amiens Man," Myra said urgently as she drove to their flat in Henley. "The Royal Academy is about to convene a session on Piltdown. Your debunking evidence will be on the table. And you will be expected to testify. Also, I have to tell you that somebody from the press, a tabloid guy from that rag *Day Break* I am sure, is poking around campus asking a lot of questions. Not only is he looking for a scoop on the Piltdown hoax, but he seems equally interested in you and, by that, I mean us."

"What do you mean by that?" Art asked half smiling.

"I mean that I am getting quite obviously 'great with child'-- your child, Art, your child. Our long affair is well known, but making babies is not quite acceptable outside marriage here in the middle of the 20th Century."

"I love you, Myra. Hope you know that. I think we have just been too busy to marry. We'll fix that as soon as we can."

"Yeah, and I love you too, despite your tendency to be an asshole sometimes!"

"Me? Not Me! Well, I did hear from one of my old students that he and others used to call me 'Professor Over-Barringer'. All part of my academic persona."

"Well, I am just glad to know the real persona and he is certainly not *persona non grata.*"

"Oh, and how's the bambino coming along? Are you getting a kick out of him?"

"Ha-ha! Well, I am sure she's a girl and sometimes she kicks like a footballer!"

"So, when she is born we shall shout, GOALLLL!"

"Art, you are too funny."

"All right! As soon as I get decompressed from the trip to America, we shall run up to Gretna and forthwith be married. But why the sudden urgency about our angel?"

"You know that pimply-faced assistant you hired last spring?"

"Billy MacAdoo?"

"Yes, he's the one. I think he has found the keys to the ice box."

"Well, do you think he knows anything?"

"Uh-huh. The very day after that creep from *Day Break* appeared at King's College, Billy was driving a brand new red MG roadster. I saw it parked outside Blackwell's Bookshop. I think that's more than co-incidental."

"That wasn't Harvey McGarvey the so-called journalist, from *Day Break* was it?"

"Yes, I'm pretty sure."

"He's the one who specializes in UFO sightings."

"Oh, yes, and now he's going to say there's an angel at Oxford. And he has an eyewitness! You hired Billy as a charity scholar, right?"

Authorities ruled the death "a tragic accident involving alcohol." However, it was at a party celebrating the marriage of Professor Arthur J. Barringer and Myra Rosenblum that one William X. MacAdoo had consumed a quantity of Glen Fiddich whiskey, generously poured by a smiling Myra Rosenblum. Thence Billy drove to his death on a country lane near Henley-on-Thames. His new MG Midget roadster was no match for the ten-ton lorry he met head on.

Somewhere on the third page of a Tuesday edition of *Day Break*, hardly read, was a short article entitled "Angel Found at Oxford!" complete with a ridiculously crude sketch made by one William X. McAdoo, now unfortunately deceased. The scholars at Oxford laughed at the absurdity. Myra and Art laughed the hardest.

▪▪

27

A few months later little Marla was born. She was feisty from day one and looked very much like Myra's baby pictures.

"She looks just like you," Art said holding his first born child. "Soon she will be throwing mud balls at me. I can see it in her face."

"Yes, and she looks like my mother, too. We must have very strong genes. Too bad Lillian couldn't be with us to enjoy her grandchild."

"Yes, and Levi too. Damned Nazis!" Art added.

Chapter 4 Life after Art

Six years passed during which Piltdown Man was exposed in 1953; Myra earned her PhD at Oxford and accompanied Art on several expeditions to Africa in search of a real missing link.

Their second child, Zoë, was born in 1956. She was much a much calmer baby than Marla and looked more like Art than Myra. Her parents agreed that Zoe would probably be better looking as she got older. "We can only hope!"

The couple also spent considerable time examining the angel mummy but never getting the incontrovertible evidence Art insisted they need to divulge the extraordinary find. One thing they discovered in 1956 was that the angel's bones were quite porous. Art had drilled out a core sample from a femur and reported to Myra, "Now I know one factor in explaining how an angel can fly."

"What's that?" Myra asked. "You know even at an eleven foot wingspan, we haven't figured the aerodynamics out."

"Exactly. There wouldn't be enough lift to allow a six-foot-five man to take off. Even soaring would be difficult. But what I think I have discovered is that an angel's bones are not very dense. They are very light and porous, but do not seem in the least bit weak. Perhaps that is due to the structure of his kind of osteoporosis."

"Guess we need an electron microscope to see what that structure might be." Myra suggested. "And we're paleoanthropologists, not aeronautical engineers."

Art laughed, "Well, isn't that ironic? Aeronautical engineers are still insisting that bumblebees can't fly!"

In the spring of 1957, Art and Myra were slow dancing in the lab as *Earth Angel,* a hit song by the Penguins, was playing on the radio. Later Myra was in a nearby room as Art was trying to uncrate a new Siemens scanning electron microscope in order to better examine the Amiens Angel bones. As Art strained to remove the bulky and heavy device from its crate, a metal strap, out the range of Art's vision, caught on a leg of the microscope. Awkwardly the aging professor yanked harder, but failed to dislodge the expensive device. He feared dropping it and called for Myra to help him.

"Help, Myra! I'm stuck with this goddamned microscope!"

Myra hurried from the adjoining room. When she got to Art's side he was perspiring profusely. In the next moment the microscope was loosened and Myra helped place it on a lab table. "Golly, Art that thing is a lot heavier than I expected!" Myra exclaimed.

Art said, "Thank you, My Love!" Those were Art's last words as he collapsed from a massive heart attack. After a minute of resuscitation attempts, she rushed down the hall and found Dr. Archibald McIver, an anatomist and an MD as well.

"Archie, come quick! It's Art. He passed out!"

When they returned to the lab there was nothing they could do. Dr. McIver pronounced Art dead. Myra quickly produced a copy of Art's will from a file cabinet. The will specified that all his worldly wealth would go to Myra and made it very clear that, upon his death, quote: "I, Arthur J. Barringer, be immediately frozen and preserved until such time as Myra Rosenblum or her heirs see fit to thaw me out."

"We need to get Art into one of our freezers right now!" Myra urged Archie to help. "No, don't bother with his clothes, we can't lose a second."

The science of cryopreservation was in its infancy and Myra was aware that it would be many years before science could successfully revive and repair a body that, in the usual sense, was dead. Myra and Dr. McIver loaded Art's body into a refrigeration crypt that had held the Louvre bog man until a few months before when it was donated to the British Museum.

A memorial service for Arthur J. Barringer was held in the Chapel at Oxford. Hundreds of faculty and students, current and past, showed up to pay their respects and give testimonials about Art's good works.

Myra spoke tearfully, "I have lost my lover, friend and mentor and my husband. Those of you who knew him from afar as an aloof and demanding scientist have praised his professionalism and high standards. Those closer to him know him for his heart and soul; a generous and good man. As he wished, we shall keep him in a frozen state until one day may find him back at a dig, back in the classroom, back in his laboratory."

The congregation gave a standing ovation that lasted several minutes.

The widowed single mother of two young daughters Myra raised little Marla and Zoe on her own while teaching at a small college in the Southern US.

A few years later she met Elliott Zimmerman, the wealthy owner of the EZ-Tel motel chain. He had the same flat-top hair cut he'd had for years. His smiling face and haircut became the logo for the chain. Elliot's hobby happened to be paleoanthropology. Zimmerman, though just an amateur, made some interesting finds by providing large grants to *bona fide* paleontologists and being handed a trowel and brush at just the right time to claim a new find. One day, the spade work having been done by Dr. Myra Rosenblum, She and Elliot "bonded." A month later, in June 1959, they married.

Their marriage was a good one based on *The Prophet's* ideal: "(to) stand together yet not too near together: /For the pillars of the temple stand apart, /And the oak tree and the cypress grow not in each other's shadow."

The whole passage *On Marriage* by Khalil Gibran from *The Prophet* was the one read at their Jewish wedding. It was a bit of humor at the reception as to who would be the oak and who the cypress. Myra said "Elliott is most definitely an oak!"

Elliot and Myra enjoyed each other's company when they were together. That was a rather infrequent occurrence since Elliot was usually on the road managing his hospitality business and Myra had her teaching and research. She also took several trips to various countries to explore different culture's angel myths. During a month-long excursion to Sudan, baby Michael was conceived.

"Myra, why did you pick the name Michael? asked Elliot who thought he should be an Isaac.

"I thought he should have the name of an angel. I was going to call him Gabriel, but that angel talks too much. Michael is the strong silent type, like you, Elliot."

"OK, Silent Mike it is," replied Elliot with a grin. "We'll see just how silent he is at 2:00 AM feeding time!"

When they were together, the Zimmerman's enjoyed day trips into the mountains with the kids. Elliot loved his Harley-Davidson and Myra learned to be less terrified riding on the back. She would never let any of the children on the bike despite Elliot's pleas that "Bikes are safe; especially when driven by an experienced rider."

One day in the fall of 1963, when Myra was in the Far East, Elliot was riding with friends on the snaky road known as the Dragon's Tail in Western North Carolina. He rounded a curve too fast, the front wheel caught some gravel, and the Harley slid off the mountainside Elliot was thrown from the bike and killed instantly. The tragedy hardly made the news since the accident occurred on November 22nd the same day John F. Kennedy was assassinated.

Myra was left with her three children: Marla 9, Zoë,7 and Michael 2. She was also left with ninety-eight EZ-Tel motels.

After the funeral, Myra met with Bob Vandervoort, the Eastern Regional Manager of EZ-Tel, and promoted him to be the General Manager. He along with her lawyer Phil Briggs would see to the business. Seven years later she sold the entire motel chain to a giant hotel corporation for just under $350 million, making her the world's richest archeologist.

Marla never spoke of the great find in the summer of '48 true to her pact with Art. Until, that is, until she had the proof that Art insisted must be iron-clad. Each summer she made a pilgrimage to Oxford and to the locked crypt in the basement of the archeology building where she continued her study of the Amiens Angel and to pay homage to Art, frozen solid, in a nearby liquid nitrogen cooled tank.

With the electron microscope that she would say "killed Art," she discovered that the porous structure of angel bones was one of the more remarkable features differentiating him from normal humans. The pores resembled geodesics, the design invented by Buckminster Fuller that heretofore was not known in nature. An angel's large bones weigh far less than normal bones.

The Archeology Department of Oxford, being wholly dedicated to discovering and preserving sites in the UK, took little notice of the American woman who seemed obsessed with pondering "a few bones found in France."

After she became rich she endowed Oxford with enough money to support many digs in the UK as well as to get an independent lab there, the "The Arthur J. Barringer Archeology Laboratory."

Myra bought an estate with a few of her millions. It was located outside of Asheville, North Carolina. It was in Asheville that she had met Anthony "Kirk" Kirkland

Johnson, a seldom read local poet, at an Anti-Vietnam War rally. That was in the summer of 1970.

Kirk's most well-known accomplishment was that of fathering, in his first marriage, James Jackson Johnson, better known as "Jimmy Jack" Johnson; a pop music icon. In the North Carolina Mountains Kirk and Myra were practically neighbors with him in Swannanoa and her place near Black Mountain.

Myra was a fan of Kirk's poetry and the music of Jimmy Jack as well. One day in the spring of 1971 she was at an academic conference in Rome. Myra was giving a paper on "The Ubiquity of Angels in Ancient Roman Culture" which was attended by Kirk Johnson. Kirk was coincidentally in Rome attending a conference of the World Poetry Society where he was about to receive their *Ars Poetica* award. Kirk approached Myra after hearing her paper.

"Hello, er, uh. Ms. Rosenblum" Kirk said a bit red-faced as he didn't know if he should address her as Dr. Rosenblum, Rosenblum-Zimmerman, or what?

Myra replied, "Hey, Kirk, call me Myra. And I have gone back to 'Rosenblum' since 'Dr. Myra Rosenblum-Barringer-Zimmerman' is several names too many. Funny to see you here in Rome four thousand miles from Asheville. Our homes are, what, three miles apart?"

They shared a laugh and Myra said, "I saw a notice about the Poetry Society conference. Surely that's why you're here and not to listen to some boring academic treatise on angels."

"Actually, I thought your paper was very interesting. I might could be a country boy, but that don't mean I'm ignernt!" Kirk said feigning the ungrammatical dialect typical of the Appalachian Mountains.

Myra laughed and said, "And just because I'm a scientist don't mean I don't read no poetry."

"Well, touché to you, and all that, Myra. Hey, tomorrow night they're having the *Ars Poetica* award ceremony. Want to come as my guest?"

"Sure, Kirk I have a feeling you're going to win something. I think your poetry is wonderful!"

"Well, jes' maybe." Kirk replied with a wink. "Hey, Dr. Myra, would you like to have dinner this evening with a Carolina Country Boy?"

"Well, I sure could use some Eye-talian food. Got any ideas?

"Where there's a pretty woman involved, I always have ideas."

"I bet you do, Mr. Johnson. I know a great place near the Trevi Fountain. My treat."

Over dinner, Myra caught Kirk up on her life story and surprised him by reciting her personal favorite of his poems:

Symbiosis: Sulphur on Pink

He fluttered by, this butterfly
Flitting along on his migration

Sulphur lit upon hibiscus pink
Tongue probing her sweet nectar
And in that instant
Their kingdoms were as one.

"Wow, I don't think very many people read my poetry, much less memorize it!"

In the background ubiquitous American rock music was playing in a next door leather store. Both Myra and Kirk had a laugh. The song playing was Jimmy Jack Johnson's *All Good Things Must End.*

Myra looked into Kirk's eyes and said with a wink, "Well, let's hope that end is none too soon."

The next evening Kirk was in his rental tux and Myra was at his side in a very fashionable gown by Leonardo Ferraro all shimmering in green and gold sequins.

After the recitation of poetry from former winners of the *Ars Poetica* laurels there came the highlight of the evening: the 1971 award winner. Kirk, of course had been notified, but, as promised, kept the secret.

Nobel Prize winning author Maya Angelou made the announcement that Anthony Kirkland Johnson had won the award "Not only for his outstanding work over twenty years, but for his exquisite poem on young love. Perhaps serendipity meant this to be as the setting of the best poem is right here in Rome." Angelou then read *Campanile.*

Saturday in the campanile

He spoke to her of love
Whispers that warmed her
Now return this Sunday morn
On the wings of wry grins
Across the nave shared secrets fly
She beams her thoughts to him
Aching with adoration for touching
Words that have no syllable
Chanting in the choir of passion
Ringing in the bell tower far above
Pealing in laughter of unbridled joy
She buries her head as if in prayer
Biting hard upon her lip
Stifling the giggling giddiness she feels
Count your beads, count your beads
Ave Maria! Ave Maria!
Through tears of joy the rapture came
Hallelujah! Hallelujah!

After the ceremony and a champagne reception following, Myra and Kirk headed to Bambini at that time Rome's most "in" disco. They frugged and twisted for hours until the traditional last song was played, *All Good Things Must End.*

"Of course it had to be that!" Kirk laughed.

"Well, not necessarily," Myra said, "Why don't you come see me at my room at the Babuino?"

In mid-morning, a ray of sunlight light was streaming through a small space between the heavy green velour curtains. The shaft of light beamed directly on Myra's Ferraro sequin spangled gown draped casually over an ornate baroque chair. The light projected thousands of tiny green and gold coins on the walls and ceiling.

Kirk said, "Next to you, that's one of the most beautiful sights I've ever seen or maybe that's just because I'm next to you."

A few months later, after dozens of dates in North Carolina, Myra and Kirk married. They enjoyed the mountains and traveling. Kirk accompanied Myra on some of her expeditions as well.

At Myra's urging, Kirk stopped drinking so heavily. They only had one major fight in their long marriage. Both had forgotten the substance of the argument, but not the memorable line Kirk uttered. That was when a drunken Kirk told her, "I've got but one friend in this wide world, and that is Mr. Jack Daniels!"

"That has to be the most ridiculous statement I have heard out of you, Anthony Kirkland Johnson!" Myra replied. She then took the half empty bottle from Kirk's hand and smashed it against the stone fireplace.

"Jack Daniels is not your best friend! I am. And I am damned jealous of all the time you spend with that false friend. You need to write again, or get yourself a very good hobby, Kirk."

Kirk seemed shocked at the outburst from his usually reticent and happy wife. After a make-up hug and some black coffee, Kirk said, "Darlin' I think my writing days are done."

"I doubt that very much, but why not get more active with your Viet Nam buddies in the Confederate Air Force thing. Didn't you fly helicopters in that idiotic war?"

A month later, Kirk got a letter from one of those buddies telling him about a Huey available for sale in Orlando. Kirk said to Myra, "I think I have an idea for that hobby you want me to take up."

"Oh, what's that?"

"The Confederate Air Force must have heard that I may have married a rich lady."

"Ok, Kirk, where is this going?"

Kirk began to sing, "To Orlando, there to find/ A helicopter I've in mind. One like I flew in the war/ Now begging me to it restore."

"How much, Kirk? Replied a skeptical looking Myra.

"Real cheap, my Honey/ Not a whole lot of money. The guy said it would be less than two-hundred thousand."

"Well, I guess that's not bad if it flies."

"My buddies will make sure it flies, Dear."

"Ok, Kirk, go for it!"

That's how the Kirkland Estate came to have a Bell UH-1 Iroquois helicopter in the barn fifty yards from the house."

Chapter 5 Truth Emerges

In the early 1980's Myra tested a small fragment of The angel's vertebra that proved through radioactive carbon dating to be close to seven thousand years old.

Using her enormous wealth she was able to be one of the first archeologists to afford a Magnetic Resonance Imaging device to scan the entire body of "Amos", her affectionate name for the angel. The MRI revealed the answer to an early question Myra had raised with Art twenty-five years before: "How did this angel die?"

The answer was that he was murdered, or died in battle, from a single arrow that pierced his oversized heart. But try as she might, Myra Rosenblum could not produce a plausible explanation for the incredible match of the Amiens wings to the nearby scapulae other than the seeming fact that they belonged there.

In 1984, she read about the breakthrough discovery of Sir Alec Jefferies called "DNA fingerprinting." She contacted Jefferies at the University of Leicester where he had been flooded with requests to speak at both professional conventions and to give public press conferences. She was finally able to get through to Jefferies and get an agreement to test "some bone fragments to see if they are a genetic match." She said "They are from a French peat bog man and we want to see if they might be a DNA fit with bones from a fairly recent find of some Neolithic bones in Amiens and also with the DNA of people from living families there."

With absolute certainty, the bones matched! Even Sir Alec was amazed at the closeness of the match. Just thinking that people living in a region separated by a few miles, but seven-thousand years, could be so closely related was nothing short of astonishing. What Jefferies didn't suspect was that the match of fragment of wing bone marrow to vertebra marrow was not so incredible having come from the same person. Or, as Myra Rosenblum now knew, she had DNA evidence from the same angel. Amos definitely had wings!

Myra had to bury her emotions while she was speaking to Jefferies. She said, "Sorry Alec, the tears are for the thousands of people of Amiens. They have suffered so much in two World Wars yet remain genetically bonded throughout history and prehistory."

All the years of study of anatomy, anthropology, and archeology had not prepared Myra to accept what she intuitively believed for years. And that was that maybe, just maybe, angels were real. Now what was she to do? This discovery would turn science on its head. This discovery would raise religious belief beyond faith and mythology. It would simply be one of the greatest scientific discoveries in history!

****

Jimmy Jack Johnson was, in his thirties in 1971, when his dad married Myra Rosenblum. He was on a world tour reprising his 1960's hits as well as promoting recent recordings. Jimmy was worth millions, but, like many pop stars, the alpha-state highs created by fame and fortune were not enough. So, like dozens of other entertainers with more ego than good sense, he blew much of his fortune up his nose with the help of scores of roadies, band members, groupies, and drug runners all of whom eagerly supported all of Jimmy's bad habits. Then nearly broke, Jimmy went into rehab and thence to the estate his father now had thanks to the marriage with Myra.

In 1985, eight months after Myra had proven to herself, with the unsuspecting help of Sir Alec Jefferies, that Amos of Amiens was an angel, she decided to retire to Kirkland in North Carolina with Kirk Johnson and do nothing but read and relax. She continued to attend meetings of the American and British Archeology Societies. And she continued to read every book and academic paper she could find on mythology and all the scientific literature on the daily life of Stone Age peoples of Northern Europe.

She spent many hours on the veranda at Kirkland thinking about Amos and how she could present her findings to the world.

Kirk continued writing poetry. He published a volume of collected poems and was nominated, but didn't win, a Pulitzer Prize. He and Myra toasted the sale of 1,500 copies to the Barnes & Noble chain. That made the book a New York Times bestseller for a little less than one week.

Myra always had a vivid imagination and that led to bizarre dreams. Crazy as they seemed to her, they were very rich in detail and often had dialog. Like the recurring dream, or nightmare, of her father's death, people from her past would appear in her dreams filling roles as if in a drama.

One dream in particular revealed several plausible answers to her many questions regarding the last days of Amos and the people who killed and buried him. Myra recalled many details of the dreams in great detail: people, landscapes, conversations all as vivid as if she were there, at times playing roles herself.

The Dream:

A tiny boy, about six years old, is sitting on a high rock. He is the image of her son Michael Zimmerman, clad in animal pelts, red-headed and freckle faced. He is a look-out for the tribe assembled the village below. His name is Mica.

In the distance two giant birds approach. Their size makes their progress toward him seem slower than that of eagles. Mica was told to watch for that sign. He knew to shout the news, "They are coming! They are coming!" He ran down the hill to tell his mother Minah and his father Ahman.

All the people gathered in the center of the village. All watched the skies while swaying and chanting, "Ah-keena macumba, Makeena, macubana,macumba!" This means: "Great Ones, we thank you for visiting us today. We praise you!"

After circling for a few minutes the flying creatures land. The Angels have arrived! One is pure white; the other iridescent purple. Down-like hair covers their bodies. The huge feathered wings, now folded, are about four feet long, two thirds their total height as they tower over all the tribe.

In the dream the purple angel is Manashi, his face looks like Art Barringer from years before Myra knew him. His luminous female companion is Leeka. Her face is that of Helen Barringer who died in the Blitz and whose picture Art kept with him always.

Manashi speaks first, "We come today to warn you. A horde of new people is coming from the east. They plunder forests and fields. They drive bison off cliffs to their death in streams. They take only a small portion of what they have killed and leave the rest to rot and foul the water. Instead of hunting deer, they burn the forest and kill the horrified animals that run to them. When they find tribes such as yours, they take the people as their slaves."

Then Leeka spoke: "These murderous people fear us winged-ones because we hold the power and knowledge and we carry messages from the Great Spirit. They have killed all of us they have encountered. We are certain we are the only two left."

Ahman, the tribal leader was shocked to hear this. "The last two? Why are there not new angels coming forth as they have forever?"

"Yes," his wife Mina added, "Surely the great change of the elders continues, does it not?"

"Sadly, no" Leeka replied, "Only after one hundred twenty-five sun cycles can the transformation take place. No one these days lives to that age. Unless that changes, there will be no more like us."

Myra awoke stunned by the plausibility of the dream. Intuitively, she now knew that "angels" were a higher form of human beings. They are the teachers; the bringers of wisdom. At a certain age they metamorphosed like butterflies from a pupa stage to the full adult human that we call angels!

In the dream and in Myra's imagination, this is what happened next in that small valley in France seven thousand five hundred years ago: The camp of Ahman, Mina, and Mica would be overrun; the angels murdered. The male, with the auburn feathers, had to be Amos, shot with an arrow. There would never be angels on earth again except in the collective memory and folklore of humankind. The dream ended with the voice of Manashi saying, *"Tell the story! Tell the story!"* And thus across the tapestry of time people did tell of angels, the Messenger of the Gods; Bringers of Wisdom.

Myra recorded the dream in her journal. She believed she knew intuitively what happened and why angels became extinct.

Myra, now sixty, shared her dreams with her step-son Jimmy Jack. He had told her of many a bizarre dream he had and not all were under the influence of drugs. Myra said,

"I believe memories are mental reconstructions of the past. Imagination is a mental construct of a potential future. In dreams, the two are combined into creative and intuitive processes that help us see things that we may never see in a conscious state."

Jimmy replied, feet up on the railing of the house's great veranda, straw cowboy hat on the back of his head, bushy long hair trailing from under it. "You sure are smart, Myra. What the hell did you see in my dad? Ha-ha, just kidding, my dad's greatest trait is dreamin'. Plus, he ain't bad lookin'."

Myra laughed, "Well, you are right about that, but long before I knew about his looks or his dreams, I was a fan of his poetry."

"Yeah. Most people don't know that he wrote or inspired several of my biggest hits," Jimmy said.

"Of course, All Good Things Must End was your biggest of all. My daughter Marla and I heard that one live at the Watkins Glen concert in the spring of '70 when I met your dad."

Jimmy broke into a spontaneous rendition of the song performing the vocals and uttering the guitar and drums verbally as well: " Budda, budda, BAH; Budda, budda, BAH, Barrranng, bring, bring Barraang...

Leave me in a comet's tail/ Tangent to the moon (budda budda bah, budda buddabah bah bah bah Barraang nang brang) Leave me in a decibel/ Ringing afternoon/ Leave me now my Baby/ As all good things must end/ (more guitar and drum sounds) Leave me in a raindrop/ Hangin' on a line/ Leave me in a buttercup'/ Baby I won't mind/ Leave me on a rainbow/ High above the range/ This you know, my Baby/ Everything must change/ Yes, and all good things must end"

There was more, but Myra was laughing, "I always liked that one, but it's hard to believe you made a million-seller out of it."

"Well, Myra, there are worse. A lot worse!" Jimmy snickered, "Hey, where is your lovely daughter Marla these days?" Jimmy had been taken with pictures of her that were on the mantle and he had seen a home video of her when she was in her twenties. They were at least thirty years old. She and Jimmy Jack were close to the same age. Jimmy could not get her out of his mind.

"Jimmy, I can't talk about Marla just now. She disappeared two years ago and, except for a few one line messages to Kirk and me every few months, we only know that she's alive—somewhere. Jimmy, I do have something very important to tell you," Myra's facial expressions had changed from the smiling one a moment before to one deeply serious.

Myra with her grey hair was swept back; her brow furrowed. "I have been very impressed by your rehabilitation. Your charitable work with the homeless has been remarkable. I know you have seen a lot and done a lot in your life, but what I am about to tell you is going to surprise you. In fact the whole world is going be very surprised."

And so she did. First she had a family meeting with Kirk, Zoë, Michael and Jimmy.

Myra began, "What I am about to tell you must remain with you until I have prepared a more public announcement."

"You ain't pregnant are you?" Kirk asked with mock seriousness. The children and Myra laughed.

"Well, what I have to say may be more miraculous than a sixty-year old giving birth."

Chapter 6 The Announcement

The story bowled them over. From Zoe's "Wow!" to Kirk's, "Holy shit!" After two hours of questions and Myra's thoughtful answers, everyone agreed not to say a word until Myra had a chance to make a presentation to faculty at Oxford and a few select guests.

Myra flew from Charlotte to Gatwick Airport and took the bus, as usual, to Oxford.

The meeting was held in the Faculty Lounge on the second floor of McAllister Hall. The room reeked of five-hundred years of mustiness rubbed over with beeswax polish.

The meeting of the archeology and paleoanthropology faculty at Oxford was also attended by her attorney, her personal physician, and other faculty members who thought she brought them together to announce an even greater endowment than she had previously made. Her startling announcement had nothing to do with money.

"Thank you all for coming to this gathering today. As you know, my first husband, Arthur, and I were collaborators on many research projects before his untimely death. You may recall that it was Art who debunked Piltdown. It was Arthur's high regard for exacting science and for his avoidance of sensationalism in the press, that he made me vow never to reveal his most profound discovery until we had more than enough proof that our discovery was authentic. What I am about to reveal is a secret discovery, made in Amiens, France, in the summer of 1948. Before I lay this out for all to see, I want to assure you that I am not suffering from dementia, as I am quite sure some will say. Dr. Clyde Davenport will speak to this point now."

"Distinguished faculty," Dr. Davenport began, "I am Dr. Myra Rosenblum's personal physician. I am here with her today to attest that she is of sound mind and body. She has recently assented to a series of tests that prove this beyond any doubt. I do not know what she is about to report to you, but I can say with 100% certainty that she is neither delusional nor senile."

Myra's attorney, Philip Briggs, in his usual stylish pin-striped suit, spoke next. "I have here a non-disclosure agreement which I would hope each of you to sign. It merely provides a good faith promise not to divulge what you will hear today until two-weeks from now giving us ample time to prepare for the public presentation and subsequent Q & A period." Everyone present signed the agreement even though there were no civil or criminal penalties attached. It was simply a "gentlemen's agreement" with signatures.

"Thank you, Dr. Davenport and Mr. Briggs." Myra then continued with her prepared speech.

"While in the midst of a dig near Amiens, actually near the bombed out railroad station there, Arthur Barringer and I found the remains of a barrow that had been covered in mud since Neolithic times. That discovery alone would have been sensational news, but that was nothing compared to what we found in the barrow. There, in a tight chamber, was a crypt with a bejeweled cover. You may recall the one that's now in the Louvre. Inside that coffin were the nearly perfect mummified remains of a king, or so we first surmised. On closer inspection we discovered several remarkable things."

Myra then began a series of slide projections of the black and white photos that were made on the day of the discovery. Knowledgeable people in the room fairly gasped and then murmured amongst themselves as Myra continued.

"Here you see the sarcophagus, inlaid with semi-precious stones. Sorry, we had no color film that day. Next we show the removal of the lid and the corpse within. Two features struck us immediately: One was the sheer size of the specimen. See Art's hand with the tape measure—right at 6 feet five inches head to toe!"

The assembled group of experts had never seen a man of that size from the Stone Age. The next slide caused a couple of professors to stand up, mouths agape.

"Yes," Myra said, "you are looking at a pair of gigantic wings next to the body. Unique to Neolithic burials? Yes, but now look closely at the next slides. We had carefully turned the body over. The golden leather-like skin was strong and broke in no place from the handling. There, on the back were projections of both scapulae. They are extremely oversized, what we might call an osteopathic deformity. Now look at the close-ups. See the rough edges of the back bones? Then check the close- ups of the bottom ends of wings, or top in perspective to their placement next to the body. The ragged cuts there match the scapula. Gentlemen, we discovered an angel!"

The audience went ballistic. Shouts of "Amazing!" "Ridiculous!" "Unbelievable!" Finally the Chairman of the Board, Peter Wembly, a short red-faced man with wildly unkempt white hair, brought the mob to order, "Quiet!

Take your seats! I am sure Dr. Rosenblum will entertain your questions."

Nearly everyone started screaming, "Professor Rosenblum! Myra! Over here!"

Wembly had to shout, "Sit down and shut-up else we will have no questions!"

The room quieted and Wembly called on Simon Weiss, an American anthropologist on a post-doc research assignment at Oxford.

"Dr. Rosenblum, this is either the greatest discovery in the history of archeology or a ludicrous fraud that makes the Piltdown Man seem alive by comparison. How do you answer that? Why should anyone believe you have found an angel?"

"Hear! Hear! The crowd shouted, and someone in the back yelled, "Yes, those are the only questions that need be answered today!"Myra then calmly spoke, "You are right. The reason it has taken twenty-seven years to reveal that 'Amos,' as I call him, is truly an angel is exactly due to the reactions I see here today. Ironically, Arthur Barringer had spent a great part of his career proving that Piltdown was a fraud. For that reason, as he said, we needed iron-clad proof that what we found was real. I could not make this announcement today without such proof.

"Last year, I met Professor Alec Jefferies at the University of Leicester. I had him do his "DNA fingerprinting" on a couple of bone samples from Amos. With apologies to Dr. Jefferies for misleading him into thinking the samples were from ancient and more modern specimens from France, the results were a perfect match: that is, the DNA samples from the wings match that of the bones of Amos' body. Amos is an angel!"

"Further, using instruments of analysis not available in the 1950's, I was able to determine that Amos died from an arrow wound; that he lived about seven thousand five-hundred years ago; and that he was approximately 145 years old when he died."

Once again the audience erupted. Wembly was growing hoarse shouting to restore order. "Take your seats, damn it all! Next question AFTER order is restored!" The formidable figure of Sir Alec Jefferies rose from the back of the room. "I see why you had to trick me Myra; apology accepted. Now when do we get to see your angel Amos?"

"We will arrange a viewing, as well as independent scientific studies, of Amos. Also, the University will need to arrange a press conference. This will no doubt entail armed guards, security checks, and whatever else needs to be done to prevent a media circus from becoming a riot. I beg you to please allow preparations to be made for a press conference and avoid discussion of what I have told you today until we have set up the public announcement."

Chapter 7The Press Conference

As Myra predicted, the word of the discovery of an angel leaked out. Myra thought the leaker was likely Simon Weiss the American archeologist at Oxford whose advances she had spurned while she was attending an academic conference in Los Angeles sometime in the late 60's. She had told Jimmy Jack and Kirk the whole story of the tabloid leak back in the '50's when a reporter had bribed Billy McAdoo into giving up some secrets including crude sketches from the Oxford lab. The day of after Billy's death an obscure article appeared inside an issue of *Day Break*that an Oxford graduate assistant had revealed the presence of a winged human in a lab at the University. Of course the article was illustrated with dubious sketches that looked like bad police wanted posters. Harvey McGarvey was nearly fired for writing the outlandish story because he had no proof and his source was, unfortunately, dead. In those days, even a tabloid had some standards.

The press conference was held at The Royal Albert Hall, since, as anticipated, nearly five-thousand representatives of the world press that were expected did show up. Myra did not disappoint them. Dressed in a full-length gown of gold and glowing like a diva, her hair swept back and twisted into a tight bun she introduced her family (absent Marla), and academic associates. When a spotlight shown on Jimmy Jack, there was much applause and whistling.

■■■

Since the academic announcement nearly a fortnight prior, Myra asked Jimmy Jack to gather some of his old roadies and show producers to set up lighting and sound fit for a rock concert. She also paid dearly for a super video presentation that not only showed the original slides seen by the Academy, but new pictures of Amos in full color.

She had a ten minute documentary prepared by a young film maker who had just begun work on an American Civil War documentary with his brother. This had been a secret project paid for by Myra as an anonymous benefactor eighteen months prior. And for a little extra drama its title was *The Amazing History of Angels*. Ben Burns worked on and off on the project for more than a year. It covered several dozen disparate cultures and historical periods. The point was: Angels have been with humanity around the globe for a very long time.

Myra took up the story when the applause for the film subsided. "Thank you for coming today, even though you are well-paid and on expense accounts." Laughter rippled through the audience.

"First, I want to say that the rumors that have already appeared in the press, contrary to the norm, are, in this case largely true." More laughter.

"In deed my colleague and late husband Arthur J. Barringer and I did discover an angel buried some seven thousand years in a barrow in Amiens, France. Much research remains to be done. Not so much to prove his existence, but to find out where he came from and even how he came to be."

■■■

Myra began as before to illustrate her lecture with slides. And like the academics, the audience fairly gasped with astonishment. Toward the end of the presentation Myra offered some theories that she offered to the world in a continuing search for answers.

While I have no doubt as to the existence of angels, I have some intuition and insight on the subject of where angels came from." At this point academics and laymen alike were on the edge of their seats to hear what Myra was about to say.

"I do not believe angels came directly from outer space. And do not know now if they had more power than other humans, except for flying, of course!" More peals of laughter brightened the hall.

"But my academic research does lead me to the potential conclusion that angels were metamorphosed humans."

Someone shouted, "Like a butterfly's metamorphosis?"

"Yes, that is what I believe. Amos, the Amiens Angel, was about 145 years old when he died. Suppose he changed when he was, say, 125 years old from an ordinary human non-angel?"

Professor Wembly from Oxford called for order. He did not have to shout for his voice to boom thanks to the mega amps Jimmy Jack's crew had supplied. "I'll start with a TV network. Go ahead down there, what's your question."

■■

Carlos Williams, a reporter from CNN, asked, "Do you know the circumstances of Amos' death?"

"I do. He was killed in battle or murdered. I discovered that his heart had been punctured by a single arrow. I think we have a slide on that." A technician pulled up the side and enlarged it to show the arrowhead close up.

A reporter from the *Times* of London was next. "Why would anyone want to kill an angel?"

"That's a very good question. In most ancient and modern societies, angels are seen as benevolent messengers of God or gods. Our word "angel" is derived from the Latin *angelus* and Greek *angelos* both meaning "messenger of the gods." In the Christian era, it's "messenger of God." But also in non-western religions the word for "angel" is consistently associated with beings that convey information from some higher spirit. So why would anyone want to kill an angel?"

I suppose it lies with the corruption of the soul of humanity or in the mind-set of a person who would kill a Gandhi or a Martin Luther King, or, who knows why—hate?; for profit?; for power?"

"Why do so many cultures have these angel messengers?" a reporter from the BBC asked.

"Well, the simple truth seems to be that they were once pretty common. Everyone, it seems saw them and, probably, were helped by their knowledge and wisdom. Things that might cause great leaps forward in human prehistory; such as language, agriculture, management of communities, mathematics. The list of humankind's most remarkable achievements is endless. Today we would call these events 'breakthroughs', 'revolutions', or 'turning points.' I believe that a 'higher power', if you will, carried crucial knowledge to people for the benefit of humankind through angel messengers."

"So, what happened to them?" asked a seasoned stringer from *The L.A. Times*.

"Another good question. And again, all I have is a scientist's intuition to go by. I think that, like other animals, chiefly insects that 'morph,' a certain set of conditions must occur. Mainly, 'morphing,' if I may coin a term, needs a certain length of time to bring about that change. Think of the seventeen-year locust or cicadas. As I mentioned earlier, our Amos morphed probably around age 125. I think factors such as global warming—yes there was global warming seven thousand years ago—or the prevalence of life-span limiting diseases and warfare may have continued to push humanity back to the average age of thirty or thirty-five in the late Neolithic. This could account for the extinction of angels. Simply put, no one lived long enough to morph."

Professor Wembly closed the press conference by saying, "Dr. Rosenblum has provided you with enough fodder for your feeding troughs to last you many weeks. As she mentioned, research will continue apace and all new discoveries will be swiftly conveyed to all news outlets. Thank you, and good day."

▪▪

Myra returned to Kirkland Hall and spent most her days answering her mail. Along with the many requests for access to Amos, there were hundreds of letters that ascribed spiritual meaning to the reality of angels. Many attributed special powers to the remains and wanted angel bones for healing miracles, icons, and talismans.

Chapter 8 The Angel Debunked

In 1986 there was a new twist to the angel story: Various authorities both secular and religious seemed very nervous about the angel phenomenon and were bent on debunking Amos as an angel. Myra was attacked in the press as the perpetrator of a fraud, especially since she had profited with sales of a million copies of her book: *Amos, the Amiens Angel.*

Myra knew there would be repercussions that would shake up science, but she was blind-sided by the furor in religion. At first it seemed that the easiest course for established religion was to simply ignore the angel. But then so many questions came up, especially among Christians, the angel had to be discredited as flesh and bone. Religious authorities wanted only those angels that existed on a spiritual plane. Biblical angels such as Gabriel, Messenger of God, or Michael the avenging warrior, could not be demeaned by a competing angel, especially not a mortal one!

First, a group of skeptical forensic anthropologists, led by Simon Weiss, claimed that their "thorough examination" revealed that Amos was a more recently mummified warrior-king of some Gallic tribe wiped out by the Roman army. The wings were attributed to an extinct eagle. Oh, and the king was a hunchback with very abnormal shoulder blades.

The debunking stories ran in all of the mainstream press. The only major paper to make any effort to debunk the debunkers was Harvey McGarvey's *Day Break.* They pointed out that Simon Weiss had received an enormous grant from a Jesuit foundation and been given a two-hundred fifty thousand dollar tenured position at Libertas University in Virginia. But of course, *Day Break* still offered a million dollar prize to anyone who could "produce a space alien dead or alive and the same reward for the capture of an angel."

Before a horrified Myra could respond, the body of Amos was transferred to the Vatican Museum, for further study. This was done through a legal maneuver that showed that the Amiens burial site was owned by the Catholic Church. The Church also claimed that the peat bog man Art and Myra had taken from the Louvre was also their property. The Archbishop of Canterbury met with the Pope and gave his blessing to the whole matter of debunking as well as the removal of the bodies to Rome.

Myra was devastated. Her attorney, Phillip Briggs, said "There's very little I can help you with here. Very powerful forces are arrayed against you. I could try to defend you, Myra, but the case would eat up most of your considerable resources."

"Well, Phil, do you believe me?"

▪▪▪

"Of course I do. Simon Weiss was paid a lot of money to discredit you."

"Yes, Simon and I go way back," Myra replied with a cynical laugh. I certainly did not expect the Church to get involved."

"Hah! It was the Christian Establishment that paid Weiss. I didn't see that coming either, but I suppose the Biblical angels must stand a better chance of surviving as spirits than would Amos as a human. That's the motive, I am sure."

"Yes, you are right, Phil. Gabriel was a very busy and talkative angel. He's the one who appears in both the Old and New Testament as a messenger of God. In the Old Testament he tells Daniel what his visions meant. Then, in the Jesus Story, he tells Zachariah that his wife Elizabeth will give birth to John. And later he tells Mary she will give birth to Jesus. He returns to tell Joseph that Mary's pregnancy was caused by God and, basically, not to worry about adultery. But he didn't stop with the greatest messages in both testaments of the Bible."

"What else did he do?" Phil asked. "He just recited the entire Koran to a Mohamed, the first hafiz, that's all!""What's a hafiz?"A hafiz is a person who can recite the Koran verbatim. They have them to this day. Scribes in the 5th Century wrote it all down.""So, The Koran is one very big message from Allah delivered by an angel to Mohamed. Hmm! Well, Myra, you sure know your Bible and Koran. I am sure this is why there's so much religious angst about a mortal angel. So what do you want to do now?"

■■

"I'm guess I am going to finally retire, write some more books, and enjoy the North Carolina Mountains with my husband."

■■■

Chapter 9 James Jackson Johnson

When Jimmy Jack was 18 he was enrolled at Georgia Tech. He was much more interested in the Anti-War movement and his garage band "Jimmy Jack and the Jumpin' Jacks" than in the courses he took in electrical engineering. When he was just 15 and in high school, his rollicking "Irish" ballad *In Condemnation of Folly* had made him richer than most college kids thanks to covers of the song by Phil Seeger and the Wyman Brothers.

In Condemnation of Folly by Clifford Ferret (Jimmy Jack wrote it under a pseudonym)

■■■

Oh, yer runnin' helter skelter
Down to yer fall-out shelter
And yer divin' fer kiver
With the fallin' of the bombs

There's a bright flash fer away
And the ground begins to sway
So yer beatin' on yer Bibles
And yer callin' out the Psalms

Well things settle down after bit
Yer lookin'fine and feelin' fit
And it looks as if yer money
Wasn't wasted after all

But ya been in there a week or two
Breathin' air with residue
Yer tongue begins to tingle
As yer hair begins to fall

And yer in this fool contraption
That ya built fer times of action
But yer filters ain't a-workin'
And yer water's goin' stale

Now ya figger time's a-waistin'
'Cause yer pulse is fairly racin'
So you go to see yer neighbor
Just to listen to his tale

But his face is not familiar
'Cause he has suffered similar
His teeth and hair and eyes are gone
His family looks like ghouls

So maybe now you'll realize
From what I got to theorize
That Shelter Plan's a folly
For the Nation's biggest fools!

The rest is history as far as Jimmy's music career went. He went on to write and record dozens of songs, many hits, and had one gold album with *All Good Things Must End.* Eventually, his stellar career succumbed to the destructive lifestyle of fame blinded by all that glitter.

Jimmy Jack's father, Colonel Kirk Johnson, a decorated veteran of the Korean and early Vietnam War, managed to use his connections to get Jimmy into the army. At first Jimmy was very skeptical having had many arguments with Kirk about the stupidity of the Vietnam War. As the war dragged on, Kirk came to believe his son was right.

Jimmy later joined the post-Vietnam U S Army. He went to Ranger Training at Ft. Benning thinking this would be good for his slumping musical career. "After all, Pops, I ain't doin' nothing else these days." Jimmy said to his smiling dad.

Two days before completing training, Jimmy fell from a cliff in the woods of North Georgia. He broke a leg in two places and, even after healing, was deemed unfit for further service. The war was over and had little need for a gimpy Ranger.

Throughout his heyday Jimmy stayed best friends with Jason Faircloth from high school and Georgia Tech, an unlikely pal considering Jason R. Faircloth, PhD, would become a world-famous physicist and electro-mechanical engineer; a pioneer in laser optics. He had scores of patents and was a highly paid contract researcher for Bell Labs. Faircloth had played a key role in the development of Magnetic Resonance Imaging. His many patents had made him one of the wealthiest scientists in America.

■■

While Jason was becoming an engineering whiz getting a PhD from MIT, Jimmy's money seemed to disappear as fast as it came in. The residuals on *All Good Things Must End* kept him going for years and, after rehab, meant he had a comfortable living.

With Jimmy and Kirk at her side Myra passed in the winter of 2013. She was 88. In her will, she set up trust funds for Jimmy Jack, Zoe, Michael, and Marla. She also specified that several millions go to The Institute of Cryopreservation Research. She wanted Art to have a chance should a breakthrough occur that would provide for his resuscitation and the repair of his exploded heart.

Kirk got the estate and a small fund as well to keep him writing poetry and supplied with Jack Daniels. Zoe used her fund to sponsor herself in various projects to save endangered species. She spent most of her time in Africa with Save the Elephants Foundation. Michael chose law and became an expert in digital copyrights.

And Marla? The family only knew she was alive and living under the radar somewhere in New York. She left an occasional tweet for her step father to assure him she was ok. She appeared at Myra's funeral and had stood unnoticed near Jimmy Jack at the services. She avoided contact with everyone and all thought she was someone else's friend or kin.

Jimmy Jack became increasingly interested in the cause of income inequality, perhaps ironic since most of his millions now were derived from his "One-Percenter" status as a "trustafarian." But Jimmy was serious. He had taken his charity work with homeless seriously, and now with the Tea Party firmly in control of America, he felt he had to work with other Progressives to turn things around.

When the Tea Party nearly claimed the Presidency in 2016, Jimmy was sixty-six. He had been the “angel” for a number of start-up businesses that did good works that benefitted all of society. One, for example, was the central hot water system for Asheville, North Carolina. There he helped fund the conversion of a power plant into a gigantic boiler that distributed hot water through pipes all over the city. It was based on the system in place for years in Copenhagen. Even though it ran on carbon fuel, all of the energy was conserved as heat, not for turning inefficient turbines. Of course, there was lots of opposition from the Tea Party that called the conversion “socialistic” since the City of Asheville was running the plant.

Jimmy moved to New York to be closer to the hub of his multi-business empire. He appointed his old friend Jason Faircloth to be Chief Technical Officer of JJJ, Inc. Already a multi-millionaire, Jimmy had made his single best investment when he purchased a small Long Island radio station which emerged from bankruptcy as WORY, Nassau, New York

■■

Chapter 10The Worry Channel

WORY had one shtick that captured millions of listeners, and later legions of viewers as it became a cable TV channel with 24/7 talking heads, experts, and "real people" with things for us to worry about. No disease, no catastrophe, no financial crisis, was out of the purview of WORY. When Ebola struck in several parts of the USA in the summer of 2015, WORY had non-stop coverage for weeks.

Jimmy's channel was also first to cover the "Geezer Riots" in St Petersburg, Florida in 2017 after the Tea Party succeeded in gutting major parts of Social Security and raising the retirement age to seventy-five. An army of seniors, waving American flags had surrounded the Federal Building and laid siege. Many were veterans of several past wars and some were also armed. Thirteen senior citizens were shot dead by SWAT Teams from the St Pete Police Department who also suffered five officers killed and nine wounded.

In 2017 the United States of America made itself a constitutional oligarchy in all but name through a series of amendments and affirmations by the extremely right-wing Supreme Court. On the surface things appeared pretty normal, but the erosion of voting rights and the complete subversion of civil and personal rights to corporate interests had combined to change America into the political likes of a Third World country run by one-percent of people at the apex of society.

Both the Democratic and Republican Parties had splintered into factions: The Tea Party officially called itself the "Conservative Reform Party (CRP)"; the old GOP was a small faction of sensible "Small government, big business" Republicans; and the left consisted of Moderate Democrats (primarily unionists) a.k.a. "Modems" and Progressive Democrats, the "Prodems." Most people still called the CRP, "the Tea Party"which the Prodems liked to call the "Crap Party."

The WORY Channel was one of the few independent voices on the air, though obviously partisan Prodem. In one of their most famous exposés, WORY ran a program on the Vortex Corporation. The series was called "Murderous Machines in Your Home."

One of the Vortex TV ads ran during Super Bowl LI. It was supposed to be humorous showing a toddler stuffing a large soaking wet angora cat into a front loading dryer. "Even a two-year-old can work a Vortex!" says the off camera narrator. The smiling toddler presses a button. Seconds later the little boy opens the dryer and out pops an extremely fluffy cat, startled but unharmed. The video went viral and generated the most hits of any commercial on YouTube up to that time. The video was monetized, of course, and the Vortex Corporations made hundreds of thousands more in profit.

WORY ran the protests from the SPCA and other animal rights groups. Outraged pet owners appeared on TV. WORY hauled in a spokesperson for Vortex to their studio for an interview with Jimmy Jack Johnson.

"We have Marvin Whitmeyer, VP of Marketing for Vortex, Inc. here today," announced Jimmy Jack

"Mr. Whitmeyer, do you think the now infamous Super Bowl ad was a mistake."

"Well, Jimmy, not really. You see kids have been putting pets into dryers since the day they were invented."

"So, you are saying that Vortex should not be liable for any of the deaths of three babies, and forty-seven cats that have died in electric dryers since the Super Bowl?"

"No, Jimmy, our products are safe when used correctly; nor, do they make people smarter. And neither can Vortex prevent parents from exercising good judgment in monitoring the activities of their children."

"But don't you think that Vortex actually promoted the misuse of their product in that ad?"

■■■

"Come on, Jimmy, didn't you think the ad was funny?"

"Well, I did, but then I'm not a two year old. And your cat survives the dryer, which to some adults, like me with a sick sense of humor, is funny. But to a two, three, or four year old this scenario looks like a good idea. And, Mr. Whitmeyer I do wish you well defending the hundreds of lawsuits pending against you and Vortex."

Soon after that interview the cable companies, now dominated by far right-wing media conglomerates, dropped WORY on the grounds that people had enough to worry about. What the corporations really had to worry about were the many revelations about false advertising, product safety, corporate greed as well as articles concerning pollution, global warming, privatization of education, etc. all dealt with on Jimmy Jack's channel.

Once when Jimmy was in New York with one of his reporters they were mugged by three hoods. Jimmy and the reporter, Sheila Davies both spent several days in the hospital. Jimmy regretted that his Ranger training and skills in martial arts had gotten rusty. He said to Sheila when they were recovering, "I am truly sorry I couldn't have done a better job defending you."

"Jimmy, for god-sake there were three of them! I hope you aren't planning to start carrying a gun. That would make you a hypocrite considering all the anti-gun shows we did."

"Yeah, and you are correct especially since I really believe that somebody like me with a gun is more likely to have that gun used on them than on the assailant. What I am thinking about is martial arts."

A little while later, Jimmy enrolled in an intense course in karate followed by jujitsu and one on Japanese weapons. He excelled in all the courses earning a black belt in each. Even though he had no intention to ever own or carry a firearm, he did see the value in becoming an expert in their use. Under an assumed name, he enrolled in a "weapons and tactics" course run by a white supremacist group in Alabama. That gave him not only skills with weapons, but a great series for the WORY channel.

WORY was losing some audience by alternating real worries with silly ones, e.g., "Tax Breaks for Oil Companies while you pay $7.00 a Gallon" juxtaposed to "Spiders—the Web You Could Die For." Most of the programming was designed to light a fire under latent "Progressives" or piss-off a lot of blue-collar voters into thinking a little more about their affection for the Tea Party.

In addition to squelching WORY on cable and satellite TV, the CRP FCC went after WORY on various trumped-up charges including use of "inappropriate language" in prime time broadcasts. Jimmy did not help his case when he published an open letter in the *Toronto Times*in which he "Respectfully" asked the Chairman of the FCC to "go fuck himself."

Jimmy then spent many millions buying up abandoned off-shore oil rigs on all coasts and turning each into a hundred thousand watt radio and TV platforms. Ignoring a cease and desist order from a Federal Court, Jimmy had a huge and enthusiastic audience that cheered him on through the Internet which was also becoming more and more restricted and controlled by corporations.

The Tea Party Congress then passed laws that extended the borders of the US far out beyond the twelve mile limit. When Jimmy refused to comply with the Draconian laws, the US Navy was sent to blow up all of the platforms. Jimmy Jack Johnson's empire was thus physically and financially destroyed.

■■

Chapter 11 The National Lotto

By 2018 the CRP was slipping badly in the polls. Tax breaks for corporations and the richest people were causing massive budget shortfalls. That's when Congress Passed the National Lottery Act of 2019. It seemed like overnight every convenience store, supermarket, depot, bus stop, and fast food store had the new lotto vending machines. To encourage patronage, there were endless TV ads featuring the latest winners screaming and thanking the Lotto Commission for its great work. Winners were required to appear on FOX NEWS to be in a constantly revised infomercial praising the Lotto. Nobody, it seemed, had the slightest objection to the Lotto Act. There was some debate aboutArticle 13.2 that read, *"Any person found to have tampered with, altered, or stolen money from an official National Lottery Machine shall be terminated by the Lotto Security Agency."* But the Act passed anyway.

Jimmy Jack played a $50 token several times a week just as every Real American was expected to do. Social Security was entirely paid for by proceeds from the Lotto. After chipping away for years at 'Obamacare,' the CRP made a breakthrough with "LottoCare." This was a scheme to pay doctors and hospitals billions from a Lotto slush fund for reducing medical bills for "most average Americans."By "average" it meant that upper class people paid next to nothing for health care and "nominal fees" paid by everyone else could result in bankruptcy just like in the 20th Century.

Jimmy was broke compared to his former wealth, but he still had a trickle of royalties and his extraordinarily wealthy best friend, Jason Faircloth, helped him with living expenses.

In the fall of 2019, Jimmy was at Jason's apartment on the Upper West Side of New York City.Jimmy parked his 2015 Indian motorcycle in Jason's garage under his fiend's Central Park West condo and took the elevator to the penthouse. Jason Faircloth, like Jimmy, was in his 60's, taller, but forty pounds lighter. He was a grey and balding African-American wearing old-fashioned wire-rimmed bifocals."Welcome, Jimmy! Did you have any trouble with the code?"

"Yeah, well I did have to remember pi to six decimal places plus the name of your cat. Where is Einstein, by the way?"

■■

"Probably using the toilet. He really likes to flush. Only took me a week to teach him that trick. And then you should have seen my first water bill after that!"

"Hey, Jimmy, check this out." He produced what appeared to be an ordinary motorcycle helmet. "Try it on."

Jimmy donned the black helmet and adjusted the straps.

"Now what?"

"Mash the button on the right side, Partner."

"OK, uh, Jeezus, Jason! I can see through stuff! It's way better than an x-ray in full color—what the hell?"

Jason said, "Push the button again and take off the helmet. Remember that class you were in with me at Georgia Tech."

"Sure do. Never would have passed without you helping with my homework."

"Well, remember that Iranian prof at Tech, Kalik Monsari?"

"Sure do. Didn't he do research in magnetic resonance?"

"Yes. He never managed to develop an instrument sensitive enough to measure the impulses in very weak molecular fields."

"But you did?"

"Uh huh. You know that in the 1960's—in our lifetime, Jimmy, the scientific community was skeptical of such things as auras, really halos of brain activity. And that was simply because they had no technology with which to measure those brain waves. Monsari was theoretically correct to say that all matter has electromagnetic properties. Different substances, elements, compounds, whatever, they all vibrate with different patterns of very minute sub-molecular level pulses. But proving that this is true would have been difficult without the sensors that could detect them."

Jason pulled up and played the Beach Boys *Good Vibrations* on his stereo system.

"So you, Jason Faircloth, soon to be the world's first African-American Nobel Laureate for Physics, have done just that: invented a magnetic resonance device sensitive enough to work with any material."

"Well, don't know about a Nobel Prize, but that is what I have done. The trick was both in the detection and the amplification of the omnipresent electromagnetic waves."

"Wow. Then you miniaturized the device to fit inside a motorcycle helmet!"

"Yessiree! And the decoding processors are in there as well. That's what you call looking through things; the images are just the result of decoded electromagnetic impulses."

"Amazing! This could make you really rich, Jason."

"Well, I hope so. Never made a penny off of the miniature laser pistol. I couldn't patent it because I was just a peon at Bell Labs when I invented it. They got all the credit, all the government contracts, and, of course, all the money."

■■

"You should make a killing with this invention. Pardon the pun. Every MD will want one of these see-thru helmets. Every hospital will want dozens. Homeland Security? You bet!"

"Yes, and in the wrong hands a lot of damage could be done."

"Such as?"

"Well, safe-cracking comes to mind. Also, there's a potentially big market for Peeping Toms," Jason chuckled."You'd have to be pretty sick to get off on those ghostly images."

"That's because you didn't mess with the dial on the left side of the helmet. Put the helmet back on. You'll see."

Jimmy pulled the helmet on again. "Now turn the dial slowly clockwise," Jason instructed.

"Oh, yeah. Not as filmy; more solid."

"The processors use predictive analytics, a branch of artificial intelligence, to filter meaningful information from the extraneous."

"See what you mean, Doc! Haha, you are standing there buck naked—this artificial intelligence sure is smart. This is a trip! Whoa, there's a $50 Lotto token hiding there in your couch! I'll just pick him up."

"Come on Jimmy, that's mine!"

"Finders, keepers!" laughed Jimmy. Then he got serious. "If you can see inside of things, I bet you could 'read' a Lotto machine, you know, for 'quality assurance,' like when it is bursting to pay-off."

"Uh oh. Now, Jimmy, don't get any wild ideas. I still have lots of testing to do."

"Come on, Doc, let me do some field-testing. I have the motorcycle. Now all I need is a brand new helmet. Just for fun, I'll invest your Lotto token in a machine. "I'll even give you twenty-five percent if I win anything."

"Fifty."

"Deal." With that Jimmy descended to the basement garage and onto his Indian and then rode out onto Park Avenue heading south

At Grand Central Station, Jimmy parked the bike and, fairly inconspicuously, entered. He was wearing the helmet, but no one noticed since the Ebola scare had many people wearing various face coverings, helmets, and even gas masks. Also, Jimmy's bright yellow trench coat contributed his anonymity since that seemed to be half the population's favorite color.

■■

■■■

Chapter 12The Grand Central Lotto

The National Lottery Commission (NLC) determined that the most ideal spot in America for the placement of Lotto machines was in the lobby of Grand Central Station in Manhattan. No less than a hundred machines lined the walls and formed an island of garish neon. The lobby looked very much like a Las Vegas casino with flashing lights of every color of the rainbow and a constant whir of spinning mechanical parts and the intermittent chime of bells signaling mostly minor winnings.

Market research had revealed that people wanted "tangibility" in the machines; not something as detached as purely electronic transactions would be. Focus groups were clear: people wanted "real machinery" not just a computer. And they wanted the pay-offs in real cash, not an automatic deposit to an account. They even preferred using silver dollar sized tokens to play the machines rather than credit cards. Each machine featured a holographic video of recent winners grinning madly and waving uncut sheets of $1,000 bills, a hundred thousand being one of the typical larger pay-outs. Market research showed that people much preferred payment in old fashioned cash rather than less tangible deposits to their checking accounts or on plastic cards. On each machine there was the mandatory disclaimer that not all plays would result in a pay-out; that ABSOLUTELY NO PERSON UNDER THE AGE OF 12 would be permitted to play unless they were accompanied by an adult over the age of 18; and, of course the warning that everyone chose to ignore: Article 13.2, ***Any person found to have tampered with, altered, or stolen money from an official National Lottery Machine shall be terminated by the Lotto Security Agency.*** By order of Mario F. Belladonna, Commissioner of the NLC.

Mrs. Lillian Paisley, an octogenarian, wearing a 20th Century earth-toned calf-length skirt, white blouse, grey cardigan sweater, and old King James basketball shoes made her way across the vast space of Grand Central terminal. She walked slowly with the aid of a cane with eyes fixed on her favorite machine which she had played daily since it appeared with ninety-nine other machines twenty-three weeks before. She had told a friend that this particular machine had "spoken to her."

In fact, it had. The machine resembled a soft drink machine, neon bright in fashionable primary and secondary colors and all had holographic screens. The hologram on Mrs. Paisley's favorite machine featured members of her own family, drawn from a Facebook database. An algorithm in the machine's computer had done face recognition of her and thus the machine was able to talk to Mrs. Paisley. "Hello, Mrs. Paisley, how are you today? Did Twinkie recover from her hairball?"

"Yes she did, thank you!"

Mrs. Paisley loved her interaction with the Lotto machine. She called it "Marvin Two" after her late husband because it always said what she wanted to hear, just like Marvin One.

"Mrs. Paisley, what have you for me today? A $50 I suppose, but I was really thinking $100."

Mrs. Paisley fished two fifty dollar tokens from her purse. The machine sighed pleasantly.

She pushed the first token into the slot. There was a hollow clunking sound that was unfamiliar to Mrs. Paisley.

"Please deposit your token," the machine said in a cold, less than pleasing tone.

"I did deposit the token!" Mrs. Paisley exclaimed.

"Please deposit your token," the machine repeated.

Mrs. Paisley was now confused. She had feared her growing dementia. She could forget something in the space of turning around. Did she just feed Twinkie or was that yesterday? Where did I put my purse? Oh, there it is on my left arm, and so on.

She produced the second token and deposited it. Again, the clunking sound.

"Please deposit your token," the now completely soulless machine coldly intoned.

Exasperated, Mrs. Paisley shouted, "I deposited my tokens! Damn you, Marvin, what's gotten into you?"

"Please deposit your token...please deposit your token...please deposit your token."

Mrs. Lillian Paisley was the sort of 'sweet old lady who wouldn't harm a fly' as her neighbors would say.But Mrs. Paisley wasn't going to let Marvin Two rob her of a hundred dollars. She raised her cane and tapped on the machine.

"Please deposit your token." Was the reply to the tapping.

Now Mrs. Paisley began to beat the machine as hard as she could with her cane.Whack! Bang!

From a corner of Grand Central Station, emerged the looming form of Harold "Butch" Gratzky, a plain clothed member of the Lotto Security Forces. Gratzky wore a bright green suit and yellow tie, in the fashion of the time.

Butch had had a very unhappy childhood: He had been a victim of an abusive father who drank excessively and beat Butch nightly. At school his obesity and acne scarred face, caused kids to make fun of him but always behind his back. They wouldn't bully him as he was 6' 2" and 270 pounds in 9th grade. Some kid from the football team, also of good size, mocked his slowness in gym class. Later the boy shoved Butch in the locker room. Butch punched his tormentor in the face and then went into a frenzy of kicking and punching the boy senseless.

The boy later died of the beating and Butch was sent to a prison for juvenile delinquents. When he emerged from prison, he was a hardened criminal invited to join a gang in Chicago. After years of working for the mob as a hit-man, he was a perfect hire by the newly formed LSA. Having a criminal record was not a detriment to getting a good paying job with the agency; it was actually an asset. The agency had a little army of bad guys: police who shot unarmed teenagers; army personnel involved in civilian massacres; and people like Butch with one or more murders on their resumes.

"Hello, Ma'am," Butch began, "Couldn't help but notice yous over here beatin' on the Lotto machine. Ya know you was causin' infractions of the law here."

"Well, the darned machine just stole $100 from me!" Lillian Paisley exclaimed in wide-eyed innocence.

Butch Gratzky then raised his government issued ZR7 laser pistol and squeezed the trigger sending a very strong beam into Mrs. Paisley's left eyewhich instantly fried her cerebral cortex causing her immediate death.

No one really noticed, either through blind indifference or fear of getting involved, that a human being had just died. Sirens wailed. The body was carried away by an EMT van in service to the LSA. Mrs. Lillian Paisley simply disappeared. Friends made calls to no avail.

Somebody picked up Twinkie. There was nothing else to do.

The Indian had quickly carried Jimmy to the west side of Grand Central Station. The bullet train from DC was screeching to a halt on track 56. Jimmy picked this time because in a matter of minutes the station would be crowded with five-thousand politicians, marketing agents, and lobbyists returning in their daily commute from the US Capital.

He surveyed the crowd. To his eyes, everyone was completely naked. For a moment he was totally distracted by the striding form of an absolutely gorgeous female, twenty something, carrying a Louis Vuitton shoulder bag. He felt creepy having stripped this stranger with his high-tech helmet and would have averted his eyes, but then he saw the contents of the bag. Jimmy could only guess, but the bag seemed loaded with at least a quarter of a million dollars in $1000 dollar bills!

Jimmy could have chatted her up, but he couldn't let curiosity or his lechery get the better of him. He proceeded to carry out his mission to "field test" the Faircloth Helmet. He perused the entire south wall Lotto machines. Nothing looked like the levers were aligning to pay-off in any machine. Then Jimmy noticed one machine, a little dimmer than the rest, with a crack in its holographic screen. Inside it, he saw a jammed mechanism and hundreds of sheets of $1000 bills just bursting to come forth.

"Please deposit your token," the machine said.

■■■

"Yessiree. Coming right up!" Jimmy deposited the $50 token.

Lights began to flash. Casino bells began to ring. The machine disgorged every sheet of money it had inside.

Jimmy had no time to count his winnings. His trench coat could barely cover it all. He was supposed to wait at the machine until FOX News showed up, but he bolted for the exit. As he was leaving, he heard the machine speak, "Sorry for your inconvenience, Mrs. Paisley. Have a nice day."

Soon back at Jason's condo, Jimmy was ecstatic."Hey, My Brother, check this out!"

"Oh, no, you didn't!"

"Did what? Well, yes, I did. Hit the Jimmy Jack Jack-Pot on a malfunctioning machine, I did. And you, Doctor Faircloth, get half. Let's count it."

There were exactly two million dollars stacked on Jason's dining room table. It took the men more than an hour to cut the sheets and count the money.

All the while, Jason Faircloth was grim faced in stark contrast to Jimmy's constant grinning.

"You know the LSA will find you. And they will kill you when they do. And then they will find me and they will also kill me."

"Aw, come on Doc! The beauty is they don't know where to look. The hologram camera on that machine was busted. Security cameras were everywhere of course, but I was just one of four hundred other men and women in yellow trenchies. They've got nothin'."

The office of Mario Francis Belladonna, Director of the Lotto Security Agency, was on the 101st floor of the World Trade Center. Belladonna was the spitting image of Supreme Court Justice Anton Scalia and had even taken the Justice's place at a CRP fundraiser in Texas when an assassination plot against the Chief Justice was detected. Belladonna had a panoramic view of the city through twelve-foot floor to ceiling windows. Seated across from his massive desk, sweating profusely was Harold Gratzky.

Belladonna began, reverting to the vernacular of his early years as a crime boss, "We go back a long ways, Butch. You was my best man in Chicago, back in the day. I could always count on you. If somebody pulled some shit on the Company, you was there to give him a swim in the Chicago River."

"Right, Boss, with a concrete Speedo!" said Butch getting a little more comfortable.

"But today, Butch, today you was sleepin' on the job."

Gratzky began to squirm a little in his chair."The day started out good. An old lady was beatin' the crap out of aLotto. You took care of that particular situation fine. But then what happened? You was supposed to follow-up! Did you ever get to the old lady's apartment? No. Did you remove everything from said apartment? NO! The neighbors already had herkitty and started making phone calls before you got there! This was not good, Butch."

"I am truly sorry, Boss. The traffic was horrible..."

■■

Mario cut him off: "New York traffic is always horrible, Butch. Truth is you are slow. You need to eat more salad. What are you now 350, 375? The Company, I mean the LSA, put you in Grand Central for a reason. It is the biggest Lotto station in the country. We do billions outta there. You been good in the past, but now you seem to be slipping."

"Because I messed up with some old lady?"

"NO, Dickweed! That was just your first fuck-up of the day! You don't even know what I am talking about do you?"

The six-foot four, 378 pound Gratzky seemed to shrink in his chair. "No, I am sorry, whachu talkin' about?"

"Let me explain. While you was movin' ever so slow over to the old lady's condo, you apparently forgot to secure and put an "Out-of-Order" sign on the machine she trashed. Hours later, a very anonymous cat in a motorcycle helmet and yellow trenchie drops a fifty in said Lotto and cleans that particular machine out of two fuckin' million!"

"Jeezus, Boss, I am so sorry."

"Sorry don't cut it, Butch. You gotta make it good. You gotta find that perp. He didn't hang around for the FOX interview and that makes him a perp even if he just got lucky."

■■

Chapter 13 Marla

Jimmy Jack Johnson was now a wanted man. At least he figured he was even though the identity of the man in the helmet and yellow trench coat was as yet unidentified by the authorities.

By chance he ran into Marla Rosenblum-Barringer at a Starbucks on 7th Avenue in Brooklyn near where he was keeping a very low profile in a brownstone on Garfield Place. She looked younger than a woman in her sixties, slim and fit, with the same blue eyes and mostly brown hair of her late mother Myra. "Hi, uh, Miss, are you Marla?" Jimmy asked.

At first she denied that she was Marla saying, "I'm sorry, but you must be mistaken. Do you know someone who looks like me, or was that just a pick-up line?"

"Well, we are in the Take-Out line," Jimmy joked.

Marla smiled. "Well you look pretty darn familiar to me, too. Except for that goatee, you are a ringer for Jimmy Jack Johnson."

"Ha, I get that all the time. What was his biggest hit—*Leave Me*?"

"Or, *All Good Things Must End*'" Marla chimed in, humming the chorus. "My mother and I saw him live at Watkins Glen, jeez, forty-five years ago."

At that moment the music box in Starbucks started playing *All Good Things Must End* which was not coincidental since the music system was programmed to play any song it detected in the ambience of chatter in the store. Marla's humming had done that.

"Ok, you are Marla and I am Jimmy," Jimmy stated. "Your Mom told me about the Watkins Glen concert. You know we are now related, sort of, since your mom married my dad. So, what's up, Prodigal Half-Step-Sister?"

"Jeez, Jimmy, I don't know where to start."

"Well, I say we start with our Latte Grandissimos at my place. It's just around the corner." They walked the two blocks to Garfield Place. Marla was a bit nervous since Jimmy signaled to someone on the second floor of a three story brownstone townhouse. A buzzer sounded and the below street level door under the stoop clicked open.

The front rooms were dark, but the room in the back opened to a tiny urban garden with lots of light and twittering birds. Fragrant herbs, lilacs, and lavender like potpourri filled the air wafting into the flat. It was an ethereal oasis with urban canyon walls all about.

"Golly, Jimmy, this place is uh,OK, kinda nice, but is this all you can afford?" said Marla politely.

"Ha ha, actually I could probably do better, but my landlord here is an old friend. Hy Mariampolski is letting me stay here awhile. So, let's sit and sip and catch up on the last forty years. You first."

"Well, let's just do the last four years. Before that, Jimmy, it's mainly a blur of booze and boyfriends, more world travel than a set of *National Geographics*, and lately being as anonymous as possible here in New York. My mother warned me that the Angel thing was a curse and that my knowledge would be a target if certain people knew who I was."

▪▪

"How so? I thought the Amiens Angel was proven to be a hoax as far as the public knew and that people just forgot about it in the Nineties. Of course, I always believed your mother."

"But then some goddamned government doctors at the National Institutes of Health in Bethesda, Maryland started a cover-up. They said the bird wings didn't fit. They pointed to the hanky-panky with the bog man from the Louvre. Then, mysteriously, the Angel wound up in the Vatican Museum."

"What the hell? Myra didn't tell me that. You mean to say that something supposedly not really an angel caught the attention of the Vatican? Why?"

"Jimmy, I don't know for sure. I think that they think "Amos," as Mom called him, really is an angel. They are probably trying to extract some secrets from him as we speak. They are likely to know he's an angel. Who knows, maybe they think they can clone an angel and have their own carefully programmed messenger from God? You know how Science is always tugging on the robes of Religion. Well now, Religion is swatting the dogs off with their own science."

"Marla, how did you learn about all this?"

"I was there when the deal went down. Mom told me I needed to keep an eye on her lab and make sure the iceboxes, for Amos and Art were kept up. I went to England fairly regularly. Well, some Vatican lawyers went to Oxford and confronted the administrators on the issue of the Louvre heist. They said the bog man was theirs since it had been leant to the Louvre before the war. But they pulled a switcheroo and took Amiens Man instead of the bog man. I was hiding near the cryocrypt where my father lies frozen. I know what they did. One of them caught a glimpse of me as I ran out of the lab. They have been after me ever since."

"Whew! All I have done lately is to lose most of my money in the battle to keep WORY on the air."

"Yeah, I followed that. Guess you are lucky you weren't on one of your oil platforms when the Navy came by."

"That's for sure."

"So, you still broke?"

"Well, not exactly." Jimmy went on to recount his recent "good luck" at the Lotto and that he was now on the run from the LSA. "Gotta lay low until this blows over."

"And I bet it's not easy cashing $1000 dollar bills, either." Marla grinned.

"Yeah, gotta run to Brighton Beach every week or so. My Russian Mafia connection pays $750 for each one but only on four or five at a time."

One day, soon after that first encounter, they walked through the Brooklyn Botanical Garden, an oasis in Park Slope. As they strolled, a golden shaft of sunlight filtered through a tree illuminated Marla's smiling face. Jimmy couldn't resist stealing a kiss. They embraced, hugged, kissed, and ended up in bed in Marla's third floor walk-up.

"I think I have been in love with you for twenty years." Jimmy whispered. Ever since I saw a picture of you on your mom's mantle.

"Well, Mr. Rock Star, I have had a crush on you for forty!" Marla, more loudly, whispered back. "Ever since I saw you at Watkins Glen. But I was just one of your million groupies!"

■■■

A couple of days later, Jimmy returned to Marla's place to find it transformed. Since neither of them had cell phones ("You can't disappear with a cell phone" Marla had said.) They hadn't communicated for several days. Jimmy paid a visit to Jason's place to his "ATM," as Jason called the periodic visits, to exchange $1000's for $100's and $50's.

Every wall and ceiling had been covered in aluminum foil. "Just because you aren't paranoid doesn't mean THEY aren't following you." Marla repeated the old joke.

She explained to Jimmy that she had seen a couple of black SUV's in the neighborhood. She didn't know who was in them or what they wanted.

"They could be Vatican Police, FBI, or if they are after you, the LSA." Marla suggested, "Or, if you are into conspiracy theories as I am, THEY are ALL of THEM!"

"Guess we shouldn't take chances. Hey, I borrowed Jason's helmet again."

"You goin' to knock off another Lotto?" Marla grinned.

"No, not for money, but to check out the neighbors."

"Hah, you just want to see what that blonde in the next apartment really looks like."

"Now that you mention it..." Jimmy was laughing. Marla threw a pillow at him.

"No, but if you want I'll take a ride around the block and see what's in those SUVs. If they are wearing green suits, LSA; black suits, FBI; and if they have miters or beanies, we'll know the Vaticanines are sniffing about."

■■■

Marla laughed, but then got serious again. "Oh jeez. Just remembered Panda."Pandemonium or 'Panda' for short was her tuxedo Maine Coon Cat.

"What about him? He likes me."

"He's got a chip, Jimmy. We have to get it out. I know how to do it. I worked with my sister Zoe when she was at the U of Tennessee Veterinarian School. They routinely inserted microchips for relocating lost pets. I'm sure our visitors out there in their SUVs can detect and read those chips. Get me your razor."

"Will this work?" asked Jimmy producing his Norelco trimmer from his travel bag.

"Yes to shave a spot on the back of Panda's neck, but I'll need a straight razor as well."

Panda purred the whole time. He loved the attention and begged to be massaged with Marla's "electric boyfriend" as she called her dildo.

Jimmy found his old time straight razor also in his travel bag; a souvenir given to him by the late George Jones. As Marla worked on Panda, who purred with the vibration of the electric razor., Jimmy broke into song. It was one he had written for George in the eighties. George said he was the King of Sad Songs, but this one was too sad for him: Jimmy sang in a country drawl,

I was cleanin' out my old electric razor

It is a Norelco 4-0-2

When I noticed all them whiskers

Turned to silver

And I reckon that it's all because of you

Now I'm takin' out my rusty old straight razor

■■■

I'm gonna run it right across my old red neck

Yeah, your Old Man's goin' away.

What the heck?"

"Stop it, Jimmy!" Marla howled, "I'm gonna cut Panda's ol' black neck if you keep that up!"

Marla deftly removed the microchip with tweezers and, put a Band-Aid dot on a stillpurring Panda. She then flushed the chip down the toilet.

She then peaked out of a corner of the foil covered window."They're baaaack!"

"Ok, time for a little neighborhood recon." Jimmy donned the helmet and his new bright blue trenchie; jumped on his bike and headed out onto 7th Avenue.

He saw a moving SUV and pulled alongside it with the resonator turned up. "Shoot, everyone inside is naked!" Jimmy thought. "Need to dial down to see what they are doing. OMG! Green Suits!"

The SUV turned south onto Garfield Place. Jimmy was glad he had moved from there and in with Marla. He was also glad that his friend Hy was on a business trip to San Francisco. Jimmy watched from the flower shop at the corner of 7th and Garfield as eight men in green suits broke into Hy's brownstone. Jimmy moved closer and ducked in under a neighbor's stoop. From the sound of things, they trashed the entire house looking for him and the two million, he supposed.

The next day Jimmy went to his mail drop in the Bronx. He hadn't been there in a week. Not many people knew he even had a mailbox at Kinko's. Pretty 20th Century. There was only one innocuous brown envelop amidst the usual anonymously addressed junk mail The envelope contained a letter that confirmed what Jimmy had suspected for a month—The Lotto Commission knew he was the Jack Pot Winner at Grand Central Station.

Dear Mr. Johnson,

Congratulations on winning the "Ginormous Pay Day" at Grand Central Station! We at the Lotto Commission know that you must have been so excited and simply forgot that sharing your good fortune with the TV audience is a requirement of the Lotto Act and therefore we expect you to show up for the celebratory interview. Our agent will meet you at Tavern on the Green at seven o'clock on September 21st to enjoy a fine meal and go over the details of the interview. Sincerely yours, Mario F. Belladonna, Commissioner.

"Wow, that's tomorrow night!" Jimmy noticed the letter was dated September 12, 2019.

Jimmy sped over to Jason's place to tell him about the latest developments.

A grim faced Jason said, "I warned you, my friend. And you know they will probably kill you at that meeting or on the way to the TV station. They use the seventh generation of my miniature laser pistol. IT is much more powerful than my prototype. The best protection from such a laser is a mirror."

Jimmy said, "I don't think they'd be so brazen. The Tavern on the Green is a very public place. I think they really do want me to testify on how great the Lotto is. And my being a still slightly famous guy and consumer advocate can only be to their advantage. Don't you think?"

"That's all pretty logical,Jimmy, still you might need these." Jason said handing Jimmy a pair of fashionable concave sun glasses. "These will help you riding your bike when you get used to them. They are high grade optically with a micro layer of titanium."

Jimmy put them on. "Sheesh, that's weird! I can't see through anything, but it's like ultra- focused tunnel vision."

"Yes, Jimmy, and remember your physics—the angle of incidence equals the angle of reflection."

Next afternoon with the Chromatics version of *I'm on Fire*playing in the background from an XM radio, Marla and Jimmy made love. The scent of lavender wafted through the open window. Jimmy kissed her and said, "Wish me luck—and watch the news tonight."

■■

Chapter 14 Tavern on the Green

Jimmy Jack then rode his Indian across the Brooklyn Bridge and made his way to Central Park and Tavern on the Green. He gave his name "Jimmy" to the hostess and he was guided to a small table in the back of the mammoth restaurant. There, sitting alone, at a small table behinda giant fern was Harold Gratzky, munching on an appetizer salad.

"You're late Mr. Johnson." It was 7:05.

"The traffic was horrible."

"Traffic's always horrible in New York. I'm Harold Gratzky, but you can call me Butch.

"What will you have? I like the bacon stuffed rib-eye and three cheese mashed potatoes."

Jimmy looked at Gratzky's enormous gut that rendered his belt invisible and thought I bet you do, Butch Gratzky.

"I think I'll go with the pasta primavera and the Tavern Salad."

■■

"Mr. Johnson, do you know why we are having this here little meetin'?" "Sure. You want to set up the FOX interview so I can scream and shout the praises of the Lotto and say anybody can be as lucky as me."

Jimmy then howled "WOOOOEEEE I WON I WON WOOOOEEEE!!"

Then he lowered his voice as startled patrons were looking their way. "Am I right, Mr. Gratzky?"

An unruffled Gratzky replied "Not exactly, Mr. Johnson. You see, you was supposed to wait for the FOX News crew to show up and catch you at the most excitin' moment of your life. Mr. Johnson, the law requires it."

Gratzky then removed a small silver colored object from the inside pocket of his bright green suit jacket.It looked like a digital camera, but Jimmy knew otherwise.

"Hold still Mr. Johnson while I take a pitcher of you."

"Gee it sure is bright in here." Jimmy said as he donned his concave sunglasses.

Butch Gratzky then quickly aimed and fired a ZR7 at Jimmy's left eye. But the concave lens reflected the beam back into Gratzky's right eye and he did a face plant into his Triple Cheese mashed potatoes.

Jimmy casually recovered the ZR7; slipped it into his pocket and strode off smiling. "The angle of incidence equals the angle of reflection. Uh huh, that works for me!"

Sirens wailed as the EMT ambulance meant for Jimmy arrived. Instead they removed the body of Harold Gratzky.

Next stop for Jimmy was the New York Public Library. Due to budget cuts it was open only one evening a week. Luckily that was this night. Jimmy went directly to the laptop carrels and deep into the internet to find an article on the ZR7, his new toy.

He learned that the range of the model 7 was 30 yards and that it could be recharged the same as a cell phone. He also learned, to his dismay, that government issued ZR7s also had a tracking device. He googled another site under the search*Removing tracking devices from the ZR7.*

"Ok, there you are you little bastard." Jimmy muttered to himself as he used his Swiss Army knife to remove the tracking chip. His military training was finally paying off.

Just for fun, he selected a copy of *Nineteen Eighty-Four* from the automated book finding system and moments later the book shot out of a large vending machine. Jimmy inserted the tracking chip into the book, left it on a library table, then casually strolled out of the building and blended into the crowd. Moments later an LSA swat team descended on the reading room ready to blow away a copy of George Orwell's greatest hit.

When Jimmy returned to Marla's apartment, she and Panda were nowhere to be seen. He found a note written in lipstick on the bathroom mirror. It simply said, "All good things must end."

■■

■■

Chapter 15 Oxford and London

At first Jimmy felt utterly destroyed by the abandonment by Marla. In all the relationships he had been involved in, he was always the leaver, never the one left. He went to a nearby bar to blur the desolation. Soon it dawned on him that Marla couldn't say anything that would reveal his or her whereabouts. He went to Jason's place to bring him up-to-date on things. Jason, the cool headed scientist said, "Well, Jimmy you know there's only one place where she was likely to go."

"And where might that be?"

"Oxford."

"Oxford, yes, of course you are right. Gotta go, Jason!"

Jimmy then took a subway to Brighton Beach and hooked up with his Russian mob connections.

"Passport? No problems. Teeket? No problems," Dimitri said.

■■

If you had enough money there were never any problems the Russians couldn't fix overnight.

The next afternoon Jimmy Jack Johnson, a.k.a. Malcomb G. Anderson, was on his way to JFK clean shaven with his new brown wig, blue contact lenses, and his prominent protruding teeth all part of the $30,000 "traveler's special package" supplied by the Russian Mafia. He stopped by Jason's place for some more traveling money.

Jason also chipped in with a special carry-on bag. It looked like the currently fashionable bright orange bags that many frequent flyers went to, but it had a nice feature that none of the other bags had: a secret compartment for the ZR7 laser pistol. A magnetic field generated in a small compartment in the bag rendered it invisible to x-rays. To TSA scanners, the ZR7 in the compartment looked like a pair of folded socks. Jimmy settled in his first class seat for the overnight flight to Heathrow.

Marla was not too hard to find once Jimmy mastered the left hand drive of his rented Jaguar and found the School of Archeology. She was, as expected, in the Arthur J. Barringer Lab. Jimmy felt a rush of *dejavu*. He had seen a picture of Myra in this same lab 50 years ago, and there she was, unchanged, in 2019. Marla was Myra in many ways, mostly in appearance and temperament and about the same age when Jimmy first met Myra.

At first Marla didn't recognize him. But when Malcomb Anderson began humming *All Good Things Must End*, she laughed. They embraced. "Kinda like the brown hair and blue eyes, but them buck teeth has got to go!"

Marla said, "Sorry I left you without a good-bye. I'm sure you know why. That other SUV we saw did have some priests in it and, I am pretty sure, at least one of the lawyers who stole Amos."

■■

"Do you think they will show up here?"

"I do. One of the last things Mom was trying to nail down in her research was the DNA triggers of metamorphosis. She was sure that some kind of genetic impulse, based on age, was the mechanism for the 'morphing' of Amos. I found a notebook of hers that had a description of an experiment she had performed on seventeen year locusts. She thought she had discovered that the aging of DNA continued whether the locusts were hibernating or not."

"So then, Arthur Barringer might be a candidate for morphing regardless of a retarded aging process in everything else?"

"Exactly! Jeez, Jimmy, you are smarter than I thought," Marla chuckled. "In addition to running away, I needed to save Art lest the Vatican scientists make that same connection and send their Mafia after him."

"Great, but how are we gonna get a five ton freezer with a body in it outta here?"

"That's not going to happen. Instead of stealing Art away in the dark of night, we are going to go public with the whole business. We are going to announce to the world that Arthur Barringer, a 131 year old man, is going to be thawed out as a stent is inserted in his coronary artery. That is sensational enough, but can you imagine what will happen if he begins to morph?"

"And where should this operation take place?"

"Walter Reed Hospital with Dr. Daniel Cannon, the best heart surgeon money can buy, assisted by the cryopreservation team from Johns-Hopkins. I have been following their work for years. They solved the biggest obstacle last year when they revived a cat somebody had preserved since the 1960's. Something about preventing cell crystallization. Anyway, it worked; and that cat is still alive and coughing up hairballs as usual."

"So what's our first move?"

"While I guard the fort here, you take that Jag into London and invite Harvey McGarvey, Jr. who runs *Day Break* to lunch. You can tell him the whole story as Mom told you, Jimmy."

Harvey McGarvey, Jr. son of the notorious Harvey Sr. had been in charge of his late father's empire of tabloids and sensational reality TV channels since his father passed in 2008 at the age of eighty-three. With the announcements in the 1980's regarding the truth of the "Oxford Angel" Harvey's star rose. After all, it was he who had scooped the story thirty some years prior. Harvey Senior's "vindication" on the early angel piece that had nearly got him fired then propelled him to journalistic prominence. His series on alien abductions were taken very seriously by millions of people world-wide.

When Harvey, Jr. took the call from someone with "new information" about the Oxford Angel, he cleared his calendar and agreed to meet Jimmy for lunch at the Thistle Coventry Hotel on Leicester Square.

Harvey McGarvey Jr. was a round man; a round ruddy face atop a round body. He was balding and about sixty years of age wearing a purple suit, orange shirt, and a solid yellow-green tie.

"Pleased to meet you, Mr. Johnson" Harvey Jr. began. "I was a great admirer of your late stepmother, Myra, and I have an autographed copy of your first album—vinyl, of course!"

"And she came to respect your father even though I am sure she hated him when he tried to expose her secret in the early '50's."

"Yes, I know, but I fought the good fight alongside my father when that entire angel debunking was going on. As you know, *Day Break* is still on the record in support of the reality of angels."

"And the reality of UFO's as well," Jimmy couldn't help himself from interjecting that.

"Of course!" Harvey Jr. replied. "Not to mention my personal favorite series on the yeti, or, as he is known in America, 'Sasquatch.'"

Jimmy felt a bit nauseous but maintained his cool. "Harvey, we need you now. We need you to break a story that will make you even more famous than your late father."

"I am all ears."

"You may recall that the Amiens Angel was discovered by Myra Rosenblum and her future husband Arthur J. Barringer."

"Yes, my father told me all about that.""Then you probably know that immediately upon Arthur's death, Myra had him frozen, er, cryopreserved I think is the proper term."

"Yes, go on."

"Recent progress in cryopreservation now makes it possible to resuscitate a person, fix whatever killed them, and bring them back to a healthy life."

"Hah! I guess we weren't so far off last year when we reported that a 57 year old cat they thawed out, Molly was her name, was about to bear kittens. Our headline was GOOD GOLLY MISS MOLLY!"

"Yes, I know about that case. The part about the kittens wasn't true though was it?"

▪▪

"Well, no, they were borrowed from a shelter, but who's interested in a cat coughing up a hairball? That's not going to sell papers!"

"I get the point, Mr. McGarvey. But I don't think you will need to embellish what I am about to tell you."

"We specialize in embellishment, Mr. Johnson."

"Be that as it may, what if after being thawed and cured of his heart ailment, Arthur J. Barringer was transformed though metamorphosis into a living angel. Does that need any embellishment?"

"Well, will he fly about?" replied Harvey, making his fat arms into flapping wings.

"I suppose he could, but why not wait for him to do so rather than giving him attributes he may or may not have?"

"All right, Mr. Johnson, we won't embellish until the wings are fully formed."The two men shook on that. Then they proceeded to enjoy a fine meal over small talk about Jimmy's career, the state of politics in America ("Ghastly" was Harvey's word for that) and the latest gossip about King William V.

■■

Chapter 16 Resurrection

Within hours of the meeting with Harvey McGarvey, Jr. Jimmy and Marla were fending off reporters and paparazzi from around the world. King William and Princess Kate called to offer any help needed to "safely and securely transport your dear father to America." The next morning the procession of the freezer from Oxford to Heathrow was watched by 2.7 billion people around the world.

Pope Xavier was glued to his TV too. He made a call to his long-time friend from Chicago, Mario F. Belladonna. Pope Xavier, formerly Cardinal Ricci in Chicago, had quickly risen to prominence in the dark days following the assassination of the most beloved Pope Francis during a papal visit to Sâo Paulo.Rumors of Ricci's association with the "Company" as the mob called itself, created an undercurrent of conspiracy theories running rampant after Francis' assassination. But with the help of the American right, Cardinal Ricci became Pope Xavier. That was certainly the first time in history that a "Super Pac" campaign had been used to assure an election of a Pope. The National Rifle Association also invested a couple of million in the campaign to elect Ricci with ads that featured a National TV super church pastor saying "Being well-armed is a God-given right! On this ground Catholics and Protestants stand shoulder to shoulder in defense of freedom! Amen!"

As the first American Pope, there was considerable optimism amongst the religious right that Xavier would help them succeed to continue the movement toward making the American oligarchy more like the theocracy they wanted. Xavier had swelled support for the "Corporation-as-a-Person" idea by declaring "Corporations as persons can be born again to serve the Lord." Big corporate money began to flow into the coffers of not only the Catholic Church, but also to conservative protestant denominations as well. Xavier wasted no time in reversing the good works of Pope Francis.

Having renovated Emperor Hadrian's villa outside Rome as a "papal retreat," Xavier enjoyed entertaining the rich and famous there. Once a month, he would have the homeless children of Rome gathered up and out to the villa for a day to romp among the gardens and have their pictures made with the grinning Pope.

"Wazzup, Tony?" asked Mario Belladonna. Cardinal Anthony Ricci would always just be 'Tony' to Mario, even though now he was Pope Xavier.

"Mario, my friend, you have been watching the news?"

"Of course, that crap is all over. I can't even watch my favorite reality shows! There's nothin' on but, 'scuse the expression, that goddamned frozen guy!"

"Mario, that's unfortunate, but there's something important I must share with you. Wasn't James Jackson Johnson one of the more important fugitives on your hit list?"

"Hell, yes! We've been looking for him for months. What's he got to do with Mr. Popsicle?"

"Heh heh! Well, Mr. Popsicle as you call him is Arthur J. Barringer the father of Marla Rosenblum-Barringer."

"So, what?" asked Mario, failing to connect the dots.

"Mario, sometimes I wonder how you got your big government job. Jimmy Jack is Marla's half step brother! Our people found them in England, but we couldn't do anything about it since the whole thing blew up in a media storm. They have five Navy Seals and half the British Army protecting the shipment of Popsicle Barringer to the USA."

"What's this have to do with Church stuff, Tony?I thought that angel was proved fake."

"Well, we did a lot to make it seem so. But I'm telling you, that angel is real, Mario. And, get this: We know how an old person must be to transformed into an angel."

"No, shit!"

"Yes, shit. And we can't let that shit happen. An angel would be a loose cannon on the deck of our ship. God knows when it would go off. Anything an angel would say would be taken as The Word straight from God Almighty. It just isn't worth the risk."

Mario was almost speechless. "So you want my guys to take out an angel? Thought you was all about the right-to-life?" Mario needled the Pope.

"Mario, we do make exceptions."

"Yeah, an angel here; a saint there," Mario goaded.

"Francis is not a saint yet. If I have anything to do with it, he never will be!"

The Pope, speaking on a supposedly secure phone, had no idea his conversation with the Commissioner of the Lotto Security Agency was being taped by the National Security Agency.

The flight carrying Jimmy, Marla, and the frozen body of Arthur J. Barringer from Heathrow to Dulles International was uneventful. Marla and Jimmy didn't need to pass customs—everybody by now knew who they were and the President herself cleared all the paperwork with one small executive order.

The Cryopreservation Team from Johns-Hopkins was waiting with Dr. Cannon at Walter Reed Veterans Hospital. Marla and Jimmy were told it would be 24 hours for the whole process plus the operation time before they would be allowed to see Art.

With Secret Service protection, ordered by the President, the couple were escorted to the Mayflower Hotel. Three hundred paparazzi trailed in the wake of the convoy. Marla and Jimmy were given the Presidential Suite and enjoyed a complimentary meal of Chateau Briand, new potatoes, escargot, and truffles. They were worn out and jet-lagged when they descended into the folds of the creamy soft covers on the king-sized bed.

Far below on the street the school of media sharks waited for any fish, big or small, that happened to swim by. Bellmen and kitchen workers were accosted. The Secret Service had to send for reinforcements. In La Fayette Park an enterprising busboy was paid $1000 by a stringer from FOX News for revealing the contents of the complimentary meal served to Marla and Jimmy.

Meanwhile, at Walter Reed, the team from Johns Hopkins and Dr. Daniel Cannon worked through the night bringing Art Barringer back to life.

■■

"It doesn't look good," Dr. Dan said to Dr. Tobias Saunders who headed up the J-H group. "He's alive, but comatose. The stent is working; good blood flow; transfusion accepted. But we have almost a flat-line on brain activity. Call Marla."

Marla and Jimmy were still asleep when the call came. Marla with tears in her eyes said to Jimmy, "He made it through the thaw-out and the heart operation, but they say his brain isn't working. Oh, hell, Jimmy! They want me to come over there right away."

An NSA helicopter whisked Marla and Jimmy to Walter Reed. Dr. Cannon greeted them grim faced. "You should know there's a slim chance that Art will pull out of this. I think there may have been a problem with the transfusion."

"Jesus Christ, Doc! Didn't you get the right type of blood?"

"Yes, Marla, we had the right blood type, of course! But my colleague, Dr. Omar Singh, an endocrinologist, said to me that he feared we may need a better match even to the DNA level."

"Yikes, well, OK. Here I am rolling my sleeve up now." Marla was quick to read Dr. Dan even before he asked for her blood.

Dr. Cannon said, "We are going to need a lot Marla. It won't kill you, but you won't want to do anything for a few days after we pull a quart and a half out of you."

"I'm OK with that; I can use the rest."Marla was fixed with an IV and rolled into the surgery. She was more than a little shaken by the appearance of her father. His skin looked pale blue. His face was drawn inward, cheekbones prominent. In a minute the blood exchange was on. Marla passed out before the thirty minute procedure was complete. She was then wheeled to a recovery room accompanied by Jimmy Jack. An orderly paid close attention as the gurney made its way to a secure part of the hospital. He pulled out his smartphone and made a call.

"Simon, here" The orderly said, "Targets B and C are on their way to a recovery unit with a Secret Service guard. 'Target A' still in isolation, could be dead already."

On the other end of that call, Mario F. Belladonna, said, "Thanks, you done good, Boy."

Belladonna alerted his team of thugs in DC and they headed for Walter Reed.

In the Intensive Care Unit at Walter Reed Hospital, changes were already taking place with Arthur Barringer's appearance. The head nurse and a young woman fresh out of Duke's revitalized nursing program were quick to notice that Art's skin had begun to change from pale blue to pale pink. They immediately called Dr. Cannon who brought Dr. Singh with him.

"Amazing!" was the first word from Cannon's mouth.

"Truly, so!" chimed in Dr. Singh.

In Marla's room, Jimmy, was singing in a whisper, "All Good Things Must End" as a lullaby to Marla. A few minutes later there was a tapping on the door. It was Simon Plumtree the orderly in bright orange scrubs.

"Brought you some refreshments, Mr. Jackson," Simon said getting Jimmy's last name wrong.

Jimmy grew immediately suspicious. Orderlies don't carry food. And why hadn't the Secret Service guy poked his head in to check up on things as he had several times in the past hour?

Jimmy said looking at the orderly's name tag, "Gee thanks, uh, Mr. Plumtree, what service! You deserve a tip."

"Uh, we don't take no tips, Mr. Jackson."

Simon was pulling his ZR7 from a pocket in his ill-fitting orderly uniform as Jimmy pulled his from Marla's tote bag. For a second Simon was utterly surprised. His shot missed Jimmy and burnt a hole in the wall. Jimmy's shot burnt a hole in Simon's face and he screamed in pain. He tried to get another laser shot off, but Jimmy second try sent the beam into Simon's eye and into his brain.

Jimmy found a linen cart in which to stuff Simon's body. In the linen closet, Jimmy discovered the body of the Secret Service agent. He then pulled both bodies out of the closet; laid them near each other with their ZR7s nearby.

Back in Marla's room, Jimmy showered and called the FBI.

"Hey, this is Jimmy Jack Johnson. You better get some guys up here quick. I just found my guard and an orderly dead outside this room!"

The FBI was there in minutes.

"Yeah, must have happened when I was in the shower. Whaddaya think happened? Why would the Secret Service kill an orderly? The guy had just left these refreshments."

"Did you eat or drink anything?" the agent asked.

"No. Why?"

"Could be poisoned. We just did an instant fingerprint check on that orderly. He is not an orderly. Not on the payroll here. He's Simon Plumtree and, get this: he is on the payroll of the Lotto Security Agency. Looks like the SS agent got suspicious and they killed each other with laser pistols. Plumtree was probably after you or Miss Rosenblum.

"Why would the LSA want to kill us? I should want to kill some of them for all the money I've wasted on those damned machines!"

As the agent was about to leave, Jimmy clearly saw the burnt hole in the wall left by Simon's poor marksmanship. The blue chewing gum in Jimmy's mouth was the perfect spackle for that hole matching the wall color almost perfectly.

They next day, Marla awoke, groggy but starving. "Hey, Jimmy, whazup?"

"Oh, nothin' much, some guy from LSA tried to kill us right here in the room."

"What the hell!" Marla exclaimed. "I thought we had all the security our tax dollars can buy."

"Well, you know, budget sequesters; seems like we taxpayers can afford only one guard at a time." Jimmy joked; then he told Marla the whole story.

"Gawd, Jimmy, did you remember to charge up your ZR7? Sounds like we might need it."

The couple donned sterile garments and masks and were permitted to visit Art for a few minutes. He had made noticeable progress not only in appearance but in other functions as well. Marla held his hand, "Hi, Daddy." She said softly.

■■■

Art, thinking she was Myra, could only offer a weak smile.

Marla wept. Her father was beginning to look just like the pictures Myra always kept. He was looking positively healthy! She held his gnarled hand. He had a pretty strong grip.

The nurses made them leave the ICU. As soon as Jimmy got his protective clothing off he began to chatter.

"Jeezus, Marla, he looks great! Even handsome. And I'm not talking about your average 131 year old guy either! Is he morphing? Is that what's happening? Holy Cow!"

Marla, crying tears of joy could only nod her head.

They had heavy guards as they returned to their room at the Mayflower. The room was electronically swept by the NSA and one bug was detected. It happened to be one of their own so it was replaced, "for security purposes" and they showed Jimmy where it was so he could be near enough to it to call for help if need be. As soon as the agents left, Jimmy flushed the bug down the toilet. "No, Marla, at this point I don't trust anybody—that is except you."

In New York, an operative with the LSA called Mario Belladonna. "Plumtree's dead. Looks like he and a NSA guard killed each other."

"Shit Almighty!" Mario exclaimed. "So where are A, B, and C now?"

"Jimmy Jack and Marla are now under heavy guard at the Mayflower. We thought the Popsicle had melted, but they increased guards there in the ICU as well, so he must still be alive."

■■

"OK, I'll call the Pope. Sounds like we may need some divine intervention."

The call to Xavier did not go well for Mario.

"You dumb bastard! Why did you only send one guy to Reed. You don't go mano y mano in a situation like this." Xavier was shouting at Belladonna as if he were a an errant schoolboy in a Catholic orphanage which is exactly where Father Anthony Ricci had met him three decades before.

"Sorry, Father, uh er, your Eminence. We will make good on this, I promise, hail Mary and hope to die."

Pope Xavier calmed down enough to apologize and said, "Look, Mario, I do trust you to get things done. I'm sending a couple of my best guys from Catania."

"Are they Sicilians?"

"No, Mario, they are Lithuanians!"

"Lutherans? Did you say Lutherans?"

"Of course they are Sicilians, you idiot! I'll let you know when to pick them up at JFK." Then Pope Xavier hung up and looked over at his aide saying, "Jesus, Joseph, and Mary! Is that guy dumb or what!"

▪▪

Chapter 17 Near Asheville North Carolina

Jimmy and Marla agreed with the NSA that moving Art to the estate near Asheville was the best choice. There were 700 acres of fields and forest and the mansion, Kirkland Hall, stood high on a mountain slope with long views and a helipad for Kirk Johnson's vintage Vietnam War Era "Huey." The family said Kirk was too old to fly anymore, but he kept the chopper in prime shape for an occasional show appearance in the Confederate Air Force.

The military plane buffs that went all over the country for air shows would borrow the Huey from time-to-time.

The Barringer party was given use of "Marine 1," the President's own helicopter to move Art, the Johns-Hopkins Team, Dr. Cannon, and Jimmy and Marla, to the estate. Three black SUVs with Secret Service agents arrived to reinforce the contingent that flew down in the big 'copter.

The Secret Service spent the better part of two weeks securing the perimeter of the grounds. They then conducted interviews and did extensive background checks with the owners of all the properties contiguous to the Rosenblum-Johnson Estate now known as Kirkland Hall.

The late Rev. Willy Garman's nearby Evangelical Missionary Center or "The EMC" was one place visited by the Secret Service.

"Good day, Suh!" An agent from Alabama named Farley beamed as he spoke to Franklin Garman who met them at the door.

A phone call had alerted Franklin so he was not surprised at seeing a Black Chevrolet Suburban with blacked out windows arrive in the driveway.

"I can't thank you enough for all the good work you gentlemen did for our family at my father's funeral. We could never have handled those crowds, much less the dignitaries that came to The EMC. We even had Cardinal Ricci here before he got elected Pope. Stayed right up there next to my own bedroom. I couldn't tell his bodyguards from y'all's"

"Well, we are here to serve and protect. Today we just want to make sure y'all are safe and you will let us know if anything out of the ordinary shows up on your property."

"I certainly will. Things have been pretty calm here since the year after Ex-President Barack Hussein Obama settled just over the ridge in Black Mountain."

Farley chuckled and asked, "Did they name it Black Mountain before or after Obama came here?"

"Long before, Agent Farley, long before, but that's a good one! Actually these days so many Mexicans live in Black Mountain they are thinking of renaming the town, 'Montenegro'!"

"You're kidding!"

"Yes, Agent Farley, I am kidding. Say, why weren't you assigned to protect Barack Hussein Obama in his retirement?"

"Well, I wanted to. I was the one who always got the gofer job to run to Twelve Bones barbeque for Obama during his several trips to Asheville. Sure do like those ribs! But, Mr. Garman, to be honest, I failed the bodyguard test.

"You failed the bodyguard test? And what was this bodyguard test?"

"Well, Reverend Garman, I know you won't repeat this. But if I can't trust you, who can I trust?"

"Mr. Farley I certainly do trust you."

"So, you see, they had only one question on the test and that was: would you take a bullet for the President? I had to be honest 'cause they had me wired up to a polygraph. If I said 'yes' the polygraph would have squiggled so I told the truth and said, 'no'."

"What happened then?"

"Well, they didn't fire me. I got demoted, and here I am in Asheville again. Can't wait to get me some of them Twelve Bones' ribs."

The other agents talked to Garman's own bodyguards; shared some shop-talk and most of the contingent then headed straight to Twelve Bones.

Chapter 18 Metamorphosis

With the assistance of Mission Hospital of Asheville, the second floor of the west wing of Kirkland Hall had been transformed. It was now a state-of-the art I.C. unit run by Doctors Cannon and Singh who had both taken sabbaticals to devote themselves to seeing their star patient fully recover.

▪▪

Shortly after arriving in North Carolina, Arthur J. Barringer at the ripe young age of 131 years began his transformation. In the first week he began to speak. His first words were, “Where the hell is Myra?”

Marla appeared with tears in her eyes, “She’s gone, Daddy. She’s gone. I am so sorry.”

“Gone where?”

“Gone to Heaven, Daddy.”

“Come on Myra. You know I don’t believe in heaven. You’re here and stop calling me ‘Daddy’.”

“Look, Art, here’s a calendar. It’s August 25, 2019. I’m your daughter Marla.”

“Who’s this fellow? Do I know you?” Art asked, looking over at Jimmy.

“No. I am Jimmy Jack Johnson. I’m Marla, your daughter’s, er uh, friend.”

“So, a sixty something man is ‘friends’ with my four year old daughter?”

“Daddy, Jimmy and I are both sixty-six, now. You have been asleep for the past sixty-two years!

I am not sure you remember the will that you gave to Mom. It provided that you be frozen until you could be thawed-out and cured of the cause of your death.”

“I died?”

“Yep. In 1957.”

“Oh, God, I am remembering now. I remember that as if were yesterday. I was in the lab. I was lifting a goddamned microscope from a crate. Heavy bastard. The radio was playing *Earth Angel.* I was dancing with my wife. Myra was helping with the electron microscope and that’s the last thing I remember. We got that scope to examine our uh, er…"

"It's OK Daddy, the secret is out. Myra, that is, Mom, got all the evidence she needed to prove that the Amiens Angel was real. And now, you are the first successful cryopreserved human being to be thawed out and cured. A great heart surgeon, Dr. Dan Cannon, whom you shall soon meet, patched you up and stented your heart. I see on the monitor your heart is performing admirably."

Jimmy spoke up, "I think your Dad needs a rest, Marla. Good to meet you Dr. Barringer. We'll see you tomorrow."

"Bye, Daddy, see you in the morning!"

That night Art felt throbbing pain in his legs and back. He informed a nurse and Dr. Cannon came to his side. "Hello Dr. Barringer, I am Dan Cannon, your heart surgeon."

"Good to meet you sir, my daughter spoke highly of you. I guess you are pretty good since you resuscitated an Old Fart like me and fixed my heart as well. Thank you very much!"

After a few questions about the intense pains, he called an osteopathic surgeon he knew from Mission Hospital, Dr. Henry Bell, to come to Kirkland Hall for a look at Art.

"Dan, I have never seen anything like this," Bell said after some x-rays came back. "I just compared the ones taken tonight from some of two weeks ago in Arthur's file from Walter Reed. Look!"

"Wow, his leg bones are both longer and thicker. No wonder he's in pain!"

"And his back?"

"Looks like a deformity of bones. His legs and arms appear to have severe osteoporosis, but that's not weakening the bone structure; it's somehow actually strengthening the bones." They too are growing like weeds. What the hell is going on there?"

"Hank, you aren't going to believe this. Our patient, Arthur J. Barringer, is morphosing."

"What?"

"Yes, he's going through metamorphosis just like the butterflies in your backyard."

"Holy, cow! I thought all those stories in the papers and TV were just a bunch of crap."

"Well, you better start believing, Hank. The best we can do now would be to raise his dosage of Percocet and let him get some sleep."

The night nurse, Ms. Leonard looked in on Art at 2:00 AM. "Oh, my God!" She screamed and called for Dr. Cannon.

Art's pillow was covered in blood. Some was still oozing from his mouth. Dan Cannon soon discovered a half dozen of Art's teeth on the pillow and the floor. "It's OK, Nurse Leonard, he's just teething. Getting a brand new set."

"Oh, wow!" was all the nurse could say.

At the dinner table the following evening, Marla, Jimmy, Dr. Cannon, Dr. Singh, Kirk Johnson, and, just arrived, Jason Faircloth chatted about current events and what was happening with Art.

▪▪▪

Marla asked Dr. Cannon, "What do you think will happen next?"

"I really can't tell you, Marla. This is all virgin territory for me. It does appear that Art is metamorphosing, or, 'morphing' as your late mother called it. I watched her stunning presentation at Albert Hall. It's on YouTube. I am just speculating, but it seems that his transformation is so rapid that it is causing him some pain—growing pains, if you will. Last night he began to get a new set of teeth in his enlarged jaws."

"Does he show any signs of wings, yet?" Jimmy asked the question that was on the minds of a billion people."

"Not yet, but there has been considerable growth in the area of the scapulae."

"That's shoulder blades!" chimed in Kirk who was getting a bit senile in his ninety-third year.

"Well, his physical state is one thing. What about his mental state?" Asked Jason Faircloth.

Cannon replied, "That's not my area of expertise; I'm just a layman in that regard. I do think his mind is working fine. The TV is causing him some confusion all relative to a sixty plus year gap in technology and history."

"Yes!" Marla exclaimed, "I was using my iPad next to his bed while he was sleeping. I woke up and he looked at what I was doing. He was astonished when I gave him a nutshell history of computing, the Internet and so on. I told him about Sputnik and that now there were thousands of satellites that could communicate with all kinds of devices, even telephones. All he could say was 'Good Lord!'"

■■■

Jason said, “Not surprising since technology in the past sixty years has surpassed everything that came before that in the history of mankind.”

Dr. Cannon made a suggestion: “I think we need a brain expert here to assess what’s happening with Arthur’s mind.” Everyone agreed.

Dr. Singh offered the name of a colleague, Dr. Francesca Biscotti, also at Johns-Hopkins.

“Sounds Aye-talian,” Kirk said with eyes closed. Everyone else thought he was asleep.

“Yeah, Pop, you’re right. Why don’t you go take a nap?” Jimmy frowned at his father.

Chapter 19An Awakened Mind

Dr. Francesca Biscotti, a strikingly beautiful forty-something Italian-American woman with a perfect figure, high cheekbones, soft dark brown eyes and flowing raven locks. She arrived at Kirkland the next afternoon looking more like a super-model than one might imagine a brain surgeon might look. She wore a purple mini skirt suit and had a bright yellow scarf about her neck all in the highest fashion. She had a sparkling bracelet on her left wrist and in her right hand she carried a yellow leather Louis Vuitton briefcase.

"Now, Jimmy, don't you get any ideas." Marla said, after the couple greeted Dr. Biscotti.

"Who, me? I don't have any ideas."

"Jimmy, your mouth was hanging open. Any minute you would have slobbered like a pit bull."

Dr. Biscotti was introduced to Art who also had a mouth agape as he managed to mumble, "Very pleased to meet you, Doctor. And to what god do I owe thanks for your visitation?"

"I am going to check your brain, Dr. Barringer."

"To see if I have one? Really, thanks for coming, I have been having some fierce headaches the past couple of days."

"Let me check some data here." Dr. Biscotti said looking at several lines of brain activity on the oscilloscope. "Hmmm, my goodness, your brain certainly is busy!"

"Yes, it should be. Marla leant me her computer pad thing. She gave me a couple of lessons on its use and I have been trying to catch up on the past sixty-years with it. Just passed the Cuban Missile Crisis. Damn, that was a close one!"

"Well, don't try to download too much information at one time." Dr. Biscotti smiled.

▪▪

She then proceeded to give him some tests of mental acuity. At first they were ordinary pattern recognition tests and tests of cognitive skills. Knowing he had been an archeologist and paleoanthropologist she tried a trick question, "What is the oldest humanoid skeleton ever found and who found it?"

"Uh, that would be 'Lucy' found by Dr. Donald Johansson in the 1970's. I'll share a secret about Lucy sometime with you, Doctor."

"Dr. Barringer, you lied to me! You said you were only up to the early 1960's googling on your tablet. Your answer is correct, so how did you know that?"

"Ha ha! Gotcha, Dr. Biscotti!" Art exclaimed. I did cheat. In my fields of study I went ahead—I guess curiosity just got the better of me. I am very much up to date in my areas. I watched my wife Myra give a great presentation at Albert Hall. It's on YouTube, you know."

"So what else do you know, Dr. Barringer?"

"Lots. It would take more time than you have for me to 'download,' as you say, all that information to you. And, FYI, I am actually a bit smarter than I used to be."

"Really?"

"Uh-huh. Take math for instance. Used to be terrible. Couldn't think that way. I really struggled with Calculus. That's probably why I chose a field closer to social science. I was OK with statistics at the level I needed. But, as I just discovered, when thinking about relativity yesterday, that I do understand Einstein's equations. Dr. Biscotti, give me a medium sized number, say 15 digits."

"OK, 907247828397654" Francesca spouted off a number consisting of a friend's phone number and her security code number at NIH. She counted off the digits with her fingers. Do you need me to write that down?"

"No. I have it. The square root is 30120554.9. See what I mean?"

"Amazing!" said Biscotti checking the result on her smartphone. I have seen a mathematical savant do that kind of thing, but no 'normal' people can do that."

"So, I am 'abnormal'?" Art feigned a sad look.

"Well, I apologize for that usually negative connotation. So I will I will say you are 'supra-normal.'"

"That's better!" Art replied smiling broadly.

"Arthur, I'd like to check your sensory perception now. You know, just to see if you are functioning well in that regard." Dr. Biscotti suggested.

"Ok, Doctor, want to check my vision?"

"Sure. That's as good a place as any." Francesca replied as she removed an eye chart from her brief case.

"That won't be necessary, Doc. I already know I can read the bottom line from fifty feet. I can also tell you that your diamond bracelet is not made of platinum and diamonds as you probably think."

"What? This was a gift from Micky McGarvey. He said it was genuine platinum and diamonds. He said he bought it a Harry Winston's in New York."

"Are you saying that playboy son of Harvey McGarvey, Jr. gave that to you? Not surprised there's fakery involved."

"Yes." A mortified Francesca replied. "Then what is this bracelet made of?"

■■

"From here, what am I sixteen feet away? I'd say it is fourteen caret white gold with a dozen cubic zirconium stones On you, quite lovely, despite its worth of maybe $500 at the Grand Bazaar in Istanbul "

A shaken Dr. Biscotti exclaimed, "Well, so much for the vision tests! Now on to hearing."

"Oh yes, my aural faculties seem enhanced as well. I listened to the Audubon Society bird calls on line. It really is amazing how they have evolved. I think I can pick up many from some distance around here. Open the window, please, doctor."

Francesca went to the window, opened it and let some fresh mountain air into the room.

"There, can you hear them?"

"Just a crow. Are there more?"

"There were five other birds singing a few minutes ago: a bluebird, a cardinal male and female, two chick-a-dees, and an English sparrow. They stopped singing when the crow arrived. The male cardinal sounded a warning to his mate and any other birds that might be attacked by a crow. Nasty predators at times those crows."

"Guess I can check off another abnormal, I mean supra-normal, trait of yours."

"I'm good at smelling, too!" Amos grinned. "When you were standing near me I detected Chanel No. 5. That was my late wife's favorite."

"Amazing! I wore that scent on my date last week with Micky McGarvey " I assure you I have bathed several times since."

"Of course you have, Francesca. But even Dove soap cannot completely subdue Chanel No. 5."

■■■

Dr. Biscotti reported to Doctors Cannon, Singh and Faircloth, "Dr. Barringer has the strongest mental capacity I have ever seen." She then told of his massive data acquisition through an iPad and his just discovered super mathematical computing ability. She also told about the enhanced sensory perception and relished them with the anecdotes "My work here is done for now, I need to get back to Bethesda," said Dr. Biscotti bidding her colleagues farewell. "Can't wait to I get my hands on that rascal Micky McGarvey! Cubic zirconium indeed!"

The assembled doctors had a good laugh as Francesca departed.

As Dr. Biscotti left the house, a wistful Jason Faircloth played *Time to Say Goodbye* by Sarah Brightman and Andrea Bocelli on his iPhone X.

"Will our angel ever cease to amaze us?" Dr. Cannon offered a reply to his own rhetorical question, "Probably not."

The next week was full of more surprises from Art although some were anticipated by the experts at Kirkland Hall.

"Did you notice his skin?" Marla asked Jimmy as they left Art to his computers, now numbering four since Marla took her 'slow' iPad back.

"Yeah, he's getting fuzzy. His body, I mean. And I noticed his eyes are always darting when you aren't speaking to him," Jimmy said, having noticed the down-like hair appearing on Art's face and hands, as well as his seeming inattention unless you had something profound to say or ask.

"Uh-huh, it's as if he gets bored with us and our petty questions about what he wants to eat, for instance."

■■

"And does he ever eat! He said, he would rather not have any meat, but that for the time being he couldn't consume enough protein without it. He had a plate of eggs and two prime rib steaks for breakfast! And he sure knows how to use his new set of pearly white teeth."

Marla added, "I'm glad he is up and walking. He was shaky at first---after all he hasn't walked for sixty-two years!"

Jimmy nodded, "Now I can't keep up with him when he starts to jog. The next thing will be the wings. Then he will start flying all over the place. That will drive the bodyguards nuts!"

Wings began to appear about a month after the morphing began. One day, as Art was flapping his fast growing wings on the balcony outside his room, he had the sudden urge to take off. Like a fledging robin just out of the nest the flight was more like a fall with a relatively soft landing. Jimmy, Marla, and the rest of the gang at Kirkland were horrified. Everyone came running.

"Good God, Daddy! You can't do that! Are you OK?"

"Yes, Dear," replied Art to Marla. "I just wanted to test my wings. I won't try that again until I get a little stronger and the wings stop growing."Art realized that he would need a lot more muscle if he were really going to fly.

The 'first flight' was recorded, however, by an ingenious paparazzi team with the aid of a tiny remote controlled drone flown off of a nearby mountain. The team hurriedly downloaded the video to Harvey McGarvey for which they were paid one million dollars. "A small price for the exclusive." Harvey would later tell FOX News.

But as it turned out, that fifteen second video was not exactly exclusive.

NSA Agent Floyd Farley surreptitiously caught the whole falling flight on his smartphone and quickly sent it off to Franklin Garman. "Get a load of this!" was the accompanying text message. In minutes the video was showing up on the cell phone of Pope Xavier. Farley's video was better than the one the paparazzi got because it was from ground level and the lighting was perfect.

"Mario? It's Tony."

Mario Belladonna took the call from the Pope. "Your Eminence! How's the weather in Rome today; hot as hell here in NYC."

"Mario, I am not interested in the weather! Have you been watching FOX News?"

"Uh, no, but I will turn it on now. It says, BREAKING NEWS: ANGEL FLIES!"

"That's right. The angel is flying and next thing we know he will be talking. The whole world will be waiting for Messages from God. No third parties needed! No churches; no preachers; NO POPE! Who will need us when they have the answers straight from God Almighty?"

"I know what you mean, Tony. Even my guys say they want to know things. Like my top guy, Butch Gratzky. He nearly died from a stroke he had in a restaurant earlier this year. Thinks he was saved by God. Said he wants to find out if God saved him or it was just dumb luck that he survived. This guy is not so bright, so I imagine there are thousands like him who also want to get closer to God."

"That's my point, Mario. This angel needs to be stopped!"

■■

■■

Chapter 20 The Angel Has Something to Say

In the next several days, the NSA decided they needed reinforcements at Kirkland Hall on account of a proliferation of drones that were shot down; a couple of hang-gliding intruders who were apprehended; and the sheer number of people camped all along the highways leading to or near Kirkland. Fifty-thousand was the conservative estimate along I-40. Traffic had come to a standstill. The NC State Police closed the highway between Black Mountain and Asheville.

In a festival atmosphere, bands played amongst the campgrounds that appeared like a skinny village in the median and right-of-way of the interstate. Signs, like letters to the angel read,

"We love you Art!" "What is God telling you?" "Deliver us from Evil!" And so on.

Marla asked her dad what he thought after he had seen the coverage on NPR, CNN, NBC, and FOX News.

"Well, my dear, I do have something to say. I am all caught up on current history, that is, of the past sixty-two years; I have read a thousand of the greatest works of literature; learnt seven languages; and I have digested a lot of scientific papers. I think I should share some of what I have gleaned from all that knowledge. I do have something to say. So shall we have some press conferences?"

"Well, Daddy, what will you talk about first?" Marla asked with Jimmy and Jason at her side.

"Probably the origin of life; why we are here? You know, some little questions. People need to know the truth. It will also help to explain me a little better."

"Are you implying that the current theories of evolution, natural selection, and adaptation are not correct? That science has it wrong?" Marla said with a shocked look on her face. Jimmy and Jason looked incredulous as well.

"They are reasonable as theories, of course. And, before you ask, 'Creationism' is bunk."

"Whew, I am glad you said that, Daddy!"

"Oh, and from now on I'm not 'Daddy' except in private. I need a new name since I have in effect been born again. In deference to you mother's pet name for the Amiens Angel, I am 'Amos the Second' or just 'Amos.' And, by the way, I am determined to get Amos the First back from those thieves at the Vatican."

"All right, I baptize thee, Amos II" said Marla giggling as she sprinkled some holy Perrier water on Art's head. The new Amos had a good laugh as well as did Jimmy and Jason.

"So where should we hold the press conference?" Marla asked.

"I think on-line would be best. But to catch the spirit the times and have real contact with people we'll let the media set up Jumbotrons along the highways from here to Greenville, Knoxville, Johnson City, and Charlotte. Put them every few miles or so. It will create spaces for millions of viewers outdoors as well as the billions world-wide on TV"

"Daddy, I mean 'Amos,' you must have studied a little PR as well as more serious stuff." Marla smiled.

"Yes, and I did some on-line shopping as well."

■■

"Oh no!" Jimmy exclaimed with a look of feigned horror on his face. "What in God's name did you order?"

"I bought three 'hotel quality' white terrycloth robes from Neiman-Marcus. They were a little pricey. Hope you don't mind, Marla; I used your credit card. I need them because beginning tomorrow when they arrive, I shall be wearing nothing but one of those robes and sandals as everyone in the world will expect. Afterall, when you cut out slits in the back for my wings they will feel a lot better than the ordinary clothes I have been trying to squeeze into."

The press conference took less than a week to arrange. The autumn leaves in the Blue Ridge Mountains were changing to crimson and gold. An army of technicians wired in the Kirkland Estate with cables and satellite antennas. A podium was erected outside the front porch of Kirkland Hall.

A relatively small contingent of dignitaries including scientists, religious leaders, and even a few politicians were allowed fifty seats in the front garden. The admitted press corps was drawn by lots and then heavily screened as well. Only four were selected.

It was a beautiful day in the mountains. The sky was as the English painter Constable would have had it: azure, with a few cotton-candy clouds. Kirk Johnson offered Amos, as he was now known, a shot of Jack Daniels before he strode out onto the porch. Amos refused, but said with a wink, "Save a shot for me after."

A surprise for the crowd and the world-wide audience was the introductory speaker, former President Barack Obama.

■■

"The man, our Angel, I am privileged to introduce has been known to you folks only through the press, which tends to embellish things, such as they often did with certain aspects of my presidency. I, too, have only known Amos the Angel, formerly known as Arthur J. Barringer, Archeologist, through the Media." The crowd chuckled. "I had not met him until twenty minutes ago. And I can tell you he is real. Just as real as my Birth Certificate." There was more laughter from the crowd and from the billion plus people around the globe who got the joke. "Without further ado, I give you Amos, a real American Angel!"

Amos stepped out of the shadows. The bright sun illuminated his flowing white hair and brilliant white robe. As a crowd pleaser to thunderous applause, Amos flared his wings to their fullest extent. He seemed to positively glow with unearthly radiance. The camera operators had a little trouble getting the light balance right which, in effect, created an aura as seen on TV.

"It is with the greatest humility that I stand today before the whole world with my fervent hope that I may share a message with you."

At this point people around the world were screaming, praying, rolling on the ground, fainting. It was as if Jesus Christ Himself had returned. And he hadn't even said anything yet. Amos waited for the initial hubbub to settle down.

"I come to you this day from a valley beyond time. I come to you through the grace of a Higher Power that created the universe and beyond; I come from a place that cannot be measured; from a time that has been lost in the aching void of eternity."

"What the hell is he saying, Marla?" Jimmy muttered under his breath.

■■■

"Hush, Jimmy, I don't know, but it's beautiful so far."

"The stars were heaped in windrows along the beachless shores of immensity." Amos waxed poetically.

"Hah, I gave him that line." Kirk smirked.

"And then through the eons a ship came upon that shore. And the shore was the planet earth."

"Holy shit, where is this going?" Jimmy said nudging Marla.

"Shush, Jimmy, he's just getting to the point!"

Amos then spoke of the origins of life. "One of the great questions of all the ages is where did we come from? The answer is,'Out there.' Way, way out there."

"Since this is supposed to be a press conference and not a speech, I'll take questions from journalists as well as from the more distinguished guests in our audience." There was a small ripple of laughter at the dig at journalists.

"A few questions will also be selected from those who Tweeted to #amostheangel. Let's go first with the gentleman from Australia."

"Thank you Amos. So, you're saying life did not originate on earth?"

"No, I said <u>we</u>, <u>humans</u>, that is, did not originate on earth. There already was life on earth for a long time when we humans came. No, I do not know exactly how, but I assume it was through a wormhole. Much research needs to be done on that. You see, we humans are vastly different from any other living creatures. We are simply not like other animals, even primates, in thousands of meaningful ways. We did not evolve from animals that were already here. We evolved elsewhere. Let's hear from a scientist on that matter."

Several hands shot up amid shouts of "Over here, over here!"

"Professor Whalen, UC Berkeley, am I right?" asked Amos, who already knew the answer from his deep knowledge of the background data on the entire guest list.

"Yes. Thank you. What you have just said is preposterous, even coming from an angel. I have been skeptical of you all along, and now I am sure you are a fraud! There is just too much evidence that evolution accounts for all diversity of species including the fact that we human primates are descended from a common ancestry with that of other primates."

"Dr. Whalen, with all due respect, what you say is partly correct, except in the case of humans."

"Ape and human DNA is very close. How do you explain that?" Whalen retorted.

"Actually, the explanation is quite simple. If I detect, say, carbon through spectrographic analysis in a star fifty light years from earth, it is carbon the same as is found on earth. Correct?"

"Yes, but what has that to do with DNA?"

"Everything, Professor Whalen, everything. You see, DNA is analogous to a chemical element or compound where life is concerned. You can't have life without it as it alone defines life. It is DNA that evolves. Not surprising at some point, given enough time and a trillion possibilities, some DNA goes on to become human DNA. No matter where it comes from it is the same. It can occur anywhere in the universe that conditions permit."

■■■

Reverend Franklin Garman asserted himself into the discussion. "Are you saying that God did not create Adam and Eve and everyone else along with all the creatures of the Earth?"

"No, Sir. You and all people of faith can believe anything you can imagine or choose to believe. You choose to believe the Bible as the 'word of God' as literal and unchanged whether written, translated or edited by humans, however well-meaning, over millennia. I certainly believe parts of the Bible are entirely possible in every sense. I also believe there is Truth in the literature of the Bible. As it says in the Bible, 'God works in mysterious ways his wonders to perform'. I believe that a Higher Power did create humankind and everything else. So, all I am saying is that a Higher Power, or a Great Spirit that most people cannot imagine, created the whole universe and not just this tiny speck we call Earth. He or She created DNA as well. If you wish to call the Higher Power 'God,' that's fine. But let's not confine God's creation to a mere fleck of dust on the outer edge on a galaxy of rather ordinary size among billions of others. My 'God,' I think, is bigger than the God you imagine, Dr. Garman."

Franklin Garman, turning purple, shouted, "You are not a messenger of God! You are an agent of Satan himself!" Garman headed toward the podium and had to be restrained by an agent of the NSA.

The next question came by Twitter sent from a ten year old girl in Iowa, "Amos, why do angels have wings?"

"That's a very good question, Britney." I asked that question of myself. I think wings are vestigial organs. That means they once had a use, kind of like our appendixes, tonsils, and toenails. We still have them but they aren't as much use as they were 10,000 years ago. I think angels once needed wings so they could fly great distances to make their rounds helping people out, sharing their wisdom, you know, how to make things, how to get along with each other better, and so on. I probably could fly if I practiced, but I think if I fly it will be on an airplane. That's a whole lot less work!" The audience laughed out loud.

A question came from a reporter with the *Pittsburgh Press*: "Amos, Sam Rockford here.

I write our science column and I am curious as to how you concluded that humans came from elsewhere in the universe beyond what you called our special DNA that differentiates us from apes?"

"Yes, Sam, I read some of your columns. It is our uniqueness that defines us. No scientist has been able to find a truly nearby genetic link to us. Not only was Piltdown not a 'Missing Link' there just isn't one. By the way, if I may change the subject slightly, I especially enjoyed the piece you did on memory. Most of your reporting is accurate when considering macro or brain-level memory. But the greater truth about memorylies in the molecular and even smaller levels of electromagnetic activity. Richard Feynman, a well-known physicist, said some years ago that quote: 'we have not yet approached the frontier of small.' My own memories probably go back perhaps fifty-thousand years in a dream state. When I was in a coma, more vague memories likely went back millions of years. If I were hypnotized I could probably describe an Ice Age village I, I mean my DNA ancestor, lived in. While conscious, I can dredge up lots of relatively current data and reconstruct vivid images of the past when my DNA was recording a great deal of old, even ancient information. This enhanced memory allows me to assess data as well as correctly predict trends. I am especially good at 'connecting the dots,' as we like to say. This is due to the fact that memory resides in the DNA we have and pass on to our children and so on down through the ever constant stream of genetic inheritance. Just as birds of a certain species build nests as their many generations have done through instinct, a form of DNA memory, so it is possible to know things from any part of our past within our sub-molecular imprinted data."

"Sub-molecular?" Sam asked with a skeptical look on his face

"Sam, you are well aware of the progress of computational power as stated in Moore's Law?"

"Sure," Sam replied, "microelectronic computational power has been increasing exponentially for years. The fact that this has actually happened makes Gordon Moore's theoretical prediction a law. The microscopic processors need to be small as the energy it takes to process information is very weak."

Amos replied, "Ray Kurzweil wrote in 2005 that by 2045, a few years from now, artificial intelligence will transcend biological intelligence due to the exponential progress in computational power in ever diminishing space. I don't entirely agree, but he has good points. He was getting close to the truth when writing about advances in nanotechnology. What I am talking about is that the seat of instinct, memory, imagination, creativity and so on, lies at a level within molecules of DNA. That's what Richard Feynman meant by the 'frontier of small.'

The audience was fairly roiling with discussions sparked by these comments. The next question came from a Catholic priest from the Basilica of St. Lawrence in Asheville. He was of the Jesuit Order and he had a pointed question for Amos:

"Do you believe, or should I say, 'have proof' of the existence or non-existence of Heaven and Hell?"

"Vicar Thomas, thank you for coming today. I knew you would have a good question for me. No, I cannot prove either. As a matter of faith, Jesus Himself is reputed to have said, 'The Kingdom of God is within you.' Likewise, I believe, he spoke often of hellfire being suffered by sinful people, but I am not sure of the geography of that place for the barbeque. I think hell comes to people who will suffer when they know they have sinned and that place is all in their hearts, minds, and souls."

"And what would you say is sin?"

"Another good one, Father," Amos said, "I do not think there would be any use in worrying about the *Ten Commandments* if people everywhere, of all faiths and beliefs, simply always held to the Golden Rule. 'Sin,' therefore, is the breaking of that rule. Just do unto to others as you would have them do unto you. Follow that tenet and you are free of sin.

Marla came to the podium to call an end to the press conference despite the cries of "What about this? What about that? Who was Amos in past lives?," etc. etc. Music over the loudspeaker was playing an orchestral version of *All Good Things Must End.*

The whole world was abuzz. For the next month, the "revelations" of the press conference were all that anyone wanted to talk about.

■■

Chapter 21 Damage Control

After the first press conference, Pope Xavier was on the phone again with Mario.

"Listen, Mario. It's coming down just as I said it would. The world can't get enough of Amos, as he calls himself. He's quoted everywhere. All I can say is 'No comment' when I get bombarded with questions. The cardinals want me to issue a Papal Bull denouncing him."

"Bull?"

"A decree, you moron! We need action and we need it now. Whatever it takes Mario!"

"Ok, Boss, you got it!"

Mario Belladonna called a meeting of his top lieutenants in the LSA to his office in the World Trade Tower.

"Guys, I brought yous here today on a very important matter. You know this angel, Amos they call him. Down south in Carolina. He's a fake, right? Like we told you."

"Yes, Boss," came the reply in unison from thirty green uniformed men.

"Guys, you know that the Lotto is the backbone of Social Security and LottoCare."

"Yes, Boss."

■■

"Without the Lotto America goes right down the tube. And without the Lotto, there goes your hundred K jobs."

"Yes, Boss."

"Well that muthafuckin' angel is about to screw the whole thing up. After that news conference last week, a reporter, who wasn't chosen, happened to ask a question about luck and somehow the muthafuckin' muthafuckah goes, 'I do believe in luck, but not of your chances of winning in the Lotto. In my opinion, the Lotto is a huge waste of money by people who can least afford it.' That was supposed to be off the record, but of course it was recorded. In one day Lotto revenue dropped 39%!"

"Jeez, Boss!" One agent exclaimed.

"Jeez is right. That angel is a bomb thrown right at the Lotto. And by the way, the angel's daughter, Marla is an accomplice for both him and her boyfriend, Jimmy Jack Johnson, who has been our top fugitive since he cleaned out a machine at Grand Central. They are targets A, B, and C. Go get them!"

Thirty green-suited agents of the LSA piled into five black Chevrolet Suburbans and headed to Asheville, North Carolina. They were heavily armed with automatic rifles, rocket propelled grenades and Glock .45 caliber hand guns. For this mission they had no need of wimpy laser pistols.

At Kirkland, all was calm. The estate was far from the highway where a hundred thousand or so people were still camped out. The main issue after the medical team had departed was keeping up with Amos' blog and the constant twitters, emails, Facebook postings. Marla hired a team of five business students from nearby colleges, interns for AmosAngel.com, to ride herd on the stampeding internet traffic.

Kirkland Publishing, Inc. was founded to publish the outpouring of books, inspirational posters, and other material emanating from the estate. Tee-shirts, available in contemporary colors, featured Amos with wings spread and quotes such as “My God is Bigger than Your God” were in such demand that a factory devoted to their production was set up in nearby Swannanoa, NC. Revenue from those shirts alone was in the millions. Amos’ first book, *Musings of an Angel* rose quickly to #1 on the New York Times best seller list. Marla’s book, *My Dad, the Angel* was not far behind. Even the reissue of Anthony Kirkland Johnson’s *Poems 1975 – 2005* went to number twenty-three on the NY Times list.

Jimmy Jack talking to Amos on the veranda noticed a concerned look on his face. Since he was cheerful most of the time that concerned Jimmy. “What’s the trouble, Amos?’

“Well, Son, it’s about the fallout from my bombshell press conference.”

“What? Your popularity?”

“No, Jimmy, it’s about politics, actually. My off-hand comment, which I regret, concerning the Lotto, just an innocuous put down of gambling, made the Lotto tank. Unfortunately this country is propped up with that damned system. I kind of kicked the sticks out from under it. You know the Feds have immediately cut benefits?”

“No, I haven’t followed that. Haven’t had time to read or watch TV.”

■■

"The CRP alliance of the religious right and the oligarchs who oppose any tax are getting together to actually make it a law that everyone must play the Lotto."

"That's real ironic isn't it?" Jimmy replied. The same folks who raised a stink at first about the Lotto now support it."

"Yes. Catholics and Mormons were always on the Lotto bandwagon, but the Baptists and other fundamentalists had to be won over."

"So, just how much is the Lotto requirement going to cost the average family?"

"My quick analysis says, 34% of every dollar they make."

"And rich folks like us?"

"A couple of hundred thousand dollars. Like 13% for people in our income range. No justice in that at all."

"So, what do think ought to be done about that? You know that income inequality has been my main social cause for twenty years."

"I know all about your good work, Son. I would suggest you run for some high public office, but the corporate money machine run for the CRP would crush you. They will find some drug dealer somewhere and more than enough of your old girlfriends to smear you from here to Kingdom Come."

"Yeah, you are right, damn it! What about Marla? Oh, yeah, they would find her lost years as well. Hey, what about you, Amos? The election of 2020 is not far away and you have about the highest profile of anybody in this wide world."

"You know I am not even registered to vote."

■■■

Chapter 22 The Kirkland Hall Raid

In the woods above the Kirkland estate, men in camouflage were picking their way through the tangle of greenbrier and blackberry undergrowth. They were hot and sweating; scratched in the face; and stung by yellow jackets."

"This don't exactly look like that 'Welcome to Nawth Carlina' postcawd I picked up at the last rest stop," muttered Harley Bernsteen to his buddy, Jake Dickinson, two of the company of LSA agents out of New Jersey sent to waste targets A, B, and C.

Below them, the NSA contingent was packing up to leave. The order, due to the efforts of a certain CPR congressman who said, "With the unfortunate downturn in the economy, we just can't afford spend money on private protection. That Angel is rich; let him hire his own bodyguards!" The President was pressured to pull out the NSA.

Kirkland was informed, and Marla searched the 'Net for bodyguards, but all seemed to have credentials that seemed more like macho bluster and less like reassuring safety. She elected to hire a couple of Buncombe County deputies and a highly recommend Major in the Highway Patrol. They would be in place the next day.

After breakfast, Marla with Panda on her lap, sat with Amos on the veranda. Jimmy was elsewhere in the house talking to his dad. Jason Faircloth was in the computer room chatting with the interns as Einstein stretched out on a table.

It was a warm day in late October. The leaves were the brightest and most colorful Marla had ever seen. A huge jack-o-lantern she had carved was grinning and looking their way.

"Dad, we need to talk. Jimmy told me you might be thinking or running for some high office. What, Presidential? That worries me. I don't feel entirely comfortable here, especially since our bodyguards are gone. I can't imagine how scary it would be if you had to go out campaigning."

"I have thought about that. But 'Nothing ventured, nothing gained,' as Ben Franklin said. I think the stakes are very high for the 2020 election. A 'watershed in American politics' as it will be known as."

"But daddy is it worth your life? Why not just support somebody you really believe in? Your endorsement would be all a halfway decent candidate would need. Then you could be named Secretary of State or something."

"You are probably right, but there is nothing better than the bully pulpit of the Presidency. I really think I could change the world, Darling."

The appearance of two deputy sheriff's cars and one from the State Patrol early the next morning dissuaded the thirty assassins from the LSA from launching an attack right away.

The cops knew Kirk Johnson well over the years. They were eager to see the improvements he had made in his Huey helicopter. Kirk may have seemed senile most of the time, but when it came to his pride and joy he was sharp as ever.

"Just like the one I flew in Viet Nam," Kirk beamed.

The deputies admired the pair of .50 caliber machine guns mounted under the cockpit. "Got these workin'" one deputy asked.

"Hell, yes!" Kirk replied. "And I don't mean will they work if they were to be activated...they do work and they are loaded to boot! Damn ammo's gotten expensive."

"Holy shit, Kirk!" Major Wilson interjected. I guess we could say that's not exactly 'street legal'?"

"Well, I guess I have some Second Amendment rights, especially here on my own property, right? And take a look over here, Mason and Jared," Kirk motioned to the young deputies to see his most recent addition to the Huey. He opened a panel on the side of the chopper revealing a hell-fire missile.

"Good Lord, Colonel Johnson,How did you come by that?" Major Wilson asked.

"You mean 'them', Wilson. Got one on the other side too!"

"Where did I get them?"

"Off the Internet. You can get damn nearly anything on that Internet. Provided you can pay. Those puppies cost eighteen grand a piece, which, by the way, is a lot cheaper than the Pentagon pays for them. I think they came from the Guatemalan Air Force."

▪▪

"Well, Kirk, you are the most well-armed 93 year-old dude in the country."

"Hey, you are probably right. Now let's got up to the house and meet the second most interesting thing out here, Amos the Angel, my step daughter's bio-dad."

Marla served a big brunch at 11:00 AM on the veranda: Cheese grits with shrimp, country sausage, pancakes, and strong French press coffee made personally by Amos. The young deputies packed away seconds. They hadn't eaten since the Grand Slams at Denny's at 6:30 AM that morning.

After everyone got selfies with Amos, wings unfurled, they had a meeting with Major Wilson regarding security.

"We may already have a problem here. I just spoke with Agent Floyd Farley of the NSA who just got back to DC. I asked him for the codes to the perimeter motion detectors and the app to put them on my smartphone. He said they never worked on account of deer and bears always tripping them. Apparently every time they viewed the monitors there were always just deer and bears. So they quit looking and turned it off."

"Those idiots!" Marla yelled.

"Well, he said, they might still work and he gave me the code." Jason looked at the codes and found a couple of transposed numbers. "That Dr. Faircloth is pretty damn smart. Now the system is working. Let me see if I can pan the side of the mountain."

Just below the last ridge above Kirkland, five LSA agents sweltering in very realistic bear costumes were making their way down the mountain toward Kirkland.

■■■

“Jeesus Kee-rist, I am about to die in here!”Harley Bear exclaimed to Jake Bear.

“You and me both!”

“Looks like we just a quartah mile away and it’s all downhill from here.”

Harley Bear pulled his vibrating cell phone from beneath his suit. “Good,” was all he said.

He then told Jake Bear, “Recon up slope spotted three cop cahs, but the good news there’s just three cops. Heh heh. I think we can handle this particulah situation.”

At the house, Marla had the interns stop selling stuff on the internet and concentrate on watching the perimeter monitors on their smartphones.

“Hey, Marla,” Julie, the intern from Mars Hill University called out. “Check this out. Two bears sitting on their butts. They look like they are having a conversation. Isn’t that a riot?”

“Ha, ha, we ought to record that for YouTube. It’s sure to go viral!”

■■

Marla responded, “Wait a second. Did you see what I just saw? I can’t believe it! One of the bears is talking on a cell phone!”

Marla ran downstairs and caught Major Wilson as he was about to take a scouting drive up the old logging road that ran up to the ridge. “You aren’t going to believe this, but an intern and I just saw two bears on the monitor. At first we laughed because they looked so comical seeming to talk to each other. Then one of them, swear to God, pulled out a cell phone!”

■■

“That’s taking camo to a new level. If they were talking to somebody, then there are at least three. You know the ‘Rule of Pests’ Miss Marla? If you see three roaches then there’s anywhere from thirty to three hundred. I’m hoping it’s just thirty. In any case, we gotta move.”

The deputies were informed and they opened their patrol car trunks where they handed out pistols and rifles to everyone with any experience at all. Jimmy, Jason, Marla, and Kirk each got a Glock 9 mm and an AK-47 automatic rifle. Amos said he didn’t know anything about guns except their history and how inane our National non-regulation policies were. Two interns, Julie and Frank, got guns since they had been hunting with their dads. The three others hid in the basement with Amos and the cats.

Major Wilson had Jimmy and Marla go to the big shed to help Kirk roll the Huey out.

Seconds later the first shots pierced the serene garden and echoed off an adjacent mountain.

Ratttatatt, rattattat. “Man down, man down!” Major Wilson yelled as deputy Jared had taken a shot to his thigh. He fired his AK back in the direction of the shots and ran to get Jared out of the line of fire.

■■

Rattattat rattatat, zizzez, zzizzzip, the bullets whizzed through the air. Wilson whipped off his cop tie and made a tourniquet on Jared’s thigh and called 911 and for an EMT and reinforcements. Outside the shed, Kirk was firing up his Huey.

Jimmy ran into the woods despite Marla’s cry, “Where the hell are you going?”

■■

"To the cave. Ask Kirk."

Kirk said, "There's a little cave just a few yards in the woods over there. Jimmy played there when he visited here when he was a kid. He'll be fine."

Jimmy slid into the cave thinking how small it looked now that he was grown. A minute later a bear with a man's head and carrying an automatic rifle fell from the top of the cave opening right in front of Jimmy.

"Son of a bitch!" Harley Bear screamed in pain as his leg broke. When he spotted Jimmy it was too late to use the Glock he went for. Jimmy shot him dead with a short burst from his AK.

Then ratttatta rattatata! Bullets zipped past Jimmy as he ducked back into the cave. Jake Bear made his way around to the cave entrance, but saw nothing. He went to his friend who stared up lifeless at the canopy of yellow leaves. Jimmy came up from behind and placed the muzzle of his rifle on the back of Jake's head.

"Drop your weapon, Motherfucker!" Jake complied. "On your knees!" He kneeled.

"I want to know how many of you assholes are out here."

"Just me now that Hawley's dead."

"Wrong answer, Dipshit!" Jimmy then shot the bear in his butt.

"Arrrhhhh, Shit!"

Next shot you die if you say the wrong number! We have been watching y'all on surveillance cameras. Got a pretty good idea, so you tell me your number. If it's close I'll just take off your kneecap; if you are way off, Jersey Boy, you die!"

■■■

"OK, OK we have 30, I mean 29 now."

"Sounds close enough." Jimmy then immobilized the second bear with a shot from his Glock to his kneecap. Something he learned from an old *Soprano's* episode.

Jimmy then returned to the shed where Major Wilson, Jason, Laura, and the two armed interns were waiting.

"They have 29, or 28 now, I had to take one out. Another I persuaded to tell me how many in the attack group."

"Nice work, Jimmy," Major Wilson said patting Jimmy on the back.

At that moment all hell broke loose: An RPG took off the upper right corner of Kirkland Hall with a deafening explosion. A dozen attackers in camo came running out of the woods from the far side of the estate, guns blazing and the staccato racket blistering the air.

Kirk fired up the Huey as he slipped an old CD into the player in the control panel. *Born to be Wild* was turned to high volume. The old man had the Huey in the air with Jimmy on board just as an RPG took out the shed. Kirk whipped the Huey around and said something Jimmy could barely hear. It was that line from Al Pacino's *Scarface*, "Say hello to my little friends!" as he cut loose with two fifty caliber machine guns. At least nine attackers were taken out. It was hard to tell exactly how many in the collective mess of body parts since there were some heads missing.

One of the attackers in front of the burning house was only slightly wounded. He came from behind the house and yelled to Major Wilson, "Drop it cop!"

He hadn't noticed Julie hidden behind a boulder in the front yard. She stood and gave a startlingly loud wolf whistle. The LSA guy turned and she cut him down with her AK-47.

Major Wilson yelled over to her, "Way to go young lady!"

Another RPG came from up the ridge. KABOOM! It hit the upper floor of the mansion which caused and even greater conflagration.

Jimmy told Kirk where the grenade had come from and the Huey swerved again.

"Here goes 18 grand," Kirk said as he released a hellfire missile. WHAAAAMMM! The explosion was deafening and the Huey, being a bit too close to the blast was briefly out of control.

"Jeesus, Dad, didn't you expect that from your experience in Nam?"

"No! We didn't have Hellfires then! They an 'aftermarket addition'."

Back on the ground, Marla and Deputy Mason rushed to the house now fully engulfed in flames. "There's a backdoor to the cellar!" Marla yelled. There was a padlock on the door which Mason blew off with his rifle.

Amos and three interns emerged staggering and coughing from the smoke. Five more minutes and they would have been dead.

The EMTs arrived and took the interns and Deputy Jared to Mission Hospital. Amos, with soot on his robe and wings, said, "I don't need any more hospitalization." But he did accept a couple of deep drags from an oxygen tank and later a shot of Jack Daniels from Kirk's hip flask.

A SWAT team swarmed into the estate. Kirk couldn't help himself but to remark, "Well, well, the cavalry has finally arrived, but the Pioneers have saved themselves."

The SWAT team did comb the hills and grounds about the estate. They found two wounded bear-men and another dead attacker and counted twenty-seven bodies altogether.

Jimmy said that there ought to be thirty. The Captain of the SWAT team said, "You won't believe this: all of them are agents of the Lotto Security Agency. There aren't thirty if you do a head count, but some heads are missing."

"Ok," Jimmy said, "Why not count legs and divide by two!"

Mario Belladonna was watching FOX News which had reporters on the ground near the still smoldering ruins of Kirkland Hall. "Jesus H. Christ! I send in a fuckin' army to do a simple job and all they do is burn down a house!"

A day later, at Mario's side, was Harold Gratzky, blind in his right eye and partially paralyzed from his encounter with Jimmy Jack at Tavern on the Green. He was the third of the three survivors of the "Kirkland Raid" as the press was calling it. The other two were at Mission Hospital in Asheville under arrest.

"Butch, I am telling you, you is the luckiest unlucky bastard I know. Twice you try to send that son-of-a-bitch Jimmy Jack Johnson to hell and twice you barely escape with your life!"

"I'll get the thun-a-bith nexth time, Bauth, I thware!"

"I am sure you will, Butch. We might have been too ambitious in that raid. Next time, one at a time. I'll give you a couple of guys from Itly to work with. I am going to have to disappear after I resign tomorrow. *US DayBreak* said all the raiders was LSA guys and even our friends in Congress have called for me to quit. Before they get too deep into things, I am going off-the-grid as they say."

Mario F. Belladonna went on FOX News to "apologize" for the conduct of a few "rogue agents" who felt that the Lotto was under attack. They simply, "misunderstood my outrage at what that Fraud, so-called Amos Angel, had said about our great National Lottery. They took it upon themselves to take action. I am very sorry. I am resigning now."

The FOX News interviewer, entirely sympathetic to Mario, raised the specter of conspiracy—on the part of the left-wing, of course. "Commissioner Belladonna, do you think the Kirkland Raid was a set-up by the Prodems to make the National Lotto look like bad guys so they can get the Lotto Act overturned?"

"Could very well be. They have been calling the benelovent Lotto, the "Looto" for years, besmirching it and even questionin' the justice part."

"Yes, all that belly-aching about people disappearing for nothing more that treason against the United States of America! You mess with the Lotto; you die. Everyone knows that. Keeps the country solvent and moving ahead. Thank you for your time, Commissioner Mario F. Belladonna. And now a word from our sponsor, EXXON MOBILE. Exxon, Clean Energy you can count on!"

■■

Belladonna did what he told Butch Gratzky he would do. First he took refuge in the Vatican Embassy. A day later he was in Rome.

Chapter 23 The Campaign of 2020

Marla told the SWAT Team Captain that they weren't saying where they were going due to leaks. The SWAT commander looked offended, but agreed saying, "After this mess I guess I don't want to know. Somebody sure wants y'all dead."

When she shook Major Wilson's hand in departing she slipped a small piece of paper in it with one word: Greenbrier.

The homeless contingent from Kirkland boarded Kirk's helicopter and took a short flight over the crowded I-40 to the Asheville Mall where they landed and each bought a few changes of clothes and personal items before many people even knew they were there. Kirk held Panda and Amos, of course, stayed behind in the 'copter with a singed Einstein still smelling of smoke on his lap.

▪▪▪

When she returned to the Huey, Marla said, "Here, Dad, three new fluffy robes from Dillard's. Kirk, your favorite Jeans and shirts from Land's End."

Jimmy and Jason hit Banana Republic and the Sunshine kiosk for some regular and concave sunglasses which Jason said were "Sizzlin!"

Kirk revved up the Huey and they made the relatively short flight up to the Greenbrier Resort in West Virginia. In many ways, this was the perfect place to hide out for a while: The Greenbrier Hotel was a shelter in the 1960's for the entire US Government in case the Cold War got hot. This is where Congress, the President, and the Department of Defense brass would go underground, literally, to run the country under nuclear attack. In the past few decades, the bunkers, tunnel command posts, and living areas were a tourist attraction for the resort hotel.

Jimmy had a good laugh at all that recalling his song, *In Condemnation of Folly.* He hummed it as he went on the shelter tour with Marla. She nudged him in the ribs giggling, "Stop it, Jimmy!"

The Greenbrier, a Five-Star hotel, was also more recently famous as the birthplace of the new Progressive Democratic Party which had returned for their annual convention a few weeks after the Kirkland folks arrived.

As the delegates met to forge the platform for the 2020 campaign, Amos appeared before them to make a speech:

"Thank you for your gracious invitation for me to address the only political group in America that I can endorse," Amos spoke with his booming baritone voice.

The convention center erupted in applause and shouts of “We love you!” and “God Bless America!”

“Good People, we live in perilous times. The Oligarchs have taken over. The rights of the people have been denied. Giant corporations and their radical right-wing billionaire allies are running the country from the Capitol to the State Houses. If you want to change anything you are thwarted at every step; your voting rights suppressed.” More applause.

“The only right we have left is the stupid one about bearing arms.” The audience cheered and laughed derisively.

“If you are fortunate enough to have traveled as much as I have, you will not wonder why people of other countries shake their heads in dismay when talking about America. The rich countries see us as stupid or unenlightened despite our great wealth; the poor ones hate us for exploiting them. They say the success of America was simply due to the good fortune to have endless resources and that, when those were wastefully expended, we bullied the weak and stole them from others.”

“I do not see America as a stupid country, but I do see it as an ignorant one and an increasingly immoral one. I do see the lack of foresight in seeing America, a small minority among the Earth’s billions, and the consequences of that kind of ignorance. I want us to shed the dark mantle of greed that controls us and much of the world. I want to see America return to the honesty, leadership, and generosity we were once known for; the Beacon on the Hill that the people of the world looked up to for hope and inspiration; the bright future of the Planet Earth and all its citizens!” Thunderous applause followed.

■■

"Good People, we CAN change this country! Good People we WILL change this country! Thank, you and may God bless America!" Amos got a standing ovation that lasted longer than his brief speech.

Someone in the crowd started a chant, "Amos—for--President! Amos—for—President!" soon it seemed everyone in the vast hall was repeating the same thing. Nearly all had read *Musings of an Angel* which was a compendium of aphorisms touching on a gamut of subjects: spiritual, philosophical, scientific, and political. Many were convinced that Arthur J. Barringer, a.k.a. Amos the Angel, was the smartest and best qualified candidate they could put forth.

In the winter and spring of 2020, no candidates of the Progressive Democratic Party came forth to challenge the one who was on the ballot of every state simply as "Amos" and only as Arthur J. Barringer where state law required a registered legal name. There were, however, legal challenges to his candidacy. Those ranged from those who challenged his citizenship; to his birth; to whether he should be disqualified for being "unhuman;" or even that he was a space alien. Aside from the legal cost of dismissing the challenges, Amos just got more popular as the critics were shown to be fools.

After the primaries the surviving candidates were Roscoe Deen, Jr. of the CRP; the CEO of the FARMCO, Bert Dyson of the GOP; Representative Martin Miller of the MDP; and Amos of the PDP.

Roscoe Deen, Jr., Governor of Oklahoma, came into national prominence when he and his state legislature adopted "Biblical Law" in that state. There were endless lawsuits over everything from women's rights (by law there, "A woman's place is in the home"); to cursing that became a misdemeanor; to students enrolled in state universities or community colleges denied the right to vote and so on. Deen was supported by 63% of the eligible voters of his state.

Centrist Republicans, a tiny minority, still called themselves "The Republican Party" and used the trademark "GOP" to identify themselves. Their candidate had the support of some big corporations and sensible business people who just wanted to make money and had no real interest in "side bar issues" such as gun rights, abortion, and whether or not the Affordable Care Act was good or not. Bert Dyson, their candidate was a farmer who had made it to the top of FARMCO, America's second biggest agribusiness conglomerate.

The moderate wing of the Democratic Party officially split with the Prodems when they became the majority of that party after the disastrous elections of 2016 and 2018. Mostly old school Democrats, they were pro-union, and pro-big government. They still had a following among minorities and immigrants although those blocks were shifting fairly apace toward the Prodem side. Congressman Martin Miller, an African-American from Detroit, was their standard bearer.

The Progressive Democratic Party had made impressive gains in the elections of 2018, but were not yet as strong as the CRP. Made up primarily of people with college degrees, academic and high tech employees, environmentalists, old hippies, students, teachers, and women in the workplace, the Prodems were ecstatic to have Amos as their candidate.

The first four-way "debate" was held in the Superdome in New Orleans. Jumbotrons projected the candidates fifty feet high on four screens around the arena. All the candidates and their families and key supporters were seated on a raised platform in the middle of the field.

The debate was moderated by Nancy Kwan, of NPR. She said, "Welcome candidates, families and friends, the fifty thousand people in attendance here and, I'm told, three and half billion people world-wide. Without further ado, here's the first question chosen at random submitted by a voter from Rock Island, Illinois: What do you regard as the main problem facing the United States today? Chosen also by random selection Representative Miller, you are first. You have 30 seconds for your answer."

"I say America's biggest problem is income inequality." Miller got right to the point and sounded like the Baptist preacher he once was. "There's too much of a difference between rich and poor. There's hardly a middle-class anymore. Working people are the backbone of America and that backbone is stressed to the breaking point! When one percent of the people have ninety percent of the wealth, the country is in serious trouble. Our country is in SERIOUS trouble." There were cheers and applause for Martin Miller as he grinned broadly, waved, and stepped back to his seat.

"Governor Deen, you have the podium."

"Hello, America. Hello World; Hello Christians everywhere!" Deen began raising his right hand and waving above his head which was topped with a shiny black pompadour wig. "I say, there's nothin' wrong with America that common sense and Christian vahues cannot fix. We <u>are</u> the richest and best country in the world. Some people, including some sittin' right here on this platform, want to run this Christian, God fearin', country into the ground. They love to say, 'diversity is a good thing.' But it ain't! What ever happened to the 'Great Melting Pot' where everybody saw themselves as Americans first and whatever their background second? My Party and I stand for reform and by that we mean reforming America back to the way it once was: strong, proud, and solidly Christian. God Bless America!"

There was loud applause and cheers for Governor Deen as well.

"You are next, Mr. Dyson."

"Hello, my fellow Americans. I hope we can make this so-called debate interesting enough that you will soon forget the five hours you spent going through security," The rotund, fifty-five and balding, Dyson began, inducing a modest amount of laughter, but less from those near the end of the lines. "The main thing wrong with America is government. It's too big. It's too wasteful. It taxes the hell out of everyone. Now, I agree with my friend, Governor Deen on many of the things his party stands for, but they haven't done a lot for business. They gave us the Lotto, but that hasn't improved sales of our products overseas. I would reduce the government payroll by half starting with the Post Office. Who needs it when we have email and Twitter? That's all I have for now." Dyson drew applause as well, polite, but with fewer shouts and whistles than the first two candidates.

"And lastly, it is now your turn, Dr. Barringer, or as you prefer, Amos."

Amos stepped up to the podium and, for effect, spread his wings which seemed luminous in the spotlight. The crowd screamed and applauded for many seconds."

Ms. Kwan had to announce, "Please hold your applause and take your seats. Amos will have only 30 seconds and you have already used 10!"

"Thank you, Ms. Kwan and thank you people. The single greatest problem with America is greed. I realize many Americans do not view greed as a problem, but greed has corrupted our entire society. Rich people enjoy what greed has gotten them; poor people envy the greedy success of the rich and are not happy with their lot in life. Ironically, rich people are not particularly happy either, despite their wealth, because greed has no bounds. If you have a big house, you want a bigger one; two cars; then three. As Gandhi once said, 'There is enough for everyone's need, but never enough for everyone's greed.' There is a vacuum of spirit in America, sucked out by greed. Greed leaves no room for love. If you are too occupied with material things, the is little room left for love. No, I cannot wave a wand and make greed go away. I can help make America a more just society where everyone has a chance to live a happy life. I agree with the Congressman that income inequality is a problem, but it is only part of the problem of greed. For that we must look into our hearts and follow the Golden Rule. If we do that, rich and poor alike, inequality and injustice will melt away and America will once again be the Beacon of Hope for the world. May God bless America. Thank you."

For a long moment, there was no cheering; no applause; just stunned silence. People were not hearing what they wanted to hear. It took a minute for Amos' message to sink in. But then the chanting started, "A-mos! A-mos! A-mos!"

Then the fights broke out. The mayhem continued for thirty or more minutes. Hundreds of police and security personnel were no match for the rioting crowds.

Little skirmishes were being fought by partisans all over the stadium. Finally, Nancy Kwan gave up trying to restore order. The first debate of the campaign came abruptly to a halt as police used all their might to simply get the candidates and their cohorts safely out of the Superdome.

Jimmy and Marla were on both sides of Amos. "Guess that's why they've never held a Presidential Debate in a stadium!" Jimmy shouted above the crowd that sounded like a howling storm.

The Prodem group made it back to their headquarters in the Omni Hotel on Canal Street a short distance from the Superdome. Back in the family suite they watched the coverage on TV. C-Span had the usual matter-of-fact reporting. NPR had more analysis of each candidate's positions. They had only a little coverage of the riot. As might have been scripted before the debate, FOX News poured on this analysis:

Sean O'Malley, their anchor, came on the air as scenes of the rioting played in the background. "As we now know, the socialist Prodem candidate Arthur Barringer, the 131 year old zombie in an Angel suit, is nothing more than a front for the One World Order. In his debate speech he tried to throw a stinking wet blanket on America's best people, the job creators; the people whom God has blessed and rewarded for their good works. He calls that success 'greed'! It is no wonder the people in that stadium tonight were outraged. Some were attacked for standing up for America. Arthur J. Barringer is a dangerous man. He is a threat to all real Americans!"

Jimmy flipped the TV off. "What an enormous crock of shit! I think this may be the lowest FOX has gone in this election year and we have already seen a lot of crap from them. Did you notice the video playing behind

O'Malley? It actually shows people with Amos signs and those who were chanting your name being beaten by thugs wearing big CRP buttons. How can anybody ever believe FOX?"

Amos spoke up, "Yes, Jimmy, we expected this sort of attack. People tend to believe what they want to believe; facts rarely trouble or dissuade a true believer. Blaming the victim is an old strategy. I did get a chuckle out of the zombie part. Weren't zombie movies and TV shows the rage five or ten years ago?" Amos then began to walk stiff legged around the room growling ominously to the laughter of his small audience.

"All the talk shows want to have you on, Amos," Marla said. "I think you should do only Bill Maher. He will challenge the 'God stuff' since he is America's most well-known atheist."

"I can handle Maher especially since he and I are the same wave-length 99% of the time. So let's set him, I mean it, up, Marla" Amos said with a grin, "And I think it would be kind of fun to appear on FOX with O'Malley, too."

"O'Malley, really? That ought to be rich! Well, if you say so, Daddy." Marla then made a few phone calls and the interviews were confirmed.

Chapter 24 Assassination Plots

With the election a month away, Amos had not campaigned far from the family's temporary home in North

Carolina during the reconstruction of Kirkland Hall. An anonymous donor from Florida leant them his palatial summer home in the mountains. Not all "One-Percenters" were greedy. It was Amos conclusion that as long as he had internet and TV exposure, he could do without the endless handshaking and baby kissing aspects of campaigning. He did agree to one last public appearance before the election.

Amos was in Cincinnati, Ohio at a fund raiser in Great American Ball Park. Amos and his entourage had just left the podium to a throng of 45,000 people chanting "A-mos, A-mos, A-mos!"

Jason Faircloth, wearing his special helmet, noticed that a security guard coming toward Amos had what he thought might be a ZR7 laser pistol. He knew immediately that something was terribly wrong: First the man was so fat his uniform looked two sizes too small. Secondly, none of them would be carrying laser pistols which were highly regulated despite the Second Amendment.

Jason yelled to Jimmy, "Get Amos down! Killer coming!"

Jimmy and Marla pulled Amos down yelling, "Shooter!"

Two NSA bodyguards wrestled the rotund man to the ground.

"Ow! Thit that hurths!" the phony security guard yelled as the zip-tie handcuffs squeezed his fat wrists.

Jimmy went over to him. "Damn if it isn't Butch Gratzky!" Jimmy said to the NSA agents.One of them asked, "You know him? Who's he?"

"A hit man from the LSA. It's a long story. Check his pocket. Has a ZR7 no doubt."

"Yep. Let's go Mr. Gratzky; you're under arrest for attempted assassination." They didn't read him 'Miranda

Rights' because the CRP dominated Supreme Court had thrown out those rights back in 2017.

Just as Jimmy, Jason, Marla, and Amos were recovering from the attempted assassination, a figure emerged from the shadows brandishing a Glock 9mm pistol. They all knew him. It was Special Agent Floyd Farley, their third bodyguard, and one who had been at Kirkland last year.

"What's up Floyd?" Jimmy asked. "You're a little late. Your buddies just took the perp away."

Amos immediately analyzed the situation from his vast mental database: He knew Floyd Farley was a member of the CRP; that he had established a friendship with Franklin Garman; and that he was probably a highly paid assassin for the CRP. It took Amos less than a second to spin and kick the gun from Farley's hand. Jimmy soon had him in a choke hold. Cincinnati police took Farley into custody.

"Jeez, Amos!" Jimmy said looking very surprised, "Where the hell did you learn karate?"

"On the Internet. There's nothing you can't learn on the 'Net. Almost have my Black Belt!" Amos replied. Everyone including Amos had a good laugh.

■■

Chapter 25 Two Talk Shows

■■

Amos accepted Bill Maher's invitation first. There was more than the usual raucous applause given for every talk show guest. The audience screamed, stomped, and shouted the now familiar, "A-mos, A-mos" chant.

Maher began with a joke, "Well here I am talking to an Angel. I don't believe in God, but I am talking to one of His messengers. Damn, I must have converted!" The audience roared.

"Now, Bill, you know there are many more words for God than there are religions. But I don't want to bore your audience with all that etymology, but I will be as clear as I can: there is a Higher Power that we cannot know. I may call that power 'God' if I chose, because, lacking other evidence to the contrary, it becomes my belief. You may ridicule belief, and some beliefs do beg for ridicule, but you also lack evidence to the contrary."

The audience shouted their approval.

"So what about the Bible, Amos? Truth or fiction?"

"Mythology and fiction, mostly, of course. But a moral guide, yes, for the most part. And what would you say about something like *Aesop's Fables*? Truth or fiction? But talking animals in fiction can tell the truth, can they not? Is there truth in Tom Robbins' fiction? Sure. And remember the pigs in Orwell's *Animal Farm*?

"Oh, yes, 'all pigs are equal, but some are more equal than others.' So you say the Bible is mostly truth presented in literary parables, fables, and myths that ring true?"

"Yes, but not in a literal way. That's where fundamentalism gets all tangled up. And I believe that my God, my 'Higher Power,' is way too busy to care about us as individuals. I'm with the late George Carlin on that. He was a great theologian, you know."

"Yes he was. I had him on my show. Definitely my favorite theologian. So, Amos, does your Higher Power speak to you, yourself being more special than us mere mortals?"

"Not in any sense I am aware of, but I do carry messages from the eons of time and infinite space. It's in my DNA. It's in your DNA. The only difference is that I have 'morphed' to another level. I am simply, if you will, just more attuned to the memory imprinted in my eons old replicated DNA. This permits my special powers of analysis; it allows me to be more imaginative because I simply have more information and genetic experience on which to base my imaginings."

"Can you correctly imagine the future?" Maher asked.

"That's a very good question, Mr. Maher. As to specific and precisely accurate events, no. I probably wouldn't have gone to Cincinnati if I had known two different assassins would be there trying to kill me."

The audience groaned and then applauded loudly.

"But I am good at looking at the current state of affairs, say the way this country has been going, and derive conclusions as to what could make things better. For example, if we do nothing to change, America, as we know it, will cease to exist in fifty years if not sooner; change our ways, as I have outlined in my book *Musings*, and we will last a good long time."

The audience stood to applause and chant, "A-mos!, A-mos!, A-mos!"

■■

Bill Maher concluded the interview with, "Well, I guess I am a convert. If not, I certainly know whom I will vote for." He then picked up the chant, "A-mos, A-mos!"

Polls after the Maher interview showed Amos with 45% of the vote, enough to win the popular vote, but still pretty close in the Electoral College.

The FOX News interview was before a hostile TV audience with nobody in the studio other than Sean O'Malley and TV technicians. O'Malley was an imposing figure, six-foot eight, ruddy face with a receding shock of red hair sprouting from the middle of his head. He wore an iridescent purple suit, solid green shirt, and bright yellow tie. One of his favorite tactics was to crush the hand of a hostile guest as a method of less-than-subtle intimidation.

"Welcome, Professor Barringer, uh, I mean Amos!" He squeezed Amos' hand hard and, to his surprise, Amos squeezed back. "Whoa that's a pretty firm grip you got there!" O'Malley winced and wrung his hands together to alleviate the pain. In a few seconds he recovered and asked, "Did you fly up to New York today by yourself or on an airplane?"

"Helicopter, actually."

"It isn't often that I get a 131 year old man on my show. And even rarer that he be an angel. I was wondering if somebody of your advanced years might just up and die at any time. We have no idea if you are physically fit enough for the rigors of the Presidency."

Amos ran through the database in his mind. He knew that Sean O'Malley would continue to attack him on any level that did not pertain to the issues of the day. Aha!

He came up with the obscure fact that Sean O'Malley liked to compete in arm wrestling contests. He was very good and at one time the New Jersey state champion.

"Sean, you raise a good point. If I am just a very old man, actually 132 now, who is known only for his wings; I just might keel over and die at any moment. By the way, didn't I hear somewhere that you were a pretty good arm wrestler?"

"That's right, Amos, I am one of the best. You want to challenge me?"

"All right, Mr. O'Malley, you might want to take off your suit jacket."

Right there, before a TV audience of millions, an historic arm wrestling event took place. Both men were lefties, so there was no issue of fairness as they squared up.

Amos feigned to be struggling and allowed Sean to get as far as 45 degrees in his favor. Then Amos abruptly pulled a screaming Sean over and out of his chair. There was a distinctive CRACK as Sean's shoulder dislocated, his arm pinned, and then O'Malley was thrown onto the floor; his mouth agape in horrific pain.

Amos was shown kneeling and consoling the figure of Sean O'Malley, writhing in pain and subsequently shouting, "I'll sue you. I'll sue you! You son-of-a-bitch! Arrrahhggg!"

Amos was escorted from the studio as EMT's arrived. The video went immediately viral on YouTube. Many right-leaning independent voters and even a good many CRP members, for whom strength meant machismo, decided then and there to support Amos for president.

▪▪

Chapter 26 An October Surprise

■■

The Press was full of news and speculation regarding the assassination attempts. Governor Deen, the CRP candidate said on FOX News, "The whole dang thing was a set-up to help Amos become more popular. I have proof that Middle Eastern terrorists paid for those so-called assassins. They didn't really intend to kill him. They don't want Angel-Man to die. Heck, no! They want him in the White House because they know he'll ease up on 'em. He'll help them build another Muslim state as if we don't have enough of them already!"

Of course, Deen had no more proof of his claim than did Senator Joe McCarthy in the 1950's when he claimed proof of "256 known Communists in the State Department." No proof then; no proof now. Deen said he couldn't reveal his source for "National Security reasons."

Some people thought Deen's claim was an "October Surprise," i.e., a revelation close to Election Day that just might turn the tide of the election.

Amos and his Party had an October surprise of their own: It was well-known that the NSA tracked a lot of phone conversations. A young operative who happened to record the conversations of American officials with foreign leaders came forward with some startling information, a recorded conversation, that had the Commissioner of the Lotto Security Agency, Mario Francis Belladonna discussing what sounded very much like an assassination plot against Amos and his family with none other than Pope Xavier!

Not since the Reformation of the 16th Century was there such turmoil within the Church. Cardinals and Bishops, rectors and vicars, and on down to the parish level, the Catholic Church was in chaos. More than half of the Church leaders and congregations came out against the Pope. The minority held the most power and for a week they held staunchly behind Xavier.

Then the other bombshell exploded. An 'anonymous' tip was tweeted in to a reporter for the *New York Times.* The cryptic message read: "Pope Xavier, Belladonna, Pope Francis, Farley, Garman, and Gratzky—connect the dots!"

The next day, the *Times* looked like a tabloid. The entire front page had nothing more than the anonymous tweet. Within hours whatever support Xavier had simply evaporated. By order of the College of Cardinals, invoking some arcane five-hundred-year-old canon law, Pope Xavier was arrested by the Swiss Guard and charged with conspiracy and the murder of Pope Francis. In their five-hundred year old history the Swiss Guard had never been ordered to arrest their commander.

The instantly famous tweet was traced to a fourteen year old girl in Iowa who denied sending it. Amos chuckled as he watched the FOX News interview with Ashley Griswold. He looked over a Jason Faircloth and remarked, "You are a genius! I don't know how you did that and I don't want to know either!" In the next few weeks before the election momentum for Amos continued to build.

Endorsements came in like a torrent. Only the 'mainstream media' controlled by the CRP and its corporate sponsors still backed Governor Deen. The negative ads continued the drumbeat: "Amos is dangerous! He's an Alien! He's a Socialist One-Worlder!" and so on.

A very important message came from the candidate of the Moderate Democrats, Martin Miller. He was on all the networks with this address: "My fellow Americans, the election of 2020 is upon us. In one week, you, the American People will have to think about the future. You will have to search your soul and deep into your hearts to choose the best person to not only lead America for the next four years, but to set our course for the next fifty years. Tonight, I have made a decision. I am throwing my support to Arthur J. Barringer, your angel and mine, Amos! I strongly urge all of my supporters, my Party, and independent voters to do the same. Please get out and vote! Thank you, and God Bless America!"

Watching NPR, Amos immediately called Martin Miller's headquarters and was soon connected to the Congressman. "Marty, I want to thank you. Your support comes as a surprise, but not entirely so. Since we have new rules on selection of the Vice-President, I want to offer you that office. Will you accept?"

Amos was referring to the recent XXVIII amendment to the Constitution that eliminated the tandem election of President and Vice President. The change was that a President Elect would choose his or her VP after the election. Conservatives proposed this change to avoid having the negative 'base pleasing' distraction of a Sarah Palin as had been the case in the 2008 election. Progressives liked the idea because it took some of the politics out of the equation for a so-called 'balanced ticket' on a scale of purely electoral demographics. The amendment thus had bi-partisan support and was quickly adopted.

Martin Miller replied, "Yes, indeed, Mr. President Elect! But we should probably keep this to ourselves until after the election."

"I agree, let's not let your personal decision seem as a *quid pro quo.* After the election, we can let the pundits have their analysis and, in fact that will be their inevitable conclusion."

By Election Day2020 the results were practically a foregone conclusion: The PDR won the Presidency in a landslide with an unprecedented 72%. Amos carried forty-eight states, all but Oklahoma and Georgia. So many Progressives won races for the House, Senate, and Governorships that the term "coattails" became obsolete. The Press said hundreds of progressives were "Swept into office on the wings of an angel!"

In the aftermath of the election, the news concerned the pending trial of Pope Xavier for masterminding the assassination of Pope Francis and the extradition of Mario F. Belladonna for complicity in that crime as well as the attempts on the life of Amos.

At Kirkland Hall the family and Party leaders were very busy selecting cabinet candidates and forming a new government. A huge wing was added to the New Kirkland Hall to accommodate the new administration in the "Southern White House." Amos addressed his colleagues:

"Now the hard work begins. We not only have to transform America; we must transform the World as well. America is a just a relatively small part of this planet. All people of the world are in this life together; every person on earth deserves to live and to pursue happiness as we would have the same for ourselves."

Amos also gave a message from the family: "I am happy to announce that my daughter, Marla Rosenblum-Barringer will marry James Jackson Johnson here at Kirkland Hall on New Year's Day, 2021."

▪▪

Chapter 26 Wedding and Honeymoon

The wedding announcement overshadowed all the considerable political news. With only a month to prepare, Kirkland became like a great oak tree swarming with migrating birds. Decorators, planners, technicians, family and friends from all over the country swooped into Kirkland Hall. Marla's sister Zoë came from Africa. Her half- brother Michael Zimmerman arrived from L.A.

The family enjoyed Christmas together for the first time ever. Everyone sat around a roaring fire singing Christmas carols. They sang loudest *Hark the Herald Angels Sing.* The week between the holidays was hectic with last minute details to be ironed out. Martin Miller, Vice-President Designate came to help Amos with the guest list. The entire Progressive Congressional Delegation was invited. As a token to the opposition, Governor Deen and Bert Dyson were also invited. Deen replied, "Not coming." Dyson said he would be in the Virgin Islands, but wished the couple well.

The wedding was spectacular. Tents erected in case of rain were not needed as the afternoon temperature was in the mid-sixties and the day sunny. Marla was resplendent in a gown of white satin topped with silk lace. Jimmy wore a shiny dark blue tuxedo as did his Best Man, Jason Faircloth. Amos wore a dark green robe. He said, "So I won't outshine my daughter." He escorted Marla from the house to a flowered extension of the veranda. There they were met by the Reverend Howard Hanger, the very progressive minister of Jubilee! a community church in Asheville. Howard read the simple vows; the rings were exchanged; "I do's" were said; the crowd cheered and the partying began.

Marla and Jimmy honeymooned in Madeira which they both loved for its ancient history, sunshine, beaches and, of course, their famous wine. At 67 years, they made love like they were 18. They both had a hearty laugh about this. Both of them had heard the story about Art's "Eros call" from their mother Myra. "I guess ol' Eros is in our genes." Marla said, giggling like her mom had sixty years ago.

"Doesn't get any better than this!" Jimmy said one afternoon as Marla unfurled a big beach umbrella and Jimmy poured the wine.

"I'm happy that one-piece bathing suits are back in style, even if they don't have prints."

"Come on, Marla, you know you are still hot. I could see you modelling bikinis for a swimsuit edition.

Oh, yeah, didn't I hear that AARP Magazine is coming out with a swimsuit edition? Maybe that's what they were calling about?" Jimmy said grinning.

"Ha-ha. I think they were phoning about an upcoming article on the First Lady."

"Yeah, probably, guess you'll be the first First Lady to be the First Daughter as well. And I will be the First Son-in-Law. Or, maybe,I should be First Lord? That has a ring to it that I like."

"All appropriate, I suppose, since Amos represents a lot of 'firsts'."

Jimmy and Marla enjoyed the beach and sightseeing for several days on Madeira. They were about to pack for the trip home next day for the Inauguration the following week when Jimmy noticed a couple of odd things. First their boutique hotel's electronic room key didn't work. Jimmy went to ask one of their Secret Service bodyguards to get another but he was nowhere to be found. He then grabbed Marla's hand.

"Marla, something's wrong." "What's up Jimmy?"

"Room key don't work, and Henry What-His-Name, our SS guy has disappeared. We got to get outta here. Pronto! Come, on, Marla hurry! We'll hide for a minute in this linen closet. Oh, shit!"

"What is it now, Jimmy?"

"Jeezus. It's Henry. Dead." Jimmy whispered loudly. "Bullet hole right between the eyes. This is like *dejavu*. Last time I opened a linen closet was back at Walter Reed when that guy came to kill Amos and us. And that closet had a dead Secret Service guy in it too!"

"Shit!" Marla replied. I guess we are being hunted again?"

"We have to assume that. Hey, look!" Jimmy had turned on his phone's flashlight app, "it's a ZR7 laser pistol bulging out of Henry's sock. The killer musta missed that."

"Guess we should feel lucky if there's only one killer." Marla whispered in Jimmy's ear. "I thought we'd be done with this. After all, Belladonna and the bad Pope are both in jail."

"Right, but there are still a lot of haters in the world. My guess: Muslim Jihadists."

"Well, they do hate Amos, maybe even more than they hate America. Do you think they are going to try to kill us?

▪▪▪

"I think they have had opportunities to do that all week. I think kidnapping is more likely. I don't know how much I'm worth, but the daughter of the President? Priceless!"

Next, Jimmy's cell phone buzzed. "Who's this?"

"Agent Wilbur Ross here. I had a message at the front desk from you saying you and Marla decided to go to Fado; that Portuguese restaurant right across the street. You aren't supposed to do that, Jimmy. I couldn't find you guys or Henry. Fado says you were never there."

"Wilbur, we didn't leave any note. We are hiding in a closet near our room with Henry's dead body. Somebody is trying to kill or kidnap us."

Wilbur Ross, a very athletic African-American, hurried to the second floor of the hotel. His gun was drawn as he rounded a corner into the hall that led to the Johnson's suite. BANG! A shot ricocheted down the hall breaking off chunks of ornamental plasterwork. Ross returned fire and a scream indicated he had hit his mark.

Things were quiet for a few moments and Jimmy and Marla emerged carefully from the closet. Agent Ross trained his pistol on them until he was sure it was them. The three were about to talk when a second assassin in a black jumpsuit came up from behind Marla, grabbed her and held a very large curved knife at her throat. "Drop your weapons, agent, or she dies now!" A bearded man with a thick accent ordered loudly.

Agent Ross complied. He'd seen video of ISIS beheadings and was not about to challenge the attacker.

Jimmy fondled the laser pistol in his pocket.

The Arab made him and Ross kneel. Jimmy winked at Marla who gave the terrorist a backward kick to his shin.

Jimmy had less than a second to zap the knife-wielding man in his left eye with the silent beam of the ray gun.

Ross said, "Good shot Jimmy! Where'd you get the ZR?"

"Henry leant it to me!"

Marla said, "Enough chit-chat, boys, we should be moving. There could be more of them."

Agent Ross called for a bellman to get their stuff and for the police to pick up the dead bodies.

Ross arranged for his dead comrade to be on the same plane they left in, flying first to Paris and then to Washington, DC.

The next day the story was all over the news. The headline that electronically crawls across a building on Time's Square in New York City said it all: "ISIS TERRORISTS MURDER FEDERAL AGENT IN ATTEMPED KIDNAPPING OF THE PRESIDENT ELECT'S DAUGHTER."

Anti-Muslim demonstrations spontaneously erupted across America. Seventeen taxi drivers of diverse nationalities were dragged from their cabs and shot or beaten to death. Amos gave an address to the country as mosques in Los Angeles and Detroit were firebombed by mobs who also lynched several Arab-Americans.

"My fellow Americans, what happened in Madeira this past weekend and what's happening in the Middle East has nothing to do with the law-abiding community of American Muslims, nor is there a connection to those extremists within the community of law-abiding Arab-Americans. Those who would make such a connection are they themselves as un-American as the fiction they write and as foolish as the talk show hosts who espouse those lies. So go back to your homes. Hold vigils for the victims of prejudice and bigotry. Thank you. May God bless America."

People out on the streets did cool down and returned to their homes. Amos had spoken and that was good enough. In the weeks that followed there was something like a serene calm in America. Everyone was anticipating the Inauguration and the State of the Union speech.

Chapter 27 State of the Union

The Inauguration of Arthur Jarvis Barringer was a low-key affair due to the extreme cold weather forecast and the heightened security prevailing since the assassination and kidnapping attempts. Amos said to the heads of the NSA, Secret Service, and FBI, "I want to fly with my own power onto an inaugural platform after circling the White House, Washington Monument, and Capitol Dome."

All three men were speechless, as they sat around a large mahogany table behind closed doors in the Presidential Suite at the Mayflower Hotel.

"Ha, ha! Just messing with you boys!" Amos said to the stern men who were very relieved and joined in the laugh.

■■

Amos continued, "No, I agree we will have to make this swearing in a lot less dramatic than the circus it has become in recent years. Millions will be somewhat disappointed, but I am sure the TV crews will appreciate avoiding ten degree temperatures we'll have here on Wednesday, January 20. I suggest having the ceremony at the Kennedy Center. That's big enough for our guests and small enough to adequately secure."

Amos' Inaugural speech was very short. After he was sworn in, with Marla and Jimmy at his side, Amos said very few words, "With great humility, I accept the trust that the American People have placed in me. I promise not only to uphold the Constitution, but to do the right thing, the just thing, and at all times to hold to the Golden Rule. For if we all adhere to that tenet, all people will be treated just as they would want to be treated. Thank you. God bless America."

For those who missed that speech and for those who criticized its "lack of substance" there were millions who could quote it verbatim. It, along with the Gettysburg Address, became a "memory assignment" for boys and girls in the fourth grade.

A week later Amos delivered the State of the Union address before a joint session of Congress:

"A week ago I swore to uphold our Constitution. That I will certainly do, but I want to do more. I will do more. Our country is not as good as it can be. Our country is weak in its dependence on foreign energy.

It is weak due to burdensome foreign debt and our balance of trade, especially with China. It is even weak in National Defense. More to be said on that later."

▪▪

At this point there was some booing coming from the CRP side of the aisle even though their numbers had been considerably reduced. As the TV cameras panned over to the Joint Chiefs-of-Staff, there were some grim and unsmiling faces.

"I pledge to you to be a reliable steward of our economy; a stalwart defender of human rights and a more just society. I promise to you that I will do everything within my power to guarantee every American's right to live a healthful life and to be free of debt from medical costs when they get sick."

Cheers from Prodems and loud applause ensued.

"Americans have historically been a peace loving people and I will tell you now, I personally abhor war. Under my command no mother will see her son or daughter die in vain for an unjust cause be that for oil, or vengeance, or hatred of another people for their culture."

Hoots of support erupted throughout the vast room. When the applause died down, Amos continued,

"We reward our friends with technology and fair trade and with welcoming arms for those who would live in peace and prosperity with us. But to our enemies abroad, I say, lay down your weapons that you may live in peace and avoid the wrath that awaits you should you continue to threaten us. We have the ways and the means to destroy you."

This time even the CRP was cheering. The Joint Chiefs-of-Staff were not so down in the mouth; some smiled approvingly.

"Now many of you will want to know more details of my 'Plan for America' as I call it. First I suggest you buy a copy of my book, *Musings of an Angel.* It's available in paperback and as a Kindle book."

Peals of laughter rang throughout the hall. Amos laughed with them for his shameless promotion of his book.

"Don't worry about a conflict-of-interest; all proceeds will be donated to charity."

More laughs from the audience.

"Seriously folks, we do have a lot of work to do here. There are several Constitutional Amendments that I shall be endorsing as soon as you here in Congress get to work.

One is for campaign finance reform. I do not think a corporation is a person under the 1st Amendment and neither do the vast majority of Americans. A corporation should not be buying elections with unlimited donations to parties, candidates, or so-called PACs. In fact, America would be better off adopting the campaign laws of Denmark. The UN has cited Demark as the least corrupt country in the world. I think their political campaign laws have much to do with that. There is no PAC in Denmark because advertising, especially negative advertising, is simply forbidden. That is an exception to their very vigorous freedoms of speech and press. The only political advertising you will see there are posters of uniform size with a picture of a candidate, his or her name, and the name of their party. Want to know more? Read their published platforms on-line or in a library. That's it. How many Americans would be very happy if all the political ads on TV simply vanished? 90% or more I would bet.

■■

Thunderous applause and cheering from the Prodems and Modems—none from the CRP who sat with arms folded across their chests.

"Speaking of betting," Amos went on "The National Lotto must go!"

Again, cheers from the left; silence on the right.

"We are a better country than to be run by a state sponsored gambling addiction. Of course, the whole system will need to be phased out until funding for health care and Social Security can be restored through traditional channels. Yes, I do mean taxation. But we will not increase taxes on poor and middle class people by one single dollar. We will tax the wealthiest Americans more; we will tax corporations very much more especially if they have dodged taxes with off-shore incorporation and loophole shelters which we shall close."

The Prodems gave a standing ovation; the CRP stayed put.

"There are many other reforms that I intend to pursue, but I will save those announcements for another day. Meanwhile, I hope that I have given you enough to think about. Thank you. Goodnight, and may God bless America."

■■■

Chapter 28 In the Caucasus

It was a bitter cold day in the village of Shovi, Republic of Georgia high in the Caucasian foothills. The snow laden pines were sagging with the weight. In a log house above the village, a wizened old woman lay dying. She was Monika Garashevili "the oldest person in the world," or so Vlademar Katavili, Commissarof the County proclaimed her to be. The short, ruddy faced man with a blonde comb-over was hoping to capitalize on Georgia's status as home to the oldest people on earth. That was in hopes of attracting tourists and wealthy people who might buy their second or third home there; enjoy the clear mountain air; and maybe live past 100.

Vlademar Katavili made his way up the slope in his new snowmobile to the humble dacha with smoke billowing from the stone chimney on one side. He struggled in the deep snow to the door and knocked loudly. An old woman came to the door.

■■

"Greetings! And how are you on this beautiful day?" Vlademar asked the unsmiling wrinkled old woman who made no reply.

"So what is happening with our dear Monika?" Vlademar asked Monika's daughter, Lena who was a child of only 101 years.

"Come inside Commissar you let out heat. Mother much same. I bring tea. She drink. She not eat for week." Lena replied.

Although no birth records existed from Czarist Russia, Georgian authorities had records on her from 1913, if she was the same Monika who married an army private named Ivan Garashevili in that year. Ivan survived the World War, only to die in the subsequent civil war that was won by the Bolsheviks. Lena was born in 1920 during the turmoil of those early days of the Soviet Union. An old orthodox Bible had this inscription written in faded brown ink: Today 25 February A.D. 1920, Monika Garashevili gave birth to baby girl, Elena Ivanevna Garashevili. Monika claimed to have been 23 years old at the time Lena was born, so she was, by all accounts, 124 years old in 2021.

Commissar Katavili was more than a little excited when he added up the years. He had watched many news programs featuring "Amos the American Angel" as he was called on TV-GEORGIA. He had laughed aloud when Amos had thrown Sean O'Malley to the floor and he had seen the State of the Union address earlier that week. Katavili thought, "Maybe Georgia have angel, too."

He wiped a shock of gray-blonde hair from his ruddy sweating brow.

"Lena, I will have doctor come. He will bring good medicine and oxygen for your dear mother."

▪▪

"She old. She dying. Go back to village Commissar Katavili, leave us in peace."

"Oh, but my dear sweet Lena, you know age of your mother, am I correct?

"Yes, she 124 years. She old. She ready to die."

"Look, I brought papers with stories about American Angel they call Amos. He was 131 years old. He changed, like butterfly, into angel."

"My mother is not angel. She old. She ready to die."

"May I see your mother?"

"OK, she sleeping."

To Lena and Vlademar's astonishment, Monika was sitting up in bed. "Lena, dear, bring me pirogues. I smell them. I am very hungry!" Monika exclaimed. Her wrinkled skin looked radiant and less like an eroded landscape. Her blue eyes were twinkling. Her gestures were quite animated.

Monika consumed a plateful of pirogues. The meat and potato dumplings were not enough. Vlademar helped Lena slice bread, boil eggs, and make tea. After consuming enough for two grown men, Monika, thanked them and went to sleep.

"I have never seen Mother eat so much!" Lena said, still in a state of disbelief.

"I must go now, Lena. I come back tomorrow."

"OK you come back, but bring no one with you."

"OK, Lena, see you tomorrow!"

Commissar Katavili sped back to Shovi nearly capsizing his red snowmobile several times in his reckless enthusiasm. After warming up in his office he paced the floor wondering who he should call first.

After being on hold for 23 minutes, by his watch, Vlademar reached Prime Minister Iraki Garabashvili at his office in Tbilisi. "Your Excellency, this is Vlademar Katavili, Commissar here in Shovi."

"Shovi? Where Shovi?"

"In Caucasus, your Excellency. Maybe you skied here?"

"No, I ski in Sochi, Russia, not in Shovi. Is it in Georgia?"

Vlademar was becoming exasperated. First the long "on hold" with that awful elevator music blasting in his ears punctuated be the universal recording, "Your call is very important to us. Please wait." Now here he was talking to the Prime Minister of a fairly small country who had never heard of his town? "This is travesty." He thought to himself.

"Did you say you are Commissar? Why do we have Commissar in town I have never heard of?"

Vlademar was beside himself. He thought, "Here I am with most important news in history of Republic of Georgia and Prime Minister doesn't know that my town exists. And he is going to believe that we also have angel up here? No chance."

"Mister Prime Minister, let me send you information about our village and potential ski resort here. Sorry to bother you. Good day."

Vlademar Katavili went through his file cabinet for papers he had regarding Amos. He found a tabloid he had saved when he was on a junket to London a couple of years ago. It was a copy of *Day Break.* In addition to the story about the metamorphosis of Arthur J. Barringer, there was the international toll-free number for people to call with "information that will astound the world." Vlademar was sure his information qualified and also noted that *Day Break* paid a thousand pounds for a story they print and ten thousand if it was a cover feature. "Very good!" Vlademar said out loud in his empty office.

Katavili asked to speak directly to Harvey McGarvey, Jr. himself.

"Hello, McGarvey here. Who's this?" McGarvey said in his gruffest voice.

"Alo, thees Vlademar Katavili here, Commeessar in Shovi, Georgia. How you are today?

"How can I help you, Commissar? Something about UFO's seen over Tbilisi last week?" McGarvey replied with unmistakable condescension in his tone.

"No, no, Meester McGarvey. I think we have angel here."

"Oh, no! Do you know how many calls we get about people seeing angels flying about? It's hundreds a week. People don't see UFO's anymore, just angels, angels, angels!"

"Beg pardon, Meester McGarvey, but do you know about old people of Caucasus region?

"Certainly. We did a piece on them in the 1990's. None proved to be more than 105, but we ran with the claims of up to 118. Sold more papers."

"Vell, vee haff woman who is proven 124. I haff seen her myself. Meester McGarvey, she morphing!"

■■■

"Assuming you are correct, just who is this woman and how may we meet her?"

"She near Shovi. I can take you her."

"So where the hell is Shovi?"

"Ess een Caucasus heells. North of Georgia. See Google Earth. You see there. Meester McGarvey, you send ten thousand pounds, OK?"

"Absolutely, if your angel is front page."

After hanging up, McGarvey summoned his son, Harvey McGarvey, III to his office. The third generation of the tabloid and TV Empire was an international playboy that the rival press called "Micky McThree."

Instead of getting angry about this chiding name, Micky adopted it as his official nickname.

"Micky, I have an assignment for you. That is, if you can take a few days off of the party circuit."

"Gee, Dad, no can do. Got a heavy date this weekend."

"Another bimbo pop singer?"

"No, Dad, this one's a keeper. She's actually a brain surgeon. You may have heard of her. She's Dr. Francesca Biscotti."

"Sounds Italian."

"Well she is an Italian-American. She was one of the doctors attending to your angel Amos as he made the upgrade to angelhood."

"Oh, yes! Our paparazzi got a great picture of her standing on the veranda at Kirkland Hall. What a looker! Hold on to that one, Son! But I can tell you that the assignment I am about to give you will get you further with Dr. Biscotti than a date ever will."

"Ok, Dad, what can possibly be as good as a date with Dr. Francesca Biscotti?"

"How about another angel?"

"For real?"

"Yes, real. At least it appears so now. I just had a call from an official in Georgia saying they have an old lady who may be morphing. You need to go there with a camera crew and get the scoop ASAP."

"Ok, I had a great time when I was in Atlanta last year. Best strip clubs in America. "

"No, not that Georgia, the Republic of Georgia. Better buy some winter clothes--- it's ten degrees there now."

Chapter 29 Monika Goes Viral

Micky and his crew took a flight to Moscow and then changed planes for Tbilisi. Micky was bit apprehensive as beside his crew in first class there were ten men with identical black overcoats. Micky leaned over to his camera guy, Phil Ryder, and said, "You think those guys are on business?"

Phil whispered back, "Yeah, they are on business all right. Putin Secret Police business."

The dictator of Russia was keenly aware of the influence the new American President was having on the whole world. The news of a possible emergence of an angel in Russia's backyard came from satellite wiretaps on

Commissar Katavili's phone both when he talked to Iraki Garabashvili and to Harvey McGarvey, Jr. Putin didn't know what to do, but he immediately thought of the potential impact an angel could have on his domain which he considered to include Georgia as with all other neighboring countries.

The plane landed in Tbilisi with no problem. But Micky did have trouble getting the Hertz car rental he had reserved. Seems all the SUV's were taken.

"Very sorry, Meester McGarvey, but all vee haff ees Fiat 500." The Hertz agent said.

"Come, on! I paid for a Chevrolet Tahoe, and you only have a Fiat 500? I could park a Fiat 500 inside a Tahoe!"

"Very, sorry, maybe you take two Fiat's for price of Tahoe?"

"Well if that's all you have, OK." Micky assented and then saw the Fiats, "Oh, what the hell is with the smiley faces?"

Both Fiats had huge yellow smiley faces, ubiquitous world-wide for sixty years, painted on their tops and sides.

The Hertz agent replied, "These for Tbilisi Happiness Festival. Mayor read report that Georgia was an unhappy country. He and Prime Meeneester declare Happiness Week and beeg Festeeval. We haff parade. These cars in parade. Do they make you happy?"

"No, they don't, Goddamn it!"

Micky and his disgruntled crew loaded the equipment in one car with Phil driving. Micky and the other two guys squeezed in the other Fiat for the three hour drive to Shovi. As they left the Hertz lot they noticed two black Chevy Tahoes leaving just ahead of them. Micky said, "5 will get you 10 that we can just switch off our GPS and follow them."

When they arrived at the grey office building or Shovi Square four hours later, delayed by the smiling Fiats getting stuck in various snow drifts, the two Tahoes were parked outside. A stern man seemed to be on guard at the door.

Micky went up to the man and presented his credentials. "We are here to meet Commissar Katavili." Micky said to the man in a black overcoat and traditional Russian fur cap.

"Katavili, busy. Go back Tbilisi."

"Spasibo, Comrade, we know how important your job is. We are from London. Have you ever been on TV?"

The big man smiled, "No, have never been TV. You from TV?"

"Yes, we are. British TV. International. We film you and you will be on a billion TVs."

The man was beaming when he posed with Micky for the camera and sound man. His superior emerged from the building with eight other men in black coats. Vlademar Katavili looked as grey as his coat and the building he stood silently before.

The Russian men put Katavili into one of the Tahoes and headed up the mountain. The head of the Russian team laughed as the two Fiats spun around in the frozen street.

Micky was determined to follow. Amazingly, the little cars found enough traction to get up the slope and arrive at the Garashevili cottage just behind the SUV's.

■■■

"Everyone stay outside!" The head of the Russian security team ordered. He and Vlademar Katavili went to the door and knocked.

Elena came to the door. She spoke in a low voice, "Commissar Katavili, you have come back. Why are many people? You promise no visitors."

"I am sorry, Lena, but these are Russian men and some TV guys from famous *Day Break* in U.K. They all insisted on meeting your dear sweet mother."

"She not here."

"What? Where did she go?"

"She say take walk up mountain."

"By herself? It is dangerous. Far below zero up there."

"She has boy from veellage with her. She be OK."

At that point nobody knew what to do. The security team leader asked Lena, "Who thees boy and where does he leeve."

"He is Petr Petrivili. He leeve in Shovi. His family reechest in Shovi."

One SUV stayed at the cottage; the other headed down the mountain to the village. It was easy for the Russians to find the Petrivili dacha perched high above a dead end lane. Micky's group slid most of the way downhill to the village. They booked lodging at Chalet Aspen, a shabby ski lodge and the only hotel they could find.

After three days of waiting and having checked out the empty dacha, the Russian contingent went home.

Their leader had reported directly to Mr. Putin that the whole matter was, likely, “a wild goose chase.”

Micky and company got in a little skiing, and spent their evenings drinking vodka. Some local girls showed up at the lodge to party with the boys until the wee hours.

On the fourth day, Micky and Phil were out on the slopes skiing when they saw an enormous bird descending in ever tighter circles from the heights. As the bird got closer, Micky shouted to Phil, “Get your camera and the crew! It’s the angel!”

They hurried to get the other guys at the lodge just now rising from bed with the women with whom they had shared the night. “Come on, she’s here! She’s flying!”

Micky also noticed a light on at the dacha of the Petrivili’s. There on the second floor, Petr was busy downloading onto YouTube a three minute video of Monika flying.

Monika, made a soft landing, folded her iridescent wings and strode toward the ski lodge. She was naked except for her covering of golden amber down. She stood 5’10, had a cascade of curly red hair and flashing green eyes. She spoke to the men in English with only a slight accent, “What brings you to our humble veelage? I am joking of course. I know it is I you wish to see. So here I am, Monika Garashevili, world’s second angel. And you must be notorious Harvey McGarvey Third?”

“That’s me, but how did you know that.”

“Petr and I did little research on Google. You best interview me queekly, Meester McGarvey, Petr has already posted some veedeo on YouTube.”

“Oh, no! Scooped by a kid!” Micky muttered to Phil.

■■

They moved into the warmth of the Chalet Aspen. The front desk man brought Monika a green terrycloth bathrobe with a C-A logo. Micky was so flustered and shivering that he hardly knew where to begin.

"It took Amos, the American Angel, nearly a month to 'morph' as we say, to change into an angel. It seems only ten days for you. Do you have an idea about that?"

"I have not had time to fully research question, but I believe that I am natural angel. Meester Amos he was induced after long time frozen. This, I theenk is reason."

With the video camera recording, Micky went on with the interview. The first question had been a good one, but Micky lacked the professional journalism skills to draw any profound insights from Monika. The interview quickly deteriorated.

"You are quite beautiful, Monika. How old are you in 'angel years'?"

"Vell, my daughter, Lena, says I look same as her great-granddaughter so that would be 35 or so. Sank you for compliment, Meester McGarvey."

"Call me Micky, everyone else does. Monika, what was it like flying around the mountains? Were you scared?"

"Yes, at first terrified, but then voice within me says, OK, Monika, just go for it! Ha ha!" Monika replied to another inane question.

The very insubstantial interview continued for twenty more minutes. Micky knew he was already scooped by the boy Petr and that many hours would pass before this particular exclusive interview could be back in London.

■■

"Micky, you are worried about your information getting to your father aren't you?"

"Yes. Monika, can you read minds?"

"Not like you think, Micky, I just analyze data een my brain. It really does not take much of that to figure things out. Go up to dacha. See Petr. He has computer. You can send all your veedeo to London queekly."

Micky did just that and within hours his interview as well as the short YouTube video from Petr got millions of internet hits.

In Moscow, Vladimir Putin was shouting at the head of the security detail he had sent to Georgia,

"So was it too cold for you to wait for angel?" Putin said in a mocking tone of voice. "I will show you cold! You are now Assistant Bureau Chief in Ulan Bator, the capital of Mongolia!"

Chapter 30 Reaction in Washington

Amos, Marla, and Jimmy and the Presidential Staff watched all the news coming out of Shovi and Tbilisi, Georgia. Amos broke the stunned silence in the West Wing of the White House.

"Monika's going to need protection. It is clear from my own experience that a number of 'special interest groups,' as I shall euphemistically call them, don't like angels. They hate what we represent and what we say. They can't stand our criticism and they want us dead."

▪▪

"I spoke with Harvey McGarvey, Jr. this morning. You know it was his son, Harvey the Third, or Micky as he likes to be called, did that first interview."

"I saw Micky's so-called interview. What a bimbo!" Jimmy guffawed.

"Monika?" Marla asked looking puzzled.

"No, no, Monika's cool. I meant that dork Micky McGarvey. All he could ask were sort of Miss America type questions: 'What's it like being an angel? What did your daughter think of you looking younger than her'? I mean, give me a fuckin' break, Micky!"

Amos added, "Yes, I would have liked to have heard more of substance, but Micky did tell Harvey that there were Russian agents on the scene when he first arrived in Georgia. Apparently they left early thinking Monika was a charlatan if she existed at all. Micky stayed, so Harvey told me, because he was having a good time waiting."

Marla spoke up, "So Putin is already aware that Monika could be a threat to him? Good God, what's next with that S.O.B.? If he isn't grabbing up his neighbors, he's crushing the opposition wherever he can."

Jason chimed in, "The only thing we have in common with Russia these days is a mutual war on Islamist jihadists."

"Right Jason, but we have gone our separate ways in dealing with that threat," Amos replied. "Putin wants to maintain the *status quo* when it comes to other countries boundaries while defending Russia's right to expand her borders as he sees fit. My position on the question of states and boundaries, especially in the Middle East, is to realign everything according to culture and ethnicity. We must acknowledge the fact that democracy isn't for everyone. I know I will be roundly criticized for putting that notion forward here and it the U.N., but we simply cannot go on pretending that America's way is best for every country or region."

"But Amos, how can you say that an Islamic State that denies so many human rights and freedoms is tolerable in this day and age?" Marla asked.

"I am sure you are thinking of women's rights, Marla. I agree that situation would be unconscionable and intolerable in the context of most of the world. But it is not so in, for example, Afghanistan, except in the Westernized capital, Kabul. The fundamentalist Islam most Afghans believe in does indeed subjugate women. This is really not so different from fundamentalist Christianity if it had its way. It's just that our fundamentalism is in a very different context. Fundamentalism is strong in America, but not so strong as to abrogate freedoms most people enjoy. The Supreme Court, as conservative as they are, could not uphold Oklahoma's 'Woman's Place in the Home' law, for example. It is ironic that Oklahoma is the only state to ban Sharia Law, but then tried to make laws pertaining to women that sound much like Sharia."

Martin Miller, newly appointed Vice President, entered the conversation, "So, Mr. President, what are we goin' to do about Monika? She will surely have an immediate impact on Russia and on the whole world just as you have, Amos."

"You are right, Marty. I am hoping she downloaded *Musings* into her brain's database. At least then we might start on the same page."

In fact, Monika, had read all thirty chapters of *Musings of an Angel.* It took her only five minutes to read the small volume, but several days to reflect upon its messages. She was now besieged by the world press. She and her daughter had to be escorted to Tbilisi by a company of the Georgian army. They now resided at the Courtyard by Marriott on Freedom Square, in the top floor suite, courtesy of Prime Minister Garabashvili. Monika enjoyed the fitness room. Like Amos, she decided to wear bathrobes with wing slits cut out. The fluffy Marriott robes were perfect. Lena liked the free breakfast and watching old movies on TV. The grand four-star hotel was surrounded by soldiers who had escorted Monika and her daughter to Tbilisi.

Amos and his family watched TV coverage showing the army and hordes of gawking Georgians and tourists who hoped to glimpse the 'Eastern Angel'.

"Publicity does have its virtues," Jimmy Jack chuckled. "Seriously, I am sure those who would bring her harm are going to have to reconsider. Getting past that army and a lot of secret police as well would not be easy."

"You are right, Jimmy, It was Myra who had the bright idea to use publicity to save Amos the First and Marla's P.R. tactics that saved me. By the way, if you haven't heard, Amos the First was shipped out of Rome this morning. He'll be at U.C. Berkeley by tomorrow night. The press is so busy with Monika that his recovery was hardly mentioned," Amos II said smiling broadly.

"I think I want to meet Monika as soon as a visit can be arranged. Marla, please see what you can do about that."

"Thanks Daddy, I'll get on that ASAP. Should be fun!"

The next day, at 5:00 AM, Marla called Prime Minister Garabashvili at his office in Tbilisi.

■■■

"Hello, Prime Minister, this is Marla Johnson calling from the USA. How are you doing?

"Who did you say?"

"Marla Johnson, President Barringer's daughter, First Lady of the United States."

"Oh, yes, yes, I see you on TV with Amos, don't you call him that?"

"Well, mostly I call him Daddy, but you are right, he is Amos."

"What can I help you with today? Oh, and you must sank your father for generous geeft of fighter planes. We already haff use them against Eeslam terrorists."

"I will let him know that. I am calling because my father is interested in meeting Monika Garashevili, your angel, as soon as possible. I think this would be a very important meeting Prime Minister."

"Call me Iraki, Marla, you shall consider it done! And how veell she go to America?

"Daddy, er, Amos, says he will send Air Force One, his plane, to pick her up."

"Excellent, First Lady, excellent!"

"Spasiba, Iraki, good-bye."

■■■

Chapter 31 Monika in America

Three days later, Air Force One touched down at Andrews Air Force Base bearing Monika Garashevili. Her daughter Lena decided she liked staying in the Marriott Hotel until Monika returned. She couldn't get enough of John Wayne and room service.

It was an unusually sunny and warm day in the high sixties, in Washington. A military guard was present. There were hundreds of well-screened journalists and TV teams ready with video equipment for the historic moment when

Monika descended the stairs and walked a few yards to meet Amos. Perhaps it was instinctual, but certainly not planned, when both angels suddenly unfurled their wings high above their heads in unison. The billions watching on live TV screamed in approval at this primeval gesture that everyone seemed to know was a sign of greeting and mutual respect.

"Welcome to America," Amos said.

"Spasiba, I am happy to be here." Monika replied.

They along with Amos' family were caravanned to Camp David, the old presidential retreat in Maryland.

"It is very beautiful here," Monika said to Amos. "Reminds me of my home in Shovi."

The two angels went inside one of the large cabins. Amos asked the family to "take a hike" and ordered the bodyguards to remain outside. Amos wanted complete privacy. Monika agreed.

"I like it here, too. Less noisy than Washington. I think we can have a good discussion here."

"I hope so. I have read your book, *Musings of an Angel.*"

"And what do you think of my musings?"

"I like it. Remind me of Khalil Gibran. *Prophet.*"

"Exactly. You must be reading a great deal as I did when I was morphing. I admit to copying Gibran's style, and maybe, some of his ideas as well."

"Maybe I write my musings as well. We need one for Europe, I think. You wrote about guns. We have no problem with guns because have no guns. Ha ha." Monika said laughing.

▪▪▪

"Yes, I think you should write *Monika's Musings*. My reflections can be somewhat America centered at times."

"Also, I do not agree with all of your philosophy."

"Tell me what you disagree with."

"I have trouble with right-to-life. How can you be for right of choice for a woman to have abortion and also be for the continuity of DNA that ensures that human life goes on forever?"

"That is my toughest question, Monika. I am definitely opposed to abortion as simply a means of birth control, but I do not see a fetus as a baby either. The 'Right-to-Life' people on the religious right in this country think that human life begins with the union of a sperm and an egg; some even with sperm and egg before that union occurred. They say all forms of human life should be protected in law that consequently forbids birth control and all cases of abortion, even for rape and incest. I would agree that the continuation of our heritage as humans through DNA is important, but not nearly as much now that the earth has eight and a half billion people. Unless we destroy ourselves *enmasse* there is little to worry about the extinction of human DNA. Furthermore, even if every last human on earth should die, there is still plenty of other DNA in the universe. Yes, even human DNA is out there."

"Amos, you are a wise angel, but I still think babies should not have to die for any reason."

"I think we should talk about something else, Monika. This is a subject that few people entirely agree on. If you still have more to say about this subject, you can share those thoughts in your own musings. Oh, and be sure to say something about the terrible state of poverty, homelessness, and the egregiously unaffordable costs of adoption in most of the world."

"Amos, you certainly have strong opinions!" Monika responded with a frown.

"Somebody has to."

"True. I have thought of going to some mountain and living as hermit. I would occasionally give advice, but only if it were asked for. You have chosen most public of forums to change world to your way of thinking. You have also exposed yourself to those who see different future and would kill you to realize it."

Amos nodded then said, "Monika, let's get back to the big house; I think they have food up there and I am starving!"

"I was hoping you would say that, the food on Air Force One was not very good and they don't give you enough of it!" Monika said laughing.

In the great room of Big Lodge everyone was eager to hear what Monika and Amos had to say to each other.

"Well, people, let me just speak for myself. Monika is a lovely angel. She and I have much in common, but we also differ in background and opinion. We are as much individuals as any of you."

"Yes, Amos is very wise man. You are lucky to have such President. We certainly agree that the Golden Rule should be the guiding light for all humanity. But enough of ideals. Can we eat? I am starving!"

As a special treat, Amos had a huge order flown in from Twelve Bones in Asheville: Chipotle Blueberry ribs, pulled-pork sandwiches, corn pudding, collard greens, cheese grits, smoked potato salad. Yum!

■■

“Now, Monika, you see what we eat Down South in the USA!” Amos exclaimed.

“Oh, my goodness! I shall never go hungry again! Was it not Scarlet O’Hara who said that? My daughter Lena she watch *Gone with Wind* three times at Marriott Hotel in Tbilisi.”

Everyone had a good laugh at that. All agreed that after that Twelve Bones feast they might never be hungry again.

Chapter 32Violence at Home and Abroad

Just as the family and guests were enjoying the roaring fireplace fire and having after dinner drinks (White and Black Russians), a newsflash came on TV, interrupting *Casablanca.* “We interrupt our regular broadcast to bring you up-to-date on the latest mass shooting rumored to have happened thirty minutes ago, but now confirmed: Forty-six people dead and scores wounded in a shoot-out near Dallas, Texas."

Amos had been briefed by the FBI, but at the time the tragedy was only hearsay.

The NBC News Anchor, Charlie Wagner, continued, "Going over to Arlington, Texas live with our correspondent, Sandy McGuire. So what happened, Sandy?"

"Well, Charlie, it seems there was another mass shoot-out here at the North Texas Gun Show. A handful of protesters came out here to voice their opinions about gun control and regulation. One of the protesters was a Sikh man wearing a traditional turban. He and a couple of other protesters went into the show. They had a megaphone and they began to recite the Second Amendment. Someone yelled 'Muslims get out!' Then the shooting began. One man shot the Sikh. A 'peaceful' protester, can you believe it, then grabbed a gun and returned fire! Apparently, at that point people just panicked and opened up with everything from automatic rifles to handguns. Another senseless tragedy involving guns."

"Thank you, Sandy. There you have it, another mass killing with guns. By our count, that's the forty-third in the past three years. Yes, that's right. And the body count is up to 763 in those forty-three mass shootings. That's almost eighteen people dead per mass shooting. Will America ever do anything about this?"

Amos spoke up, "If I have anything to do with it, we will. Let me offer a suggestion. I will appreciate your comments on it. Suppose we view the dependent clause in the Second Amendment to our venerable Constitution. Few people seem to know that 'the right of the people to keep and bear arms shall not be infringed' is preceded by a dependent prefatory clause in the same sentence which says, 'A well-regulated militia being necessary to the security of a free state (comma) the right of the people to keep and bear arms shall not be infringed.' Clearly the Founding Fathers intended for people to have guns to protect the community and nation from, at that time, marauding Indians and the English, French, or whoever may have threatened us. But, I am certain they expected the populace to be trained to use guns in combat. The country at that time was highly opposed to having a standing army, but highly in favor of citizen militias. Few members of the NRA are aware that their iconic figure, 'The Minuteman,' who fought at Concord Bridge was a certified, documented, and regulated militiaman.

"Nice history lesson, Professor." Jimmy said with a chuckle. "So what would you propose to do about guns?"

"Gun owners and the NRA in particular are afraid, so they say, of the Federal Government regulating gun ownership. Well, then, why not have the NRA, or a competing gun organization, do all the regulating."

Marla jumped in, "Mr. President, the NRA regulating guns? Wouldn't that be like having oil companies regulating off shore drilling?"

"Not exactly. You see there would be regulations enacted into law. It's just that the enforcement would be left up to certified organizations such as the NRA. They would be granted a kind of Federal franchise with a set of rules for them to go by. They would be required to train people as a prerequisite to gun ownership. To own a gun you would have to be a member of the organization, pay dues, show up for meetings on safety, for example. No one convicted of a crime of any kind would be allowed to join the organization. No one with a history of mental problems could belong to the organization or own a gun. People who are organizational members would be forbidden from trading, lending, or selling guns to anyone who was not a certified member. In the case of violations, say, having a gun without certified membership, that would be a civil contract violation, not just a slap on the wrist from the organization. Then the NRA, for example, would do the confiscating of the offender's gun, not federal, state, or local law enforcement. If a gun were used in a crime, the perpetrator's membership, or lack thereof, would be a factor in sentencing. The investigation would include sourcing the gun. Further violations, including trading in illegal guns, could result in indictments or civil litigation and penalties for those involved."

"Sounds like you have thought a lot about this issue, Mr. President," Vice President Miller responded.

Then Monika spoke, "Most people in world think, if they think about it all, that Americans are crazy and dangerous people. It is certainly less civilized way to live with millions of guns in your midst. It creates culture of violence that corrupts much of world."

"I tend to agree with you, Monika," Amos said. "The escalation of violence in the civil wars raging in Africa and the Middle East is stoked by young jihadists who can't get enough of American video war games. It is sad to say that I, a lover of peace and non-violence, am forced take a stand. Unfortunately, that is, with violence as well. As President and Commander-in-Chief, I am sworn to protect the people of the United States."

"What is latest from United Nations on your radical plan to realign all states in Middle East?" Monika said as she revealed that she was not as yet up all current events.

■■■

"The plan is not getting very far. Russia is the main obstacle. Even with extremist Muslims in several areas of Russia, such as Chechnya, Putin dislikes the precedent that might erode his gains in the Black Sea and the Caucasus. He would never allow an Islamic State within Russia. He has enough problems with Iran, especially now that Iran is allied with the USA."

"Theese thinks make head hurt," Monika replied in an exasperated tone. "I thing I need sleep."

Marla spoke up, "Meanwhile the wars rage on. I'm with Monika, let's all get some sleep."

Chapter 33 Monika Meets Putin

■■

Over a few more pleasant days at Camp David, Monika and Amos had many discussions on such topics as their origins, the future of the human race, the history of religion, etc.; the usual 'shop talk' among angels.

Amos asked, "Monica do you believe, as I do, that we humans came from somewhere else?"

"Yes, I have vivid dreams of other times and other places. I think, as you once said, DNA holds memories forever back in time."

Amos smiled and said, "Have you ever read the work of American Astronomer Vera Rubin?"

"Oh, let me think, yes yes. She is discoverer of Dark Matter also called dark energy that fills ninety-five per-cent of space."

"I found a great quote from her, Monika. She said, 'Each one of you can change the world, for you are made of star stuff and you are connected to the universe.'"

Monika said, "It has been wonderful meeting you Amos. Perhaps we can change the world!"

"If you help me, I am sure we can. I do recommend that you avoid American TV and turn down all the offers you have from our talk shows."

"Don't worry Amos, I have seen enough of them to last thees angel's lifetime. I think I return to Georgia."

Monika was returned to Tbilisi on Air Force One. She went immediately to see her daughter Lena at the Marriott who was watching *Gone with the Wind* for the fifteenth time.

"Lena, can we watch something else this evening; maybe *Sound of Music*?"

■■

"I have seen that one many many times. Have you seen *Doctor Zhivago*? You like. About Russia when you were young."

"I read book when I was in America. OK we watch."

The next day, Monika hoped to return to Shovi, but a phone call ended that plan. The phone in the suite rang. Monika answered, "Alo, who this?"

"Iraki Garabashvili, here."

"Oh, Mr. Prime Minister, what a surprise! How are you today?"

"I am fine."

"Are you rested from your visit to America?"

"Yes. Can you arrange an escort back to Shovi?"

"Well, no, I cannot. My good friend Vladimir Putin has invited you to Moscow. I have made arrangements for that visit. Your daughter is welcome to stay at Marriott. I think she like it there."

"I would like to meet Mr. Putin someday, but I want to go back to Shovi now."

"I am sorry, Monika, but that is not possible. Mr. Putin insists on you seeing him tomorrow."

"With respect, Mr. Garabashvili, I insist to go back to my home tomorrow. I can see Mr. Putin later."

"With respect to you, I must tell you that your dacha is no longer in Shovi. It is here in Tbilisi."

"What? Did you do this?"

"Monika, 'Angel Cottage' is now main exhibit at Happiness Museum. It will be featured in Happiness

Parade at the beginning of Happiness Week in August this year."

"This is outrageous, Mr. Garabashvili!"

"Monika, the cottage, your home, was being destroyed by tourists taking little pieces for souvenirs every day. Mayor and I have this idea. We brought the little dacha on truck here to save it as well as to display it."

"I still don't want to see Putin."

"I think you will when you see KGB at the Marriott. You want Lena to have a restful stay here, don't you?"

"OK, I see what you are saying: If I don't see Putin, Lena would be made uncomfortable, is that right?"

"Yes, my dear Monika, pack some fresh robes, your plane departs at 10:00 AM."

Roughly one million Muscovites lined the roads and streets leading to Vladimir Putin's Presidential Palace all hoping for fleeting glance of the Eastern Angel. She arrived at the palace at four o'clock with just enough daylight left to make a stunning appearance on the grand balcony.

Wearing a sable hat and ermine robe, a gift from President Putin, Monika waved and spoke to the 100,000 people in the square, "Greetings Russian people! I come to Moscow today to meet with great President Putin. I carry message from President Amos in America, 'Peace be with you' Spasiba."

Putin said nothing until they were back inside the warm palace. "Monika Garashevili you are looking very good. You like your fur?"

"Da, Mr. Putin, spasiba."

■■■

"Tell me, Monika, what did you and President Amos discuss?"

"Oh, the usual angel topics."

"Such as?"

"The origin of life in the universe; the future of life on earth, religious beliefs, you know, little things like that."

"Religion? What do angels think about religion?" Putin was uncharacteristically smiling.

"Amos and I agree that, on the whole, religion is good for humanity. People are given hope; they are taught at an early age right from wrong. In most places in the world religious organizations do much to provide food, medicine, and hope for people who might have none of those things."

"I, too, agree that religion is a good thing. I opened churches again. They are national treasure full of beautiful art."

"Interesting, Mr. Putin," Monika replied, "but you are atheist, right?"

"Monika, I am too busy for religion. I will say that as former Marxist I agree with Old Karl on one point. He said, 'Religion is opiate of masses.' Religion is very useful for every state be they a so-called democracy, monarchy, or oligarchy. The habit forming drug of religion keeps people happy; they believe in after life and are better able to withstand troubles in their daily lives. One of the worst tyrants in history, you would agree, was Adolf Hitler. The Nazi's embraced the Church and the Church supported them. Here in Russia we too like Church for all it does for us. We especially like Orthodox faith because their leaders either like me or stay quiet."

"Well, well, Vladimir Putin, Man of God," replied Monika with a cynical smile.

"So, Monika, what does the American Angel see as the future of life on earth?"

"We agreed that the planet has no future without much more cooperation among nations."

"Who could disagree with that?"

"Greedy people do disagree with that. They fear that a more democratic world means less profit for rich. They do not want to share to wealth of this planet with people they say are of lower classes. They are Oligarchs. America has them. Russia has them. Prime Minister, you are one of them!"

"You are, as I feared, a 'One-Worlder'. Only an individual's self-interest can create wealth. This was a hard lesson for Russia. That's why we discredit Lenin and Communism. Russia has much wealth like America. We won't share that wealth; we will exploit it for ourselves. By 'we' I mean the managers of resources and strong people with gifts of management skill; politicians like me."

"Oligarchy will fail, Mr. Putin, because it denies the potential of millions of people to grow and prosper and make everyone, including the rich, better off."

"Changing subject, Monika, what says U.S. President about our mutual enemies, radical Muslims?"

"He says you are stumbling block to solution to all problems in Middle-East"

"Oh, yes, he has said in United Nations that disputes be settled by realignment of nations and even creation of new nations. So, Chechnya now new nation?

Never. Muslims there just make base from which they bomb Moscow. Never!"

"I think not, Mr. Putin, if Chechnya was independent they would have no reason to attack Russia. They might have an Islamist state. They might impose Sharia Law there. We, that is, rest of world, should allow this to happen. Likewise, there should be a Palestinian State; a Kurdish State from both Turkey and Iraq; and separate Sunni and Shia States out of Syria, Iraq and Arabia. Rather than spending trillions on endless wars, why not spend few billion on simply relocating people with distinct ethnic, cultural, and religious backgrounds. That is what worked in the division of India and Pakistan, although with more help from the U.N. it could have been handled better and without so much bloodshed. As recently as the 1990's the 'Balkan Tinderbox' wars were resolved when N.A.T.O. intervened as a referee in a bloody boxing match to separate combatants and to create and realign ethnically cohesive states."

"Russia will not be weakened by the further dismemberment of our country!"

"Well, you certainly dismembered Ukraine, did you not? And was it not your position that Russians living there were mistreated and should rightly be part of Russia?"

"Monika, you are idealist. I suggest you go back to Georgia. Do not speak of oligarchy in Russia again. I know you want peaceful life. You and your daughter can live in peace comfortably. But if you decide to take a public path such as President Barringer has done things could become uncomfortable very quickly."

■■

Chapter 34 Monika Embraces Happiness

Monika returned to Tbilisi determined to find a way to defeat Putin. Instead of being intimidated by his thinly veiled threats, they only strengthened her resolve. She spoke to her daughter in the Marriott Hotel, "Lena, we must leave."

"Are we going to dacha in Shovi?"

"No. Dacha is no more in Shovi. In Tbilisi now. In museum."

"Where we go? Will we have TV?"

"Lena, I am not sure, but we cannot stay here."

"I will miss John Wayne and Scarlet O'Hara."

"Yes, but we will see them again, I promise," Monika said, wrapping her wings around Lena in a hug as she might have done with only her arms when she was a young mother and Lena a child ninety-five years ago.

The next morning, Monika called Iraki Garabashvili. "Alo, Mr. Prime Minister, I must see you soon. I have some ideas I would like to share with you."

"Monika, what a pleasant surprise! First you see American Angel; then it is off to Moscow to pay homage to Czar Vladimir Putin. Now it is me, just Prime Minister of Georgia, a humble man who would be duly honored with a visit from you."

■■■

Within the hour, Monika was in Garabashvili's chambers. "Welcome, Monika! Please to sit down and tell me these ideas. Georgia needs all the ideas she can get."

"Mr. Prime Minister, you and our Mayor are brilliant men. Your Happiness Festival is world famous now. All it took to make it so was the appearance of two smiling Fiats in the video made by a boy named Petr in Shovi."

Iraki Garabashvili looked puzzled. "I know the video; the world knows video, but was it not all about you circling the village and then landing. Then there was the wonderful interview with the man from London. Were our smiling Fiats in the film?"

"Oh, yes. They were in the background in several scenes. They made people very happy. There was much comment about them on internet which led to the whole world knowing about the Tbilisi Happiness Festival. Now these festivals are blossoming everywhere. Albania and Moldova have Happiness Month."

"Interesting, Monika, so what is your idea?"

"Well I think you could be the World Ambassador of Happiness with some publicity behind you. I would help you."

"This is good idea, Monika, how would you help?"

"From America I had many requests from TV for me to do interviews. I turned all down. I was interested in proposal for documentary film, but I think video boring just about me. It should also be about our great country and also about you, Iraki, and Happiness. I would say it would be beginning of world-wide Happiness Movement!"

"This is very good idea, Monika!" Iraki said beaming. "Where will this documentary be made?"

■■■

"In Hollywood USA where all great films are made. Iraki, would you please go with me to Hollywood?"

Monika made a call on a borrowed phone to Universal Studios in California. It took her only a few minutes to get connected to a top producer given her position as the most sought after person in the world.

"This is Max Steinmetz, who's calling?"

"Meester Max, eet ees Monika. Angel from Georgia."

"Yes, yes. And how are you today?" replied Steinmetz, a ruddy faced, cigar smoking caricature of a Hollywood mogul.

"I am fine. I am calling today to say I have reconsidered your offer to make film about me."

"Well, I am happy to hear that. And does my offer of ten million US dollars sound reasonable as consideration for an exclusive documentary."

"No, Meester Max; not enough. I want feefty meelion."

"Fifty million?" Max sputtered.

"Not for myself alone. I want money for poor children in Georgia and elsewhere to help them be adopted eef they are without parents."

"Yes, well, I think I could raise that much especially with the adoption angle."

"Meester Max, I also have special favor."

"And what might that be?"

"You have heard of Happiness Festival?"

"No, what's that?"

■■

"Een my country, we have Happiness Festival. Our Prime Meenester, Iraki Garabashvili and Mayor of Tbilisi think of this. Very good for country to be happy for a week every summer."

"A whole week!"

"Yes, one whole week," Monika replied with a laugh and Max Steinmetz laughed with her. "Otherwise Tbilisi and all of Georgia remain unhappy for feefty-one weeks!" More mutual laughter.

"So, what is this favor that you want?"

"To put in documentary at least feefteen meenutes of Happiness Festival. It will be theme of the video. It must have Iraki Garabashvili, lots of smiley faces, the big parade, tanks and armored personnel carriers with smiley faces, pretty girls, and bands. Like Rose Bowl Parade, you see?"

"So, you want the documentary to also be an infomercial and travelogue to promote tourism in Georgia?"

"Yes, and part with Shovi, my village, as a ski destination. And cottage where my daughter, Lena, and I were born, which is now in a museum in Tbilisi, Eet must be returned to Shovi so will be authentic documentary."

There was little the Russian KGB could do to harass or intimidate Monika now. She had out-flanked them with happiness. Monika called Amos on a cell phone she borrowed from a tourist in the hotel who was happy for the selfie with her.

"Alo? Amos?" Eet ees I Monika. I am coming back to America."

"Dear Monika, you are certainly welcome! Is this a holiday or business trip?"

■■

"You could say some of both. Lena and I had to leave. I say more later. Making film in Hollywood. We talk later, OK?"

Amos turned to Jason Faircloth, now the Chief Technical Officer of the United States, and said, "Did you get that?"

"Yes, Mr. President. She must have borrowed a phone to make that call. It was made from a Starbuck's Café near the Courtyard by Marriott Hotel in downtown Tbilisi. She made another call from there to Max Steinmetz at Universal Studios in Hollywood about an hour ago."

"What is that girl up to?" Amos said grinning broadly.

"Our man in Tbilisi says Monika is under pressure from Moscow to be like a Victorian child, seen but not heard. She's under virtual house arrest in the Marriott. Government agents follow her everywhere."

"If she is talking to Steinmetz she will be seen and heard aplenty."

In a week, Monika and Lena, and Prime Minister Garabashvili were headed to Hollywood, with a stop in Washington to meet President Barringer.

"Welcome again, Monika, and is this your lovely daughter Lena?" Amos said to the pair in the Delta Sky Lounge at Dulles International Airport.

Humpbacked and wizened, Lena leaned over to whisper to Monika, "Mr. Amos is very handsome, but he's just like all politicians to say I am lovely. Lena not lovely, but better looking 102 year-olds hard to find." She said this in Russian with Georgian dialect, but Amos heard and understood every word.

■■

"Monika, Lena is very wise and I would say she does not look a day over ninety!"

Everyone laughed. Then Amos asked Monika if she would step into one of the private conference rooms. He said to one of his Secret Service bodyguards, "Please see that Ms. Garashevili is comfortable. Get a John Wayne movie on the TV and some Stolichnaya vodka for the young lady."

In the conference room, Amos embraced Monika. "I think about you every day."

"And I think of you as well," Monika replied smiling broadly.

"Why are you going to Hollywood? Not exactly the place to be a hermit guru."

"Amos, I had to leave. Putin's KGB is everywhere. Putin himself said I should not speak out. He said he could make life 'very uncomfortable' for me and my daughter. He was most concerned that I might expose him as tyrant leading an oligarchy of rich people."

"You discussed your opposition to oligarchy with him?"

"Yes, I did."

"You are very brave, Dear Monika. I saw your public appearance in Moscow on YouTube. You are more popular than Putin and he knows it. He might have had you killed right there in Moscow by a so-called 'Islamist Terrorist' paid by the KGB, but he probably thought threatening you would be enough to keep you quiet."

"The threat just made me stronger. I think that our very public exit from Georgia would be best thing to make us safe. I brought Prime Minister Iraki Garabashvili with me. We make documentary film in Hollywood."

"Yes, I spoke with him when you changed planes in Paris. He's at the Georgian Embassy now and I will see him tomorrow morning. Monika, how did you get the Prime Minister to drop everything and accompany you to America?"

"Amos, you know Iraki very good friend of USA, especially since you gave him twenty fighter planes to combat terrorists. He use some already and he sent soldiers to fight ISIS in Syria. He is very excited about the documentary we will make. It will feature his Happiness Festival. You know he had smiley faces painted on those jets?" Monika could not hold a straight face and began laughing out loud.

Amos chuckled too and then had a flashback to the days of his romance and marriage to Myra Rosenblum. He thought Monika had the same sense of humor. In the next instant, Amos embraced Monika. They hugged and kissed and almost ended up on the conference table making love, but a rap on the door squelched that passionate encounter. Both angels rearranged their robes and looked presentable when Amos opened the door for the Secret Service.

■■

Chapter 35 An International Crisis

The agent said, "Mr. President, we need to get back to the White House right away!"

After arranging to have Monika and Lena put up in the Airport Marriott, Amos was rushed by helicopter to the White House. On the way, Vice President Miller briefed Amos, "We have a crisis developing in the Caucasus. You know those planes we gave to the Republic of Georgia? Well, five of them disappeared from their base soon after the PM left."

"Well, it so happens that PM Garabashvili is going to be at the White House in about an hour. Does he know about the planes?"

"Probably not. We still don't know where they are."

"Is Jason Faircloth there?"

"No. He had to take his cat to the vet this morning."

■■

“Well, find him and get him and Einstein back to the White House ASAP.”

“Uh, pardon me for asking, but what can Jason do in this situation.”

“You’ll see Marty, you’ll see.”

An hour later, Amos, Jason, Jimmy, Marla, and Marty, and the Joint Chiefs of Staff were assembled in the ‘Situation Room’ in the basement of the White House. They were all glued to TVs with CIA and military intelligence links and well as to commercial TV news. “Breaking News!” crawls on all the networks carried the grim reports that Islamic Jihadists, probably from ISIS, had raided an airbase in Georgia and captured five American built fighter planes. After a heated discussion in the room abuzz about what to do about the missing planes, Amos called for order.

“Gentlemen and Ladies, we are facing the first international crisis of my administration. Some in the press will be howling about supplying Georgia with such firepower when they seem to be currying favor with Russia. But Georgia has sent combat troops to Syria against ISIS. There is always a risk that our weapons may fall into the hands of our enemies. This is why I ordered Jason Faircloth to devise a fail-safe plan to deal with situation we face today.”

The Chairman of the Joint Chiefs of Staff, Army General Henry Aaron Robinson, replied with a gruff voice, “Mr. President, why have I not heard of any fail-safe plan for our weapons exports?”

A chorus of “I haven’t either!” came from the commanders of the other services.

■■

“Gentlemen and lady, it is not that I don’t trust you, but there have been leaks of classified information. It is far too easy these days for hackers, spies, and whistleblowers to spill the beans with all manner of electronic devices. Jason, let’s give the Chiefs a little demonstration.”

Jason Faircloth produced a remote controlled toy helicopter which he flew around the room. With the little copter hovering at the far end of the room, Jason said, “Hey, watch this!” He then depressed a button on the remote and the toy blew up with a fairly loud flash and BANG.

Secret Service agents burst into the room, guns drawn, yelling “Everybody down!”

“Don’t worry, fellas, Jason here was showing the generals his new toy. We’re fine. Please resume your duties outside.”

“What the hell was that?” a stunned General Robinson asked.

“Well, people, Chief Technical Officer Faircloth and I decided it would be a good idea to be able to render any weapons we gave away inoperable at any time we feel they are being used against us. All of those Georgian Air Force Planes have a wee bit of C-4 explosive tucked into a small crevice in every one of them.”

“Great idea!” exclaimed Air Force General Marybeth Morgan. “So, how does this work in real time with real aircraft, Mr. President?”

“You will soon see.”

Amos then ordered the Secret Service to fetch Prime Minister Garabashvili who was on the verge of a nervous breakdown.

■■

"Welcome, Prime Minister. I am sorry that we must meet in such dire circumstances."

"Oh, yes, Meester President," Iraki Garabashvili said visibly shaken.

"Things very bad een Georgia. Traitors have stolen planes you sent. BBC had peectures of these planes flying over Tbilisi. I receive message say they destroy whole ceety eef I don't withdraw our forces from Syria! Oh dear God, what can I do?"

Now everyone was glued to BBC TV. Their reporter showed the planes circling Tbilisi. One image of a low flying jet clearly showed the smiley face that had been painted on only a few days before for the upcoming Happiness Festival.

Chairman Robinson muttered, "Jeesus, would you look at that!"

The reporter confirmed what Garabashvili had said. The terrorists were planning to destroy Tbilisi. Panicked citizens were already in a gridlock of cars trying to escape. Two Russian fighter jets had just arrived from the other side of the Caucasus. They were immediately shot down by the Georgian defectors.

"Oh, my God!" exclaimed Garabashvili. Even Putin cannot help us!"

"Don't worry, Iraki, we can take care of this situation. Jason, do you have the coordinates?"

"Yes, Sir! Here's the phone." Jason handed Amos a red smartphone. "The app is up, just enter your password, Mr. President."

Amos entered his secret code. On the screen five dots appeared moving slowly in formation across the

Google Earth terrain map of the Tbilisi area. "Ok, Jason, what's next?"

"Just tap your finger on one of the dots."

Amos tapped the screen and the dot disappeared.

Moments later, the BBC reporter, live on the outskirts of Tbilisi, shouted, "One of the terrorist hijacked planes just blew up!"

Next he reported in amazement that the four other jets had also been blown out of the sky.

The crowd in the Situation Room all cheered. Prime Minister Garabashvili, with tears streaming down his cheeks, said, "Sank you Meester Amos, you have saved my country! You have powerful new laser weapons from space, don't you?"

Everyone else in the room facing the Georgian PM nodded in agreement. This was a rumor that would be perpetuated for a long time.

■■

Chapter 36 Monika and Amos

Once the crisis had abated, Prime Minister Garabashvili returned to Tbilisi. A mob of cheering Tbilisites met him at the airport waving smiley face flags. For that day, perhaps, Georgia was the happiest country on earth. The story that Iraki Garabashvili was happy to spread was that he had stood up to terrorists with the help of his good friend the President of the USA; that he had 'authorized' the President to shoot down the Georgian planes from space. The Happiness Festival got an early start.

Monika had watched the crisis unfold on her TV at the Marriott Hotel. As a Georgian, she was deeply moved that the threat was past. As a woman, she felt a growing affection for Amos. Monika was falling in love.

In a few days Monika arrived in California with Lena. They were met at LAX airport by a smiling Max Steinmetz.

"Greetings, Monika, and to your lovely mother, er uh, I mean daughter."

"Alo, Meester Max, good to meet man behind so many great films. I am looking forward to working with you to create documentary."

"Thank you. I have you booked into the Hollywood Marriott. We'll get started tomorrow morning at about ten."

An excited Lena said to Monika, "We very lucky. You have fitness room; I vill haff *Gone with Wind* and John Wayne!"

The Tabloids and TV jumped on the Monika documentary story, as they say in the South, "like a duck on a June bug." Every night there were progress reports. Most sounded like this:

"Harry, we are now into Day Three of *Monika: the Documentary*" an exuberant Liz Garcia gushed.

"So, what's new, Liz?

"Well, Harry, a boy showed up on the set today. His name is Petr Petrivili. He is from the same village in the Caucasus that Monika comes from. Our sources say he will play Monika's childhood sweetheart Ivan Garashevili. I think that's the man who married Monika and fathered Elena, Monika's daughter."

"Great report, Liz! Folks, stay with FOX for all the latest Angel News!"

One regular viewer of Angel News was Amos. He was glad that another angel was getting more air time than he was although paparazzi and reporters were ubiquitous every time he stepped out of the White House. Amos managed to get a secure cell phone in Monika's hands so they could communicate without fear that every word or text would appear on TV the next day.

▪▪

When the documentary was finished several weeks later, Amos invited Monika and Lena to join him and his family at Kirkland Hall before she was to return to Georgia.

Monika and her stooped but otherwise healthy daughter arrived in Asheville two days later. The throngs of gawking tourists, paparazzi, and world-wide TV lined the interstates all the way to Kirkland. North Carolina had to declare a State of Emergency simply to handle the millions of people who were camping along the route. Amos had arranged for the Garashevili's to fly to Charlotte International and then to Kirkland via Marine One helicopter.

They were greeted on the lawn by Amos' entourage. Monika looked radiant in a fine purple silk robe with her long red hair cascading over her shoulders. She and Amos greeted each other with the now famous wings-on-high salute.

Amos visited Monika in the guest house next to Kirkland Hall. With Lena in the recreation room watching John Wayne movies, Monika took Amos by the hand and led him to the master bedroom. They didn't speak as no words could quite capture their feelings for each other. At that moment touching spoke volumes. The robes were flung in a heap as the naked angels embraced. In the bed they made love for hours.

"Looks like Amos and Monika had a lot to catch up on," Marla said to Jimmy Jack as they sat on the veranda of Kirkland Hall."

"I imagine so. If I hadn't been laid in 63 years, I'd have a lot to catch up on, too! Do you think we should check up on them?"

"Nah, I'm sure Lena will bring the angels back to earth sooner or later."

■■

■■

Chapter 37 Double Trouble

Marla called from the Kirkland balcony when Amos and Monika emerged from the guest house, "Mr. President, better come to dinner and listen to the news. Florida is about to get slammed by a huge hurricane!"

As science predicted, storms had been trending worse for years. This one dubbed Hurricane Delilah, Category 5, was headed straight for Miami. The family gathered in the Great Room at Kirkland Hall to watch the news on a 96 inch TV

"Winds are already picking up down here," said a reporter standing on the sand at South Beach. "Gusts are over fifty miles an hour and the Delilah is still a hundred miles away."

The anchorman responded, "Well Mike, you take care and don't take chances with what looks like a Cat Five storm."

"I'd like to get out, but all the streets are gridlocked and I-95 is a parking lot all the way to Daytona. They can't get a helicopter here. Even if I could get to the airport no planes are leaving. Guess I'll have to ride it out like two million other people around here."

Amos knew this would be the worst storm in American history, making Katrina, Harvey, and Irma seem like ordinary thunderstorms by comparison. He picked up the red phone and called the governor of Florida.

"Randy, this is the President, I am declaring a state of emergency now."

"Good! Looks like Andrew and Katrina put together."

"Yes, and their child Delilah is a very naughty girl."

"I'm mobilizing the National Guard in Florida, Georgia, and Alabama. My weather advisors just said the surge could be as high as twenty-five feet. People need to get into high rises or the third story apartments now. Get the message out, Randy!"

"I'll do my best Mr. President."

When the Governor's message got out on all media outlets, panic ensued. It took more than an hour to get northbound access on the southbound lanes of I-95 and US 1. Several crashes soon had those lanes closed and backed up as well. In downtown Miami chaos prevailed as people scrambled to get as high up in the office builds as they could.

Four hours later Delilah hit full force. Winds hit 200 miles per hour at the peak and then the predicted surge came in. South Beach was obliterated. Many buildings came completely down. In downtown Miami glass blew out of many high-rises. Panic swept through the tens of thousands of refugees who had gone there for safety.

Early reports the next day had estimates of more than a hundred thousand missing or dead and tens of billions in property damage. Delilah passed over the peninsula and out into the Gulf of Mexico where she gained strength and wreaked more havoc up Florida's West Coast.

The next day was sunny and only slightly breezy over South Florida. The President made the ritual fly-over to personally inspect the damage. Marla and Jimmy Jack went along.

"Oh, my God!" Marla exclaimed. "I have never seen anything like this—not even in TV disaster movies. Where is South Beach?"

"She's gone, Darlin', just gone," Jimmy responded.

Amos was on a cell phone with the Governor when Marine One, the White Hawk helicopter lurched violently to the left. Everyone was slammed against the right side of the copter.

"What's that about, Captain?" Amos shouted.

"Evasive maneuver, Sir! Somebody just fired a missile at us!"

The next moment a second missile struck Marine One and the copter began a rapid decent. With the ground rushing up, the side door blew off. Marla screamed. Amos grabbed his daughter with one hand and took Jimmy by his belt and leaped out of the smoking helicopter. Amos unfurled his wings and made a spiraling glide to the ground. A mile away Marine One crashed in a fiery explosion.

▪▪

Amos, Marla, and Jimmy Jack took shelter in a mostly destroyed warehouse near I-95. Amos and Jimmy tried their cell phones, but the nearby towers were rendered useless by Delilah.

In Washington the scene in Florida played out in real time. Jets were scrambled from Homestead Air Force Base but there was little they could do now. A news helicopter from Orlando had just filmed the attack on Marine One. They did not see the President escape. At this point everyone believed the President was in the crashed copter.

Al-Jazeera released a statement from ISIS saying they were responsible for shooting down the President's helicopter. Vice President Miller was on TV immediately.

"My Fellow Americans," Martin Miller began. "Today may be the saddest day in our history. Not only have we seen the natural devastation in South Florida, but we may have lost our Great Leader and President Arthur Barringer known to you all simply as Amos. While the death of the President has not been confirmed, we do know that Marine One on which he and the First Lady and First Son were passengers did crash amidst the ruins caused by hurricane Delilah.

We have confirmed that Marine One was shot down by a terrorist surface-to-air missile. I can assure you that in addition to the massive relief effort on-going for the hurricane victims all of our armed services are in action at this time to attack and destroy the invaders."

The Press Conference erupted with screaming reporters.

"Mr. Vice President, do you know how the terrorists got to Miami?" a stringer for the Miami-Herald asked.

▪▪

"As yet, we do not. But we have an idea. There was a general warning in affect for all watercraft to avoid Miami hours before the storm hit. The Coast Guard reported a high speed boat, a so-called 'cigarette boat,' headed directly to the beach in some very rough seas. The captain of the Coast Guard boat blasted a horn and broadcast a verbal warning to get into port. The warning was ignored and, meanwhile, as you can imagine, the Guard boat had other things to deal with at that time.

This morning, despite a curfew to prevent looting, there were dozens of people out on the shore and in the streets of South Beach picking up debris as well as looting. Someone took video of the wreckage and posted that on YouTube. Several blocks into what was the City of Miami Beach the cigarette boat was found. A few moments ago a military unit searched the boat. A National Guardsman found radical Jihadist literature scattered about. So that's how we think the terrorists got to Miami."

In Miami, Amos, Marla, and Jimmy Jack were holed up in the warehouse.

"What's next, Mr. Prez?" Jimmy asked.

"We stay put for now. I am pretty sure ISIS or Al-Qaida is behind the missile attack."

"And probably Delilah as well!" Marla offered some gallows humor.

"I would guess they have a base." Amos suggested. "It's probably in the Bahamas and they planned the attack on authorities whenever a storm was predicted to hit South Florida. Presidents and Governors and a few Congressmen always flyover the day after a big storm. Terrorists will say it's not bad luck, but the 'Will of Allah' that brought devastation to America."

▪▪

As Amos guessed, there was an ISIS base on a remote Bahamian island. It was discovered by satellite and taken out by a drone that very afternoon. But the landing party was alive and well. The terrorists reached the burning copter ahead of the National Guard andNavy Seals. They found no Presidential party, but tossed in a grenade for good measure thus destroying more evidence at the crash site.

Amos was holding his head in both hands. A trickle of blood streamed down his face from a cut on his forehead the result of shrapnel during the missile attack.

"Are you hurt Daddy?" an alarmed Marla asked.

"No, it's nothing. I'm just concentrating on some trigonometry."

"So you're working on some math equations having survived a terrorist attack?" Jimmy said looking incredulous.

"Yes, just trying to figure out from where that missile was launched. We were flying over that power plant over there about two miles away. The missile came straight up from there. The copter went down about a half mile east of here. I think, just an educated guess of course, that the terrorists arrived by boat and planned to take out the power plant, but Delilah made that unnecessary. Their next target was any politician, me or the Governor, who happened to be flying over today. They probably hadn't counted on the storm being this massive, but they made the most of it."

"So where are they now, Genius?" Jimmy said grinning.

"Well, did you hear the explosion about 10 minutes after the crash?"

■■

"No, I didn't, but you have that extra keen hearing."

"I would say the terrorists went to the crashed helicopter and didn't find us. They probably threw in a grenade in frustration or just to cover up evidence. I think they are looking for us right now."

"They are a hunting party with plenty of firepower." Marla added.

"The only weapon we have is my Z71. Never leave home without it." Jimmy said. "And its range is less than thirty yards."

"We may need that, but not for poking the brains out of Jihadists. More likely it can be used as signal when the good guys coming looking for us."

There was movement in a nearby building. Amos whispered, "Marla and Jimmy, be absolutely quiet. Go to the back corner of this building then up to a solid piece of the roof and wait."

Amos concentrated his hearing and heard some low conversation in Arabic, a language he had mastered in lessons from Rosettastone.com.

"Ahmed, go to the warehouse. It is the only building standing in this area. The Devil and his spawn may be hiding there from the wrath of Allah."

A bearded man armed with an AK-47 soon could be seen by Amos making his way toward the warehouse. A Coast Guard helicopter appeared circling overhead. Jimmy and Marla made no sound, but waved their bright yellow jackets to get the pilot's attention.

On the ground outside the warehouse, Ahmed heard a strange voice. Amos had raised a long PVC pipe to his mouth an in an unearthly loud tone spoke these words in Arabic, "Ahmed, listen to me. I am the messenger of Allah. You have been deceived by Satan. Lay down your weapon and pray for the mercy of Allah! Allah akbar!"

The terrorists in the other building fired their last SAM on the circling helicopter. It missed, but it did reveal their location. A Navy jet swooped in and blasted that location.

Ahmed, the terrified terrorist, laid down his weapon and fell to his knees. Amos picked up the rifle and waited for the marines to arrive.

The helicopter landed and soon Marla, Jimmy, Amos and Ahmed, in handcuffs, were aboard.

Back in Washington, Monika tearfully greeted Amos at Andrews Air Force Base. There wings on high created a private shield against the paparazzi cameras with long lenses. They had just enough time for one deep kiss.

Chapter 38 Monika's Headache

The Presidential Party went to Camp David to recuperate from the trauma of the past several days. Monika and Amos spent a day and a night in one of the cabins talking and making love most of the time.

"You know, my dear Monika, I am falling very deeply in love with you." Amos declared as he lay on his back staring up at the rustic open beamed ceiling.

"Oh, I do love you as well, Amos."

"Would you marry me?"

"Well, I suppose we should marry, if for no other reason than to get incessant press from gossiping about us twenty four and seven." Monika replied with a wry grin.

"Would you be comfortable if I made an announcement at dinner this evening?"

"It's good. I am ready, Mr. President. But can a Georgian Angel be First Lady?

And what about Marla? Will she be unhappy not being First Lady?"

"Don't worry, Monika, we have already set many precedents and, my daughter? I think she would very much like not living in the fishbowl of the Whitehouse."

That evening at a large dinner party that included, to some surprise, a couple of progressive-minded journalists Amos rose to propose a toast.

"Dear people I want to thank several folks for our rescue in Florida especially Sam Baker Captain of the Coast Guard, General Morgan of the Air Force, and the heroes of TV station WSVN who bravely flew into enemy fire and helped direct the military to destroy the terrorists."

After a big round of applause, Amos remained standing.

"My close encounter with death has made me even surer of just how precarious and uncertain life can be. It made me reflect on the future. And it made me even more aware of the people most precious to me. And that includes Monika, the Eastern Angel."

■■

More applause, and some tears from Marla and Monika.

"I want to announce this evening that my Dear Monika has accepted my proposal of marriage. We have not made any specific plans, but, rest assured it will be a memorable event when it happens."

Everyone stood again in joyous applause, whistling, and shouting.

A happy Elena, said, "I have prayed my mother to marry for hundred years."

Everyone including Amos and Monika laughed hard at that.

Later that evening, back in their cabin, Amos was embracing Monika in their king-size bed. He made some moves of foreplay, but Monika pushed his hand away. "I am sorry Amos, but I have headache."

Amos, looking a bit chagrined, replied, "Monika, you reject my advances with the oldest cliché in the book of clichés and we aren't even married yet?"

"No, no, Amos, I really do have headache and it is very bad. Oh, my God!"

Amos massaged Monika's temples and found some Tylenol which Monika reluctantly took. It had no effect after an hour. At 1:00 AM, Amos called for a doctor. Monika had a high fever and was barely conscious.

The doctor told Amos, "We have to get her to Bethesda ASAP!"

Amos called for a helicopter and Monika and he were on the way to the hospital within minutes.

■■

The entire entourage was wakened by the helicopter and some orders being shouted above the noise.

"What's happening?" Marla asked

"Don't know." Jimmy replied. "I think I heard 'Bethesda' as they were taking off."

"Good Lord, somebody is in trouble. Are Amos and Monika still in their cabin?"

A Secret Service agent replied, "No. They went on the chopper."

At the hospital emergency room, Monika was wheeled in on a gurney. She was immediately hooked up with an IV and wired to a monitor. Her vitals were stabilized and soon her temperature stopped rising.

Amos informed the staff on duty, "Monika was fine early this evening and then complained of a severe headache."

Dr. Francesca Biscotti had been up late watching the news and thinking about the announcement of the forthcoming Angel Wedding. "How wonderful!" she thought

Within an hour of seeing the TV news she arrived at NIH. Much of her research had been on headaches and brain activity. Dr. Biscotti looked at the blood work as well as the electronic information. Then she ordered an MRI.

"Mr President, I see a tumor in the brain of Monika." She told Amos

"Oh, my God, no!" Amos replied.

"I'm afraid so. It may be operable, but I cannot say for sure."

■■

When Jimmy and Marla arrived at the hospital a couple of hours later, Amos was in deep despair.

"Monika has a brain tumor." Amos matter-of-factly told Marla and Jimmy.

"Oh my God! " Marla exclaimed.

"Can they get it?" Jimmy asked.

"Dr. Biscotti says she doesn't know. I think that's Doctor Code for 'probably not'."

"Daddy, it's not like an angel to be pessimistic or cynical. There have been a lot of advances in brain surgery, especially with lasers."

Monika's vitals were stabilized and, over a week Dr. Biscotti and a team of brain surgeons developed a plan. They would use Faircloth Helmets to explore Monika's brain in 3-D then use lasers to destroy as much of the robin's egg sized tumor as they could without harming nearby areas of the cerebral cortex.

At a hastily arranged press conference Amos said, "Under the circumstances I cannot fulfill my duties as President. Until the critical situation with my fiancé is resolved Vice President Martin Miller shall act in my behalf."

The press had a thousand questions, but Amos, grim-faced, turned away without answering them.

That evening, the team of brain surgeons headed by Dr. Francesca Biscotti began the extremely delicate process of opening Monika's skull and moving tissue away from the tumor."

Dr. Biscotti was making steady progress when she found some extra dense grey matter.

■■■

"Would you look at this!" she exclaimed to a colleague. "I mean touch it. Is that familiar?"

"No." offered the masked surgeon next to her. "It's thick, dense, not spongy like any grey matter I have ever encountered."

"And check out the monitor. Look what happens when I probe with my finger."

"I see that. It's spiking! That isn't supposed to happen under anesthesia and that part of the brain is not supposed to have tactile sensation."

"Something's going on with Monika's brain that none of us have ever seen."

All five surgeons agreed. The next amazing thing was with the tumor itself. A half an hour ago it had been the size of a small egg. Now it was as small as a lima bean.

Dr. Biscotti said, "I think we need Dr. Singh here ASAP."

Omar Singh who had been the expert endocrinologist attending Amos' resurrection, was working in an adjoining building and awaiting the results of the surgery on TV along with about three billion other people world-wide. He arrived in minutes and was in contact with his colleagues in surgery within twenty minutes.

Singh said, "Monika's blood shows extremely high levels of endorphins. There are very high levels of tryptophan and some new hormones and proteins I have never seen before. I am not prone to guessing, Francesca, but I think the shrinkage of the tumor is a direct result of a conscious, or unconscious, self-created cancer fighting biochemistry."

■■■

"You are saying, in effect, that Monika's biochemistry may be curing her cancer?"

"Well, we just might leap to that conclusion." Dr. Singh replied smiling broadly in his sing-song Indian accent.

A further review through the MRI Faircloth helmets showed that the tumor had completely disappeared. Monika was given some antibiotics that were probably unnecessary, sewed up, bandaged, and sent to the ICU for observation.

"What's the word, Dr. Biscotti?" Amos looked hopeful due to the appearance of a radiantly smiling Francesca.

"She's doing quite well. I would like to say our surgery was successful, but, it seems, Monika mended herself!"

"What do you mean?" An incredulous Amos replied.

"Just that. Dr. Omar Singh said, "You may remember me from when you were a patient here. I have detected unique compounds in Monika's blood. She was, in effect, creating her own cancer-fighting drugs in her own body. That, I believe, caused the tumor to shrink rapidly. We saw a miracle happening in front of our eyes."

"Wow! If Monika gets strong enough to donate some blood, maybe those miracle drugs could be reproduced from her? That could be a cure for cancer!" Marla was practically shouting.

"That's exactly what I was thinking." Dr. Singh replied. "The chemistry of the human body is vastly complex and a human angel's apparently even more so. It may be too early to say that this is a direct path to curing cancer, but it seems that it might be."

■■■

Amos was overjoyed. He said, "You know I was thinking that I may have something special going on regarding healing when I recovered so quickly after the attack in Florida."

"Yeah," Jimmy responded. "You took a hit when our 'copter went down. Your face had blood on it. I forgot all about that. The rescue guys picked us up and there was a little blood on your face, but no wound."

"That's right. I don't even have a scar. I certainly will contribute as much blood as I can for cancer research. I cannot think of a better legacy."

A day later the Presidential entourage was down at Kirkland for a week of recreation and reflection on the amazing recent past events as well as to plan a forthcoming wedding.

Chapter 39 An Angelic Wedding

▪▪

Security was tighter than ever as the world's most anticipated wedding took place at Kirkland Hall in June 2022. There were a huge number of international celebrities including Pope Francis II who was as progressive a pontiff as his namesake had been. Also in attendance was the Ayatollah Ibrahim Allah Akbar, Supreme Leader of Iran, now an ally of the US, Most Reverend Ivan Sheradnadze the Metropolitan of Tbilisi, Iraki Garabashvili President of Georgia, the entire Prodem and Modem caucuses of the Senate and House of Representatives, nearly every A-list Hollywood celeb including Max Steinmetz. The list went on and on.

One of the most controversial figures at the ceremony was Amed, the Jihadist who had tried to assassinate the President in the Delilah Raid. Amos had pardoned him. Amed truly believed now that Amos was a messenger of Allah. The presence of the many Muslims at the wedding further strengthened that conviction.

The Reverend Howard Hanger administered the vows on the veranda of the enlarged Kirkland Hall. He then read the passage from the Prophet *On Marriage*. The crowd cheered loudly as both angels unfurled their wings and ascended a special set of stairs erected three stories above the mansion. There Amos and Monika delivered a brief speech:

"We are wed here today angels of the East and West." Amos began.

"Yes, and we hope with all our hearts we unite peace loving people of whole world." Monika continued

"Assembled here today are the leaders of many nations and religions. They may differ from one another in beliefs, in customs and in culture, but they share, as do we, a common attachment to the Golden Rule." Amos replied.

▪▪

"This is the foundation of World Peace." Monika added.

With that both angels dropped their robes to gasps from the crowd. They were nearly naked. With their natural down covered bodies shimmering in the bright sun, Amos and Monika unfurled their magnificent wings and soared from their perch.

"Hooray! Bravo! Hallelujah!" were the shouts from the crowd below. The couple circled the crowd twice, then for the benefit of the million or so people gathered along I-40, they glided once down the highway and then to the Asheville Airport. Jason Faircloth met them on the tarmac with fresh robes. They boarded Air Force One and took off for an undisclosed location.

Thirteen hours later the newlyweds arrived in Tokyo. Monika and Amos had learned something about each other that neither had expected: They could read each other's minds.

Monika first described the phenomenon as thought transfer. "It is like two smartphones that share information just by being near each other. Amos, did you say anything to me about honeymoon in Japan?"

"No, but I was thinking about where we might go."

"Well, I had this message from you. It came like daydream. We were flying around Mount Fuji at sunset."

"Yes, yes." Amos replied I wanted to surprise you, but that seems impossible if you are reading my thoughts. And the flight around Fuji? Exactly as I was imagining. How romantic would that be!"

Monika then said, "Let me try something." She closed her eyes and got a wrinkled brow as she beamed a thought to Amos."

■■

"Oh, no! Pachelbel's *Canon?* A bit overused, but very lovely none-the-less. And who's playing it? Let's see. Could that be Yo Yo Ma with the Tokyo Symphony? Brilliant Monika! How did you know the great cellist was in Tokyo?"

"I googled it. Then I sent Yo Yo message on his Face Book site. He said he would get the symphony up to Mt. Fuji tomorrow, which is now today. He said he can't wait to see us circling mountain while he is playing."

Later that day, despite Secret Service objections, the couple boarded a helicopter which took them near the top of Mt. Fuji about an hour before sunset. Halfway up the slope, Yo Yo Ma and the orchestra set up on the stage normally used for the Mt Fuji Jazz Festival. As the sun neared the horizon, the couple leapt from an outcropping of rock and began a wide spiral around the summit then a slow descent to the site of the musical performance. The scene was videotaped from many angles and was instantly transmitted by satellite around the world. Billions saw the spectacle on TV and millions of them could not help being moved to tears of joy.

After the concert, Monika and Amos were taken by limo to a secret hideaway located on the lower slopes of Fuji and provided by the prime Minister of Japan. They made love for hours wrapped in each other's arms and wings. As the sun rose, Amos whispered to Monika, "This is the happiest moment of my life. I love you so very much my sweet Monika." Tears of joy were running down his cheeks.

"You didn't have to say that, Dear Amos, I have already read your thoughts. I love you too!"

■■

Chapter 40 Nine Months Later

On Valentine's Day, 2023, Monika and Amos were in the maternity ward at Walter Reed Medical Center. Marine One helicopter had brought the First Lady and President in her first hour of labor.

Amos was pacing the floor and recalling the birth of Marla, his first child. "I guess it doesn't matter how many times you go through this, the anticipation and apprehension is the same." Amos confided in the obstetrician, Dr. Felix Hanson.

Dr. Hanson replied,"Know what you mean, Mr. President. It's the same with me and I have five kids. By the way, the First Lady said she felt the same as you. Her first born Elena she said, I think, was born 102 years ago, she remembers as if it happened yesterday. Uh-oh, there goes my beeper. Gotta run. Mr. President, an orderly has a gown ready for you if you want to be present in delivery."

Amos donned a green gown and two secret service agents hurried with him down the corridor. Amos went into the bright yellow room a saw his beaming wife in apparently no pain at all. They had decided against ultrasound which was largely unused lately due the ubiquity of Faircloth helmets. Jason Faircloth himself had volunteered to "take a peek at the fetus" in his words. Amos admonished him, "Too much technology, Jason. I know you love it, but we want to be surprised.

In the last month, even at Christmas, Monika was getting awfully big. "Great with child was an understatement. Huge was a better description."

■■

Amos had suggested, "Gee Monika, maybe you have two in there?"

"By the frequency and placement of kicking" she said, "I think your intuition may prove correct."

They didn't have to wait long. Dr. Hanson had very little work to do as out popped two red-headed babies, a girl and a boy, in rapid succession.

Both were fat as Raphael's cherubim and soon were nursing with abandon. As she was wheeled back to the maternity ward, Monika exclaimed to Amos in a whisper, "This is even better than Fuji!"

Later that day, Amos, Monika, and the twins, Margo and Jack, were delivered back to the White House. Paparazzi were screaming for a photo-op which the President assented to. One hundred were screened and admitted ten at a time to the Press Room. There was virtually nothing else on the news for days after the photo shoot.

Amos, of course had much to do being President and Monika was glad to be watching the twins grow.

Amos had taken the Evelyn Wood speed reading course on line and was able to accomplish in a few hours work that would take other presidents days with a lot of reading matter simply skimmed over. Still, the President of the United States had little time for family. Sure he stuck his head in the nursery once a day to say, "How's it going. Have everything you need?" And so on

One day about six months after the twins were born, Amos was in the nursery when little Margo jumped from her mother's lap and landed down on the thankfully thick carpet. Amos quickly picked up his baby girl and said to Monika, "My goodness! No tears; she's just giggling. I haven't held her in what, a week?"

"More like two." Monika said in a chiding tone.

"And she's so big. Is Jack this big?"

"Almost. She's 5.1 kilos and he's 4.9"

"Golly, they've doubled their weight in six weeks!"

"It seems they have. You need to visit more often, Amos. And, while you are here, I have other news that may surprise you."

"Oh, what might that be? As President of the United States, I get to be surprised almost every day."

"Ok, now I surprise you again today. These little cherubs as you like to call them really are cherubim!"

"You mean, uh, baby angels?"

"Oh yes, and there goes theory about angels being real, but cherubim, not. Also the theory that humans have to become one hundred twenty-five years to change to angels? Well our children don't need to morph. They just needed angel parents!"

"Monika, how do you know this?"

"I know. I am with them all day every day. I talk to them every day. I say, "Who do you love?" Both of them say "Mama."

"That's pretty early for speech isn't it?" Amos said looking puzzled. "Anything else?"

"Yes." Monika said handing Jack to Amos. "He's ready for diaper change."

Amos awkwardly unfastened the soiled diaper and crudely affixed a new one getting the tape in the wrong place so Jack's diaper was askew.

"You need much more practice Amos," Monika laughed. "Before you put his shirt back on, look at his back."

"Bumps! I see and feel lumps!" Amos also was laughing now. "The little bugger is budding wings!"

"Go back and be President, Amos. But come back more often, especially when they start flying around."

The next month was chaotic for the First Family. It proved impossible to keep the 'White House Cherubs' as the twins had come to be called, a secret from the public. A White House maid had spilled the beans when she couldn't stop grinning when she was home with her family. Tywanda Washington really tried for many weeks to contain herself, but failed to do so.

Tywanda couldn't help saying to her husband over and over, "Those babies are soooo cute. They are soooo sweet. They are soooo precious!"

Her husband Reggie said, "Are they soooo cute and precious because they are white or because they are angel babies?

"No Reggie, they aren't white—they pink! And you know what? They <u>are</u> angels, too, just like their parents."

"What you sayin'?"

Tywanda caught herself and stumbled on her words. "I mean they are angels just like our babies were angels when they was small."

"Well, you never said that 'bout them. Our kids was rug-rats, devils, and a big ol' headache, 'specially when you was workin' two jobs to feed them. That White House gig came just in time, Girl. You can thank Mr. Barack Obama for that."

Reggie really knew what Tywanda was talking about when he found a book she had checked out of the DC Library. The title was *Little Angels: Seraphim and Cherubim* by Myra Rosenblum-Zimmerman.

When Tywanda returned from work the next evening, Reggie had his feet up on the coffee table reading *Little Angels.*

"Ty, Baby, I been readin' your book 'bout little angels."

"Well, it's good to see you reading. Did you learn anything?"

"Yes I did, Ty" Reggie said in a matter-of-fact tone. "What I think I really learned is that our White House has a maid that helps care for a couple of cherubs. Is that right?"

"Oh, Reggie, I am not supposed to tell anybody about them. Not even you. You gotta keep this ultra secret, OK?"

"No, Tywanda, Reggie can't do that. Reggie knows what Reggie knows. This is knowledge worth a whole lot of money, Darlin'. You always said I should grab opportunities that come my way. Well this is opportunity and it don't knock but one time."

"Reggie, don't say nothing! You know I'll get fired if they know I let the cat out of the bag."

"Uh-huh, well, maybe this cat just makes an anonymous call to that rag, *DC Confidential* or even FOX News. Shit, they paid some kid a thousand dollars to say what Jimmy Jack was eating in the Mayflower Hotel. I know the boy that got paid. How much would they pay for this tip?"

Two days later, Reginald J. Washington was looking at the biggest check he'd ever seen in his name or anybody else's: $50,000. The day before the whole world knew about the twin angel babies.

Marla Johnson got a call from Harvey McGarvey, Jr. "Couldn't you just have rung me up with your cell phone to tell me about your little half brother and sister. Look what I have done for your family and this is how you repay me? Somebody got the biggest scoop since your step mother Monika appeared."

"Mr. McGarvey, with all due respect, neither I nor Jimmy Jack knew anything about the cherubs." Marla said."I had to watch FOX news just like everyone else to hear about them."

Jimmy Jack was grinning about Marla's expression 'with all due respect'. He said, to Marla, "Ask him about Micky and Francesca." Jimmy read online that their engagement had been broken off by Dr. Biscotti. "Tell him we want the very latest gossip on that."

Marla switched to speaker phone. "To change the subject to the second most talked about event lately, whatever happened with Micky and the lovely Dr. Francesca Biscotti?"

"Marla, I don't know what happened. Micky came to my flat one night, quite inebriated. Thank God for Uber that he wasn't driving his Ferrari. He said just two words before he passed out on the kitchen floor.He said 'cubic zirconium.' What did that mean?"

■■

Marla had the speaker on and she and Jimmy could barely stifle their laughter. Marla said, "Harvey, I actually know more about that than I do about my baby sister and brother. I'll tell you sometime. Gotta run, have a nice day. Good bye."

Harvey threw his iPhone 10 at the wall. "Damned ingrates!"

▪▪

Chapter 41 Conspiracy

Every radio, TV station, and internet news and social media had non-stop discussion about the Angel Family. Most of the "news features" were entirely made up. Some went so far as to say the tots were already flying months before that became a reality. Brilliant computer graphic artists took the original paparazzi video from that early session in the Press Room and managed to animate the babies, age them by three months, and had them flying in no time. Only a very trained eye could detect that the scenes were entirely fake.

At an important press conference supposedly dedicated to Amos' breakthrough agreements on Middle East national realignments and peace, all the questions were about the babies.

"Mr. President, congratulations on ending 70 years of stalemate and war in the Middle East, but what our audience really wants to know is: Are your cherubs flying yet?" One top journalist stooped to ask.

Amos replied, "Thank you, Mr. Haywood. Yes, the wars have ended and peace is at hand. And no, the babies aren't flying yet. Their wings are only about six inches out so far."

Another reporter called on asked, "Are they talking?"

■■■

“Walking and talking,” Amos replied. “I think I will turn this session over to the mother of the cherubs since you are clearly more interested in them than in World Peace. Monika, they are all yours.”

“First Lady,” Sam Rockford here.”

“Yes, Mr. Rockford you are still Science Editor for *Pittsburgh Press*?”

“Yes I am and still fascinated by Amos, and yourself, of course. And I guess the world is now fascinated by your children. Amos said the children are both walking and talking. That’s pretty quick development. Can you tell us more?”

“Of course. I should add that they don’t just walk; they run. And climb up drapes like cat. They also hide and think it is funny that we can’t find them. And they talk. They are both getting quite good in English as well as Russian. Next year, when they are two, we shall get them going in Mandarin Chinese. The other day Jack was looking at an email from my doctor, Felix Hanson. First he says, “Felix is a nice name.” Then he asked me, “Mama what’s a gynecologist? They are so funny!”

“And they are, what, seven months old?” an incredulous Rockford replied.

“First Lady! First Lady!” Sally Munson from CNN begged for attention. “Are your little angels always little angels or do they give you any aggravation? Are there any signs of sibling rivalry?”

“Well, Sally, you have kids so you know, some conflict is inevitable. Last week they were fighting over their iPad. I was trying to get them to understand concept of sharing. Margo looked up and said to me, ‘Mama why don’t you get me an iPad and give the old one to Jack.’ I decided it was easier to do that than to explain benefits of cooperation at that point. I'll wait for another opportunity to teach sharing."

The audience, especially parents, were laughing heartily about this anecdote. All were astounded at the rapid physical and intellectual development of the cherubs.

The Secret Service, at the insistence of the President added two more agents to protect the family. An investigation was in progress to determine who had leaked information about the twins. Before it was discovered that Tywanda Washington was the source, Reggie was enjoying the big payoff for his tip to FOX News.

Reginald Jerome Washington was fifty years old, a very good saxophone player in a jazz band that had seen better days. Twenty years ago the quartet, "R.J. Washington & Friends" had recorded the biggest jazz hit of that time since Dave Brubeck's *Take Five in the 1960's.*It was the jazzy instrumental version of *All Good Things Must End.*

Reggie had a crack cocaine habit that ate most of his income and even some of the small salary Tywanda brought home. He also had a soft place in his heart and wallet for some of DC's needy hookers. With fifty grand in his new bank account and a shiny black BMW he slid through East DC as bro, 'Tweety Pie' Williams said, "Like a black snake searchin' fo' a mouse."

Reggie and Tweety Pie who always wore a bright yellow hoodie, hence the nickname, engaged the services of a couple of foxes working out of a hotel in Anacostia. One of the hookers, Charleigh Lynn Freeman said, "Hey, Reggie, you are so fine, whachu doin' payin' for all that crack when you could be doin' Sierra Snow for nothin'."

■■■

"Whachu mean by that, Charlie Brown?" Reggie laughed at his own joke with her name.

"I mean a smart guy like you should be working for my boss. And no he's not my pimp. I got no pimp. He's the biggest coke dealer in DC. He even had the Mayor working for him. You could have all the snow you want and even get paid for it just by running kilos across town. You could make a hundred thousand a year easy."

Charleigh handed Reggie a card that headlined *Import Associates, Silver Spring, MD.*

Reggie had gotten use to big bucks real fast. He didn't have to think too long about his next move. He met Ernesto Juarez at his office in a warehouse in Silver Spring after he made his appointment by phone.

"Hello, Mr. Washington, what can I do for you today?" Ernesto said with just a hint of a Latin accent.

"Mr. Ernesto."

"You can call me Ernie, Reggie"

"Mr. Ernie, I need some work. It's hard makin' a livin' blowing a sax."

"But easier when you blow cocaine. I am I right?

Reggie chuckled, "Ha-ha. You got that right, but that shit is expensive. As I told you on the phone, I was referred by uh, er, your employee, Charleigh Brown, I mean Freeman."

"Did you fuck her?"

"Er, uh, yessir I did."

"Was she any good?"

"Yessir, Mr. Ernie. She very pro-fessional."

"Glad to hear that she's doing well at her chosen profession. I guess she told you I need a delivery guy?"

"Uh-huh, she say about a kilo a week cross town?"

"Exactly. I pay good and you get to sample a little of merchandise as well. Deal?"

"Deal. The money will be good since my wife's about to lose her job."

"That's too bad. Where does she work?"

"The White House."

"You're kidding!"

"No Sir. Obama gave her the job. Been there since 2010."

"What does she do there?"

"She 'sposed to be a maid, but she really more like a nanny to those angel babies."

"That's pretty fucking amazing, Mr. Washington. I mean, Reggie, so she has a very high security clearance I assume?"

"Oh, yes sir, the highest. She been there so long the guards just wave her through."

"Uh-huh. So why is she about to lose her job?"

"She told somebody about the twins turning into cherubs. 'Sposed to be a big secret. The White House police are investigatin' the leak and I do know they will find out it was her and fire her ass."

"Interesting! Well you have a good day, Mr. Wash, er, Reggie. I'll be in touch real soon."

■■

As soon as Reggie left the warehouse, Ernie was on the phone to Franco Escobar, cousin of the late Pablo Escobar of Colombian Cartel infamy.

"Franco, its Ernie in DC. You were talking about President Amos and his shitty ideas about drug legalization and how that could kill most of our business? Carmino Ramirez out of Atlanta said we ought to kill him, but you said kidnapping would be better. Then you said maybe take his babies—real kidnapping, ha ha!"

"So what's your point, Ernie? You know I was just speculating, right?"

"My point is I think there is a way to get into the White House and grab those twins."

"Snatch babies from the best guarded house in the world?"

"Si, Senor! It could even be easy with an inside connection."

"You got an inside connection?"

"Si, Senor."

"Take the next plane to Mexico City. I hope to hell this conversation was not taped."

"No problemo. I used Skype to make this call. Paid twenty-five dinero for their new 'Call Anonymity' app. It scrambles all conversations instantly at my end and unscrambles them at yours. It works great!"

"Ernie, you are smarter than I thought." Franco said laughing.

The conversation ended on that note. Escobar called his top lieutenants to his palatial hacienda outside Mexico City. His latest mission was to figure out a way to stop the President of the United States from making any more drug policy reforms.

Amos had sent the "Sensible Drug Policy" (SDP) reform bill to Congress in his Presidency's first year. Then dominated by Prodems, SDP sped through both houses. It effectively legalized marijuana for any purpose, not just for medical use. The jails and prisons were emptied of tens of thousands of people convicted of minor crimes involving that natural drug. At first there was an uptick in unemployment. Not only were hundreds of thousands of mostly young people freed, but thousands of prison guards, drug screeners, and low level drug dealers were unemployed. The new law also specified that prior convictions of violations of old drug laws could not be used to discriminate in the hiring of anyone. Amos made a speech that had an ironic twist to that old bumper sticker phrase, "Freedom isn't Free!"

Within a few months, as Amos predicted, the economy began to bounce back. Hemp factories alone employed several hundred thousand people in manufacturing. Everything it seemed could be made from hemp-based fibrous material that was strong as steel. Materials were long-term biodegradable. Also more medicines appeared that were derived from cannabis. Detroit could make lightweight cars out of that material and they could get 60 mpg. Hybrid models topped 100 mpg.

There was vocal opposition from the religious right which had been the core of the prohibition movement a hundred years before. Marijuana remained illegal in Oklahoma for a year before its laws were overturned in the Supreme Court. Governor Roscoe Deen justified the prohibition in a thundering speech in Norman, where many students in the audience wore tee shirts bearing a large five leafed plant and the words SOONER or LATER!

Undeterred, the Governor spoke, "Marijuana dope fiends like to say the drug is 'natural' and 'created by God.' Well I am telling you, some things were created by Satan, not by Our Lord God Almighty. Things like rattlesnakes, Ebola, and marijuana are the work of the Devil. And we don't believe in the products of Satan here in Oklahoma." OU Students booed loudly and the State Police had to help him dodge a barrage of eggs thrown by students amidst a cloud of pot smoke.

Speaking of products, Jimmy Jack Johnson took immediate advantage of the new freedom of marijuana use. He had trademarked four brands of packaged and pre-rolled joints. The packs looked like cigarette packages and were called *High Points, Greensboros, and Goldsboros* all for the towns at the center of North Carolinas booming new industry. He also trademarked *Rushmores* with a package design featuring the usual Mt. Rushmore presidents with the addition of one more head: the Zig-Zag paper guy. Zig-Zag dropped their lawsuit for trademark infringement in an out-court-settlement. The likeness of President Arthur J. Barringer was inserted in place of Mr. Zig-Zag. The American Tobacco Company, now called AT&M Co, bought the use of those now most popular brand names for twenty-five million dollars.

Amos was not satisfied that he succeeded in legalizing pot. His next target was cocaine. He argued, "By legalizing cocaine the War on Drugs could be ended. The enforcement of draconian drug laws has cost this country a trillion dollars and countless lives over the past fifty years." Further, he said "Cocaine would be regulated and heavily taxed, but would be at a cost to the consumer less than the illegal product costs now. The federal and state governments would have a steady revenue stream while not bearing the high costs of prisons and jails. The cartels will go bankrupt!"

It was this speech and the pending law that further raised the hackles of the drug lords. They were determined "to do something about that 'asshole' President."

Ernesto Juarez, Carmino Ramirez, and Franco Escobar met in a penthouse room in El Gran Ciudad de Mexico hotel. They enjoyed the company of half a dozen Romanian prostitutes and a meal of Kobe steaks washed down with several bottles of twenty year old *Chateau Montelena* cabernet. After dismissing the six scantily cladwomen, the trio got down to business.

Franco Escobar spoke first, "I had some guys check out Reginald Washington's story. It is true. His wife Tywanda does work in the White House. And, get this: she has access to those babies alone for several hours every Wednesday when the First Lady attends to whatever First Ladies are supposed to do."

"So all we need to do is get Mrs. Washington to carry the babies out to us?" Carmino asked looking very skeptical.

"There's got to be more to it than that." Ernie added.

"You're right, Ernie, it is a little bit complicated. First we get Reggie to kidnap Tywanda. That part's easy since she is his wife." Franco explained. "He will take her to my East Coast office in Anacostia to meet his new boss. That's you Ernie."

"What are we going to do with her? Say she will die if she doesn't swipe the babies?"

▪▪▪

“No, no. We will just give her a little drop of tranquilizer in her drink as a toast to Reggie’s new job. When she’s knocked out we will make a very good neoprene mask from her face. We have a 3-D printer for just such disguises. When she comes to, it will be like nothing happened. Reggie will drive her home and scold her for drinking too much when she met you, Ernie.”

“You’re brilliant, Franco! And I already know who you want to wear the mask of Tywanda.”

“If you say Charleigh Freeman, your girlfriend, you’d be right. She’s an actress, a model, and she has played maids in several movies or so you told me.”

“Well, they were Pornos. She’s a real good Naughty Maid.”

The meeting ended with that comment. Carmino went back to Atlanta and Ernie to DC.

■■■

Chapter 42 The Crime of the Century

The next weekend, Tywanda was off work. Reggie said he had a surprise for her. She didn't know what Reggie did for a living, but was impressed by his ebullient spirit; his pride in his car that he was always polishing; and by the nice diamond ring he gave her.

"Now I want you to meet my boss." He said. "I'm his best employee and he wants to meet you at his boss' office in Anacostia this evening."

"Well, that's real special, Reggie. I am so proud of you!"

■■

The couple drove to Anacostia. Tywanda looked skeptical as Reggie pulled his Beamer into the parking lot of a nondescript warehouse. "Is this it?" Tywanda asked.

"Sure is Darlin'." Reggie replied. "Mr. Escobar like to keep a low profile. This is a high crime area and he don't want no bad guys to be attracted here. It's nice inside. You'll see."

Then Reggie and Tywanda went to the door and were buzzed in through the reinforced steel door.

"Oh my goodness, you are certainly right Reggie." Tywanda said as she looked around at the Baroque interior. The contrast with the bland exterior of the building was startling. There was a plethora of plush red and gold furniture and an immense crystal chandelier dripping down from the thirty foot ceiling to just twelve feet above an enormous azure and crimson Tabriz carpet. "It looks like a king lives here. What does this man do for a living?"

"He's in the import business. You, know, rugs and antiques, all very expensive shit. Mainly sells it to rich lobbyists and Congressmen."

"And what does a brother like you do for this king?"

"I'm just a delivery boy. But I do get a commission and tips. Most of Mr. Juarez' customers like to pay cash. It's a tax thing I think."

"Sounds sketchy to me, Reggie."

"Well everyone cheats on their taxes a little don't they?"

From somewhere in the back of the warehouse, Ernesto Juarez Ricardo appeared wearing the latest wide striped double breasted maroon suit. In an earlier time he would have looked like a clown, but he was the height of fashion at the end of the first quarter of the 21st Century.

"Greetings, Tywanda, Reggie has told me a lot about you. What's it like working in the White House?"

"Except for Wednesdays when I tend to those babies, my job is really pretty boring. I sweep, vacuum, and mop. I rarely see the President or First Lady and then I bow my head out of respect."

"So, you don't see First Lady Monika even on Wednesdays?"

"Not usually. She's most often already gone. A Secret Service lady cop watches them for a few minutes before I get there. She's glad I am there because those kids are a handful."

"That's very interesting Mrs. Washington. Let's step into the dining room. I have catered in some food from the Mayflower Hotel."

Tywanda had never seen anything as posh as Franco Escobar's dining room. Not even in the White House was the furniture this grand. Chippendale chairs from 1750 and an 18th Century mahogany Philadelphia dining table, Queen Anne style, was set with Limoges plates and antique silverware about which Ernie said, bragging and holding up a spoon, "My boss likes nothing but the best. Some of this shit was made by Paul Revere himself!"

The meal consisted of truffle stuffed pork chops, two inches thick, and varieties of steamed vegetables each with exotic flavoring. Tywanda especially liked the artichoke heart and chestnut salad and curried mash potatoes.

■■

Ernie kept Tywanda's glass full of *Chateau Marcella* lightly spiked with a tranquilizer. One minute she was chatting with only a slight slur in her voice, the next minute she fell out of her chair and on to the floor."

"Jeez she didn't make it to dessert." Ernie muttered to Reggie.

"Yeah, I was looking forward to the sorbet. I thought you was goin' to wait and hit her with a shot of Napoleon brandy after desert."

"Well, that was the plan if the Sleep-Eze in the wine didn't put her down. Get that gurney in the next room, Reggie."

Reggie quickly returned and loaded his loaded wife onto the stretcher and wheeled it as Ernie directed into a room in far corner of the warehouse. There a technician scanned Tywanda's face. Ten minutes later a perfect rubberized replica of Tywanda came out of a side chute on the big Builder Extreme 3-D printer.

That is fuckin' amazing!" Reggie exclaimed. "I can't tell Tywanda from the mask.

"Good. If you can't, neither will the Secret Service." A grinning Ernie Juarez replied.

Reggie then wheeled Tywanda to his BMW, and strapped her in. He drove back to their home in North DC before she even woke up. When she did come through she said, "Oh Reggie, I am sorry, I think I had too much to drink. You know I don't drink. Why did you let me do that?"

Reggie, high on cocaine, said, "Listen up, Bitch. You almost spoiled a great evening with my boss. We didn't have no dessert 'cause you pass out. Now here's a slap to sober your ass up!"

■■

Reggie smacked Tywanda hard across her left cheek. “Don’t hit me Reggie! Please don’t hit me again!” Tywanda begged, “Please forgive me, Reggie! I won’t never do that again!”

While the Washington’s were at the dinner party, one of Ernie’s men, Chico, had walked into their house through the conveniently unlocked door. He easily found Tywanda’s closet and removed one of several White House maid’s uniforms and a pair of her shoes.

His car actually passed the departing Washington’s as he made his way to the warehouse palace. Minutes later Charleigh Freeman arrived in her green Jaguar.

“Good timing!” said a smiling Ernie as the stunning prostitute came through the door. “And here if it isn’t Chico Gonzalez with your costume for your role in our little drama next week.”

Charleigh sidled up to Ernie and gave him a prolonged deep kiss. “You know I like acting almost as much as I like fucking.”

“Yeah, that’s why you like your profession, Charleigh. You get to combine your favorite activities and get paid well for doing them.”

“So what’s the gig? You said I was going to perform at the White House? Doesn’t Monika satisfy Amos enough?” Charleigh asked as she casually picked up a banana from a fruit basket.

“Well that’s a good question, but that has nothing to do with your role in this play.”

Charleigh, removed the peel with her manicured hands tipped with high luster red polished nails. She then placed the entire fruit in her mouth while making some orgasmic sounds as the banana disappeared.

■■

Ernie took Charleigh aside for a moment into a coat closet. He began to outline the plan as Charleigh groped his crotch. "Later, Baby, later." Ernie said pushing her hand away.

At first Charleigh Freeman was reluctant to get involved. "You are talking death penalty here, Ernie."

"No we're not. That was banned two years ago by the feds under the leadership of our Great President Amos. Fifteen years at the most. And look what you'll have when you get out: I'm talking ten million cash. And that's <u>if</u> you get caught. We have plenty of ways to get you out of the USA. So that's not likely to happen.

"Do we let the babies go if the Prez drops the cocaine reform law?"

"Sure, Baby, who wants to see a couple of dead cherubs?"

"So what am I to do with my other skills, Mr. Juarez?"

"Nothing, Baby. You can save some for me later. This gig is all acting. Chico, show her the uniform."

"Wow, a real White House maid uniform! Gosh I wish I could play Naughty Maid in this!"

"As I said, later, Baby. Now let's see if it fits."

Charleigh got naked in ten seconds and was into the bright blue uniform before Ernie and Chico could catch their breath. "Jeesus, Charleigh, how's it you get better looking all the time?"

"I work out and I stopped using coke. It's all weed for me now. The uniform is a good fit. What's next?"

■■

"You know our so-called Progressive President has taking it upon himself to legalize that which we depend on for our lives and our lifestyle. We have spent millions buying Tea Party congressmen to stop the Prez on the grounds that drugs are immoral. That was working until Amos got so popular that the laws went through on marijuana and next he's going to make coke legal as well."

"No shit?" said Charleigh who admitted, "I don't watch the news much."

"So here's the plan. We obtained your uniform from Tywanda Washington, you know, Reggie's wife. She's been working in the White House since Obama put her there."

"That motherfucker said he was single!"

"Reggie said that?" Ernie replied.

"Well, I guess that proves that 'too good to be true is too true to be good.'" Charleigh said with a frown.

"Whatever that means?" Ernie said looking perplexed.

"So how's this going to work?"

Ernie handed her the mask, still a bit warm from the 3-D printer. "Try this on, Charleigh."

"Oh, my God! Am I Tywanda Washington?" Charleigh asked as she looked in a baroque mirror.

"The spitting image. She was here tonight. I swear I would not be able to tell you apart except your chest is way too big and those nails have to go."

"Not my nails, Ernie! I paid $275 for them this afternoon. I can wrap the boobs, but please don't make me ruin my nails!"

■■

"Don't worry, you'll have plenty of money and time to get those nails back."

"The rest of this gig is simple. Here's a floor plan of the White House. Chico pulled it off the internet for me. You go to the second floor of the east wing after being waved through security. You'll see a lady Secret Service Agent outside the nursery. Give her a needle of sodium pentothal. It's the new stuff. She'll go down in a second. Then you go in and grab the babies, give them shots, and put them and a couple of changes of clothes into this duffle bag. You go back the way you came. When you get to the gate, tell the guard that the First Lady didn't need you this evening. If he asks what in the bag, you say 'Miss Monika is giving some of the kid's outgrown clothes to Goodwill.'" Ernie said and then handed Charleigh a large green Land's End duffle bag.

Next Wednesday the caper was on. Tywanda Freeman got off the New York Avenue bus and went directly to the East Wing of the White House, waived to the Marine guard, Captain Fred McClusky, and passed through the gate. Fred paused to ask her. "What's in the bag, Ty?"

"Nothing now, Freddie. The First Lady is giving some of the babies' outgrown clothes to Goodwill."

"You ought to put them on eBay. Bet you could get a year's salary for them." Captain McClusky suggested.

"Probably so, but Miss Monika wouldn't go for that unless I gave the money to charity. Oh, and I'll be out soon. First Lady gave me the rest of the day off."

Tywanda Freeman was waived through the gate. Then she pulled out the floor plan to find the nursery in the East Wing. She was beginning to perspire under the mask so she ducked into a restroom to check her alter ego and take a pee. Up one more floor and down a hall she saw a large uniformed blond woman. "That's Agent Sheila Gibson." Charleigh thought to herself. "You're a lot bigger than I expected."

"Hey, Tywanda, how's it going today?" cheerful Agent Gibson asked.

"Same ol' same ol'.'" Charleigh replied. "First Lady said I could take some of the kid's outgrown clothes to Goodwill."

"Yeah, I was wondering what's with the bag?"

Tywanda Freeman then began coughing non-stop. Agent Gibson was patting her on the back when Charleigh whirled around and stabbed her in the neck with an injection of a powerful tranquilizer. Sheila was down in a second. Charlie opened the nursery door, threw in the duffle bag, and dragged the unconscious agent into the room. The cherubs were nowhere to be seen.

"Jack and Margo, where are you at?" Charleigh called loudly.

Silence. The twins were hiding. "Come out come out wherever you are!" Charleigh said getting nervous about the time and having no clue where in the large room the cherubs might be. Charleigh then remembered the First Lady's press conference that she'd seen on YouTube. She knew they were crazy about technology so she said, "Tywanda's got a new iPhone 12. It has hologram 3-D graphics. First one out gets to play with it."

Immediately Jack appeared from high up in the drapery while Margo popped out of a closet and came running with her tiny wings flapping. Both were wearing red pajamas with cut-out slits for their wings. Charleigh could not tell them apart except for Margo's slightly longer red hair.

For a minute Charleigh was so mesmerized by the utterly adorable little angels she nearly forgot her mission.

"Where's the iPhone 12, Mrs. Washington?" Margo looked up at her and asked in a polite tone.

"Oh, yes it's here in my big bag. Who wants to go in the bag and play with it first?"

"Me! Me!" They both shouted.

"Well, I always say 'ladies first' so that would be you, Margo." Charleigh said.

Margo leaped into the bag, saw the iPhone and started to play with it. After a minute, Charleigh reached into the bag and pricked Margo with the tranquilizer needle. Next she invited Jack to sit on her knee. "What have you been up to today, Master Jack."

"I was building a nest on the top of the curtains." Jack said, pointing to the drapery where a couple of items of clothing seemed to sticking out about nine feet above the floor, "I won't let Margo up there. Hey, is that Miss Sheila lying on the floor? Is she sick?"

"No, Jack, she's just taking a nap just like you are going to right now." Charleigh then pricked the needle into Jack's thigh. He was out without a whimper.

Charleigh then put Jack in the bag with his sister and lightly covered both with several outfits from their closet and dresser. The bag weighed close to forty-five pounds which was another surprise as she had counted on about twenty-five pounds at most. "Little buggers are heavier than I thought they'd be." And then she muttered aloud, "Damn good thing I work out five days a week."

With the duffle bag strapped over her shoulder, Charleigh made her way back to the entrance and waved good-bye to Freddie who said, "Bye-bye, Tywanda. Good luck with eBay, I mean Goodwill."

A large black Cadillac limo was on the curb half a block from the White House. Tywanda quickly became Charleigh as she removed the sweat drenched mask and said to Reggie behind the wheel. "Jeesus, I thought I was going to die. Why didn't somebody tell me those brats weigh over twenty pounds each?"

Reggie accompanied by Chico riding shotgun sped the limo to the warehouse in Anacostia where Ernesto Juarez was waiting.

An hour later, Agent Sheila Gibson awoke just before Monika returned to the nursery.

"Hi, Sheila, where are the twins?"

"Monika, I just woke up here on the floor. I don't know how I got here."

"What are you saying? I am gone less than two hours and you are sleeping on the job?"

"First Lady, the last thing I remember was seeing Tywanda. She had a coughing fit. I was patting her on the back and the next thing I know is I am lying here on the floor."

"Oh, my God! Tywanda wasn't supposed to be here today. I gave her the day off.

■■

Chapter 43 Forty-Eight Hours

Monika called Amos immediately. "The children are missing!"

"What? Are they hiding? That's their favorite trick."

"No, Amos. They have been kidnapped by our nanny, Tywanda Washington. Look at the security video. I'm sure you will see."

Amos went to the White House security office. Sure enough, there was Tywanda wrestling with Sheila

Gibson; pulling her into the nursery; and five minutes later coming out with the huge duffle bag now stuffed with some lumpy things. Amos was sure the lumps were the kids."Can anyone tell me why nobody seemed to notice these events? Why do we have security cameras if nobody is watching those monitors?" This may have been Amos first display of angry emotion since he arrived at the White House.

"I am so sorry Mr. President. It won't happen again."

"You mean the next time my children are kidnapped? Oh, well, get the FBI here to analyze the tapes."

Through the Skype Anonymity App, Franco Escobar had issued a dire warning to the Speaker of the House on his voice mail. "We know you don't agree with the President on the legalization of cocaine. We have taken the President's children to encourage you to see that won't happen. Shelve the bill now; else the twins will die. Defy us and your family will be the next target."

That message was front page news and every TV channel had 'The Crime of the Century' as the 24/7 story.

The FBI came to the White House and also sent a swat team to the residence of Tywanda Washington.

"Open the door! Hands in the air!" the team leader shouted.

Tywanda open the door. The agent shoved her hard inside. Other agents searched the house.

"Please, Officer, I meant no harm. I love those babies. I guess I just couldn't keep a secret. I apologize. Guess I'll lose my job over that?"

"What the hell are you saying? You kidnapped the babies and you are apologizing and think you may be fired? Are you nuts?"

"Officer, please, I don't know what you are talking about."

Tywanda was led away in handcuffs and taken to the DC jail.

Amos himself went to the interrogation room where the terrified Mrs. Washington was shivering in the cold bright room.

"Tywanda, you know what you have done. We know what you have done; so all I want to hear from you is the truth."

"Mr. President I am so sorry I told my husband Reggie. He sort of coaxed it out of me."

"Coaxed what?"

"That little Jack and Margo were cherubs. I know it was supposed to be a secret."

"Oh, yes, I suppose he's the anonymous tipster that FOX News paid for that information."

▪▪▪

"I know that was bad, but I didn't take the babies. I was right at home all day. The First Lady gave me the day off."

"Well, we have video and eye-witnesses that say it was you who did this." Amos spoke sternly, but his intuition was tending to side with Tywanda.

Amos left the DC jail with a contingent of Secret Service and FBI guards. They returned to the Security Room to review the tapes once again. It was Amos who noticed the first detail that would exonerate Mrs. Washington.

"Blow up that right hand." Amos ordered a technician. He then pointed to the image of Tywanda's right hand. "See the bright red nail-polish? That's not Tywanda Washington. I just saw her and she has no polish on her nails."

"Maybe she removed the polish?" An FBI agent suggested.

"Possibly," Amos replied. "Please run a spectrophotometric analysis of Tywanda's face in the video. I suspect you will find the face to be mask; likely produced from a 3-D printer."

The tests proved that the Tywanda who took the babies was not the trusted nanny Amos knew. Whoever was behind the rubber Tywanda mask was the perpetrator.

Tywanda was brought from the DC jail to the oval office where Amos, the Attorney General, several FBI detectives and Jason Faircloth heard her story of the past several weeks.

"Mr. President I don't know anything about what happened today, but I am afraid that my husband Reggie did more than let the cat out of the bag about the kids being angels."

■■

The part about Reggie and the trip to the Escobar Palace were most interesting. Tywanda didn't know exactly where the palace was; only that it was inside a warehouse.

The next day, at the warehouse in Anacostia, the little angels were having the best time running and hiding. They would come out just long enough to eat and use the potty. Reggie, Chico, Tweety-Pie, and Charleigh had all they could handle trying to corral the quick and mischievous twins. They would giggle taunt their captors; climb the drapes; and throw fruit with great accuracy at the kidnappers. Chico and Charleigh had the best laugh when Tweety Pie took a bowl of oatmeal in the face. Reggie was laughing at him when Ernie returned.

"Jeezus H. Christ, what the hell is going on here?!" Ernie exclaimed

The grand foyer and dining room were in shambles. Jack was giggling as he swung from the great chandelier Margo was hiding on top of a Philadelphia highboy.in the dining room. "Why aren't these brats tied up? Chico, get a ladder and grab the little bastard. Charleigh find the other one in five minutes or I will personally whip your ass. Reggie, get over to Walmart and Pet Smart and get these supplies." Ernie ordered and handed Reggie a note and two hundred dollar bills.

The DEA and FBI had several ideas where the children might be held captive. They had staked out both Ernesto

Juarez and Franco Escobar's warehouses. Both had been raided in the past, but a tipoff from an insider at the FBI had meant both places were drug free at the time of the raid. The tipster turned out to be former FBI agent Farley now in prison for the assassination attempt on the President.

It should have been an easy call to go to Anacostia, but a hundred false leads had to be checked out. Another series of dead ends was due to the fact that there were four other drug cartels operating in the DC/Baltimore area. Of course they would have the same motive as the Escobar Cartel.

It was near the end of the forty-eight hours that criminal databases have shown to be a time limit for recovering victims of kidnapping alive. Beyond that time, most victims were either found dead or not at all.

At 1:00 PM the second day of the abduction, Reggie and Tweety-Pie were at the Walmart Super Center at 99th and H Street buying baby food and then, next door, at Pet Smart purchasing a kennel cage for a large dog and the largest fishnet they sold.

The men returned to the warehouse with their purchases. Inside, a circus was unfolding. Chico was on a tall step ladder trying to grab Jack. That cherub made a trapeze out of the chandelier and was swinging it in a great arc. Chico, wobbling like a drunken sailor in high seas, was about to topple. Ernie was chasing Charleigh with his belt off and ready to"whip her ass" literally as he promised for not finding little Margo.

As Reggie and Tweety Pie entered the foyer, Chico fell off the ladder as Charleigh ran screaming away from the menacing Ernie. "Come back here, Bitch!" he yelled.

■■

At that moment, Ernie's pants dropped below his knees, tripped him, and he fell face first into an Empire marble side table. Ernie was knocked cold.

Charleigh ran over to check him out. Ernie wasn't breathing. She called Reggie, who was helping Chico who apparently had broken his arm in the fall from the ladder and was screaming in pain. "Reggie, Ernie ain't breathin'!"

Reggie checked his pulse. "Shit, Charley Brown, he dead!"

Jack came down the ladder and Margo emerged from the dining room. Both were crying.

"I am sorry Mr. Chico got hurt," Jack said in his tiny voice.

"And I am sorry Miss Charleigh almost got spanked." We saw a man on TV who said spanking was bad. Mr. Ernie shouldn't have tried that." Margo said.

"Yeah, and look what happened to him!" Jack replied.

Charleigh, Reggie, Chico, and Tweety Pie could not stop laughing. Perhaps it was the relief of tension. When the convulsive laughter subsided they decided they had to make a run for it. They knew the FBI, DEA, and the Escobar Cartel would be looking for them. "Get the combo for the safe; it's in Ernie's wallet" Chico said.

Reggie swung the fishnet over Jack's little body as Charleigh grabbed Margo.

"We goin' to kill'em?" Tweety Pie asked nonchalantly.

"Hell no!" Reggie replied, "We just put them in the cage. That will give us enough time to get the hell out of Dodge."

■■

Reggie set up the large wire dog cage in a back room. Margo and Jack were tossed in along with a bottle of water and a box of Animal Crackers. "Thank you, Mr. Reggie." The twins said in unison."

Chico opened the safe despite the pain in his left arm. Inside they were delighted to find so much cash they couldn't take time to count it all. Each of them filled a pillow case with hundred dollar bills.

"I suggest the four of us head in different directions and stay low as we can for as long as we can." Charleigh said.

"No, Baby, we got to stick together. Let me go wichu." Reggie replied.

Chico said, "I am heading to Mexico soon as I get my arm fixed."

"I'm going to my Momma's. I ain't runnin' wich y'all." The image of the 400 pound Tweety Pie running anywhere made Charleigh laugh.

Reggie flipped the keys to his Beamer to a smiling Tweety Pie. Chico took off in his Chevy truck. Charleigh and Reggie peeled out in her dark green Jaguar.

The FBI had a fairly good idea who the perps were at this point. They had narrowed the search to two warehouse locations: Ernie Juarez' warehouse in Silver Spring, Maryland and another in Anacostia The bust in Silver Spring did not turn up the twins, but did result in the arrest of a dozen low level drug smugglers.

Then the White House got a call. FBI agents had a tap in place in the event the kidnappers had more demands. Amos took the call. "Hey, Papa, it's Jack."

Amos, clearly surprised began to weep, "Yes, Jack, is your sister with you."

▪▪▪

“Yes. She ate all the Animal Crackers. We’re in a cage. It looks like the zoo on the box.”

“Is anyone watching you?”

“No. They are all gone. Miss Charleigh dropped her phone on the floor when Mr. Ernie hit his head. I wanted to give it back to her, but they were putting us in this cage and that made me mad so I kept the phone. It is an awesome iPhone 12. And, Papa, it has a hologram screen!”

Within minutes the FBI Swat Team descended on the warehouse, broke down the door and found the cherubs. The cherubs were fighting over whose turn it was to use the iPhone.

The FBI got the kids from the cage and returned them to the weeping angel couple. Amos held Margo and Monika held Jack for the paparazzi in front of the White House. Next to them was Tywanda Washington. Amos had one arm around her thus showing the whole world that the stories of her being the kidnapper were laid to rest.

Amos spoke to reporters, “I want to thank the FBI and other Federal Agencies for their great detective work in getting our beloved children home safely.”

The manhunt for the real perps continued. The first to be arrested was Tweety Pie Williams. His bright yellow hoodie and his 400 pound girth were easy to spot in the Pet Smart surveillance camera video. The cops were just going to his momma’s house to ask her some routine questions and who should be in his customary place of the couch? Tweety Pie, of course.

Chico was picked up by Maryland State Police on I-95 due to improper tags on his truck. Searching for drugs, they discovered over one million dollars stuffed in a pillow case in the truck bed tool box.

▪▪

Reggie Washington and Charleigh Freeman got as far as West Virginia before the Jaguar started to heat up. Reggie opened the hood and smoke and steam billowed forth. He checked the dipstick. "Sheeit, Charleigh, she's bone dry! Did you ever have an oil change?"

"I did, just three or four years ago. Synthetic oil. I remember 'cause it cost me $107.98. They said I might never need oil again."

"Oh, damn! Well, I think the motor's fried, Baby."

They began to walk west toward Grafton. Reggie stepped behind a tree on Route 50 to relieve himself as Charleigh thumbed, or rather "legged" a ride down. They were picked up by a grinning teenager in his dad's pickup truck. His grin faded when Reggie appeared.

"Uh, er, where yuns going to?" the kid asked

"Our car broke down. We just need to get to AmTrak." Charleigh said to the kid. "We can pay you for the ride. I'm Peggy and this is my cousin Ralph. What's your name?"

"Caleb Trickett. Nah, you don't need to pay nothin.' It's just thirty miles up the road to Grafton."

"That's real sweet of you, Caleb." Charleigh said giving Caleb a firm squeeze on his thigh.

In Grafton, West Virginia, the couple had to wait awhile for the National Limited heading for St. Louis. AmTrak service had been restored to many cities thanks to Amos' Transportation Act of 2022. Since they had to wait for the next train, they called a cab and went to the Walmart to get several outfits, clean underwear and socks. They also picked up two roller bags big enough for all the clothes and the two million dollars they had been carrying in pillow cases.

Once in St. Louis, Charleigh bought a track phone and made a call to Jose "Joey G" Gomez, the boss of the Escobar cartel's Mid West franchise.

"Hey, put me through to Joey." She ordered the body guard who picked up the phone. Joey G came on the line. "It's me Charleigh Freeman, you know, Ernie in DC's girlfriend. Remember me from last fall? I'm here in St. Louis now."

"Si, mostly I remember your sweet ass and that blow job you gave me. That was un-for-get-able! So, now you come back? Did you kill Ernesto 'cause I heard he was dead?"

"No, Baby, it was an accident. Did you hear anything else about what went down in DC?

"Are you shitting me? That's all that's on the news. You and some brother, uh, Reginald P. Washington are in a nationwide manhunt. I don't want you or him anywhere near me."

"You gotta help us, Joey. Can't you put us on a truck to Mexico? I can pay you."

"How much?"

"In one of your St. Louis Steak Trucks? Say $25,000?"

"Peanuts, Charleigh. I need a quarter million and some head."

"OK, Joey, you got it."

A black limo picked up Charleigh and Reggie and took them to Joey's office in a warehouse, as expected. Charleigh went into Joey's office and came out fifteen minutes later. "She muttered to Reggie as she passed him coming out of the restroom, "Couldn't get it up!"

Joey emerged from the office, red-faced and perspiring and said to Reggie, “That bitch has lost her touch. I think I’m going to need more than a quarter mil to get you to Mexico.”

“Like what?

“A million, that’s what.” Then Joey turned to one of his body guards. “Ricky, check out this motherfucker’s roller bags.”

Ricky unzipped both bags and lifted the lids. At first he just saw clothes, but then he went deeper into the first bag. “Jeez, Boss, there’s a whole lotta dinero in here!”

“While you count it, I want Sammy and Rafie to take Miss Freeman and Mr. Washington to the back room.”

Ricky summoned Sammy Alvarez and Rafael Santana to the office and gave them the instructions.

Charleigh and Reggie were taken to a stark grey backroom in the far corner of the warehouse. Joey could barely hear the muffled gunfire as Charleigh and Reggie were both shot between the eyes.

Chapter 44 All Good Things Must End

Holidays at the White House in 2023 were especially joyful. The President's popularity was in the 80% range; the family had survived a kidnapping and other crises. All of the President's legislative initiatives had passed; Constitutional amendments were wending their way through the approval process in the states; Amos was planning the State of The Union speech for 2024. Everyone assumed he would run in the 2024 election and certainly win a second term.

As the family sat in the great room with a roaring fire, carols were playing from Sirius XM radio and everyone sang along. They were especially vocal when any carol mentioning angels came up.

In January President Arthur J. "Amos" Barringer delivered the State of the Union to a joint session of Congress.

"My fellow Americans, three years ago today, I assumed the greatest mantle that can be bestowed on anyone on this dear planet, that is, the Presidency of the United States of America. When I took office, by the grace of God and eighty-five million votes..." Here the audience erupted in applause. "America entrusted me to lead this great country into the future.

I believe the state of the union is stronger than ever. The economy is growing at a sustained rate of 5-7% a year. Unemployment is at 3.3%, the lowest in history. Instead of wealth being concentrated in the hands of a few million people at the top that concentration has diminished to the top 25% controlling 80% of our wealth. We have a way to go toward income equality. I am not talking about levelling as some of my critics have said. A tier of income levels will always exist and that is essential to a capitalist economy. I do, however, believe in a level playing field where everyone has and deserves an equal chance at moving upward in the pursuit of happiness, as it is written in our Constitution.

I will soon propose legislation that will guarantee that every working person will be able to earn a living wage. This will mean a minimum wage of $20 per hour which is the norm in Western Europe. I will also encourage businesses with large low tax incentives to adopt my 'fair compensation guidelines.' These voluntary guidelines should end the gross imbalance between the overcompensation of managers and the people who work for corporations.

The guidelines work as follows: Every worker is paid $20 per hour. His or her supervisor will be paid $30/hour plus one dollar per hour for each person supervised. That supervisor's boss shall be paid $45 per hour plus ten dollars per hour for each first level supervisor managed and so on up the ladder all the way to CEO. The corporation implementing these wage and salary guidelines will be entitled to a corporate tax reduction of one million dollars for every 100 employees."

The audience rose and both sides of the isle gave Amos a standing ovation.

"We have also taken a dozen initiatives in pursuit of world peace. The Middle East has been realigned thanks to the sacrifices of a dozen nations in the region as well as the UN. For the first time in eighty years there is peaceful co-existence and no active conflicts in that region."

Another prolonged ovation ensued.

"The Gun Association and Control Act passed in the House and Senate, albeit without unanimous approval."

This time only the Prodems, Modems, and GOP Republicans applauded. The minority of thirty-five CRP holdovers, sat with arms crossed over their chests. The standees then mocked the CRP by crossing their chests before taking their seats.

"We have diminished the National Lotto Act's contribution to revenue by 50% and it is on its way to complete elimination by 2028."

Again, the applause was limed to liberals and moderates with the CRP abstaining.

"Crime in the USA has declined 65% due almost entirely to the reform of our drug policies. Our rates of imprisonment are now at the levels of other countries. The number of known addicts has increased primarily because all addicted persons can be treated under the Affordable Care Act at far less cost to taxpayers than was the case under a system of punishment and incarceration."

Another time the entire audience applauded.

"With all these accomplishments, I can say, without equivocation, that my term in office has been successful."

A huge and sustained standing ovation erupted with all but a few of the most reactionary CRP congressmen still sitting.

Then came a shocking announcement:

"My fellow Americans, this will be my last State of the Union address."

There were audible gasps and groans from the Prodems followed by shouts of "Four more years! Four more years."

When the audience quieted, Amos continued, "The American People have changed course, the country is becoming less greedy. The people have made this country a more sustainable place to live. Crime and poverty are down. Peace prevails. But my success is somewhat due to the cult of personality that has naturally grown up due to my angelhood."

A female member of Congress stood and spoke up, "We love you Amos! Please don't go away!"

"I cannot deny that charisma has had much to do with my success. I am sure that if I chose to run I would be re-elected. The Constitutional term limits would be eliminated and I could rule like a king forever. But George Washington saw the dangers inherent in one-man rule. It is not a good thing, no matter how benevolent the ruler may be. Therefore, I will step aside after the next election and my term ends."

Amos then made his way through the crowd of well-wishers. Someone hooked a smartphone up to the speaker system and through it played *All Good Things Must End*.

Chapter 45 Denouement

Amos' family was shocked at the State of the Union Announcement as they watched it on TV. Monika was the only one with whom Amos had confided. When Amos returned to the White House, the family accompanied him to a West Wing conference room. Vice President Miller and Jason Faircloth were present.

"You surprised us, Daddy. Is there more to it than you said this evening?" Marla asked.

"Well, there is a little more, but the public doesn't need to know that. And, I really do believe that the tendency to worship me can be a dangerous trend for the country."

"So, what else?" Jimmy Jack said, looking toward Monika, "Are you pregnant again?"

Monika replied, "Yes, it is true. But that is not only reason Amos wants to stop being President."

A smiling Amos gave his wife a kiss and hug then said, "There are still forces of evil in the world. We have survived assassinations, kidnappings and God knows what's next? It may be a tired phrase, but I really do want to spend time with family. Jack and Margo hardly know me. That will change soon as I plan to hand most of the day-to-day Presidential stuff over to you, Marty." Amos said looking over at Martin Miller.

The next month the entourage flew to Asheville to spend most of the spring at Kirkland. The estate was now a sprawling compound with cottages large and small for the various guests and Secret Service agents. Thousands of native azaleas were bursting forth. Monika said, "Flame azaleas are my favorites."

Zoë returned from Africa and took a position at the Asheville Nature Center. She was offered the directorship, but declined saying, "I'd rather be with the animals all day. I would rather clean cages than deal with bureaucracy."

Michael moved his copyright law practice to Kirkland. He had almost enough work just handling cases related to Kirkland Publishing and the unauthorized biographies of Amos and Monika.

Jimmy Jack and Marla were based at Kirkland, but spent most of their time traveling to third world countries. Wearing disguises, like radically different hairstyles, they were able to go unnoticed almost everywhere. India was a favorite destination. The couple fell in love with India as they thought the pace of life and spiritualism was saner than America.

Back home rich and famous people paid a great deal of money for cryopreservation in hopes of becoming future angels. There were several scandals involving quack preservationist who disappeared after accepting enormous sums of cash for "enrollment and maintenance fees."

In his 95th year, September 2024 Kirk Johnson passed away peacefully in his sleep. A few weeks before his death a reporter asked Kirk if he thought he should be frozen when he died so he could come back as an angel. Kirk replied, "One lifetime is enough, Son. And if I fly, it will be in my Huey!" *All Good Things Must End* was played at his funeral.

The grieving of that month turned to joy with the birth of another cherub. Monika said he had to be named Gabriel because he seemed to be talking the day he was born.

Big brother Jack and his sister Margo were not-so-little angels anymore. They were three feet tall at 18 months and nobody could contain them as they delighted in flying around. Monika had difficulty getting them to practice Mandarin Chinese and they still liked hide-and-seek even more than video games. They enjoyed playing with their new baby brother and making him laugh.

Monika and Amos undertook several world tours on behalf of peace and seeking ways to eliminate hunger and disease.

Martin Miller was nominated unanimously by the Prodems for the November election in 2024. He won by a greater margin than Amos had in 2020. By the time of his first State of the Union, the widowed President Miller announced his engagement to Dr. Francesca Biscotti. She became the darling of the press immediately. They married in June. Francesca was certainly the most stunning First Lady since Jacqueline Kennedy sixty-four years before.

Amos accepted the Nobel Peace Prize for 2024 in Oslo, Norway in December. In his acceptance speech he said, "Where there is hunger, there can be no peace; where there is poverty there is conflict; and where there are greedy people there will always be needy people. The world needs a better system for sharing the bounty of our planet." Shortly after that speech, Amos took a call from Bill Gates who promised to devote millions in Microsoft money and time to develop *Food Share*, a program to track and redistribute agricultural products from places with abundance to places where starvation was the norm.

Over the next several years, Amos and Monika spoke at peace conferences, wrote a half dozen books; and continued advising the government on many issues, foreign and domestic. They lived for a few months in the dacha in Shovi after Lena passed away at 105 years and was buried in the village graveyard.

Monika said she was happier in Shovi than anywhere else. The cherubs enjoyed playing in the woods and picking blueberries and wild mushrooms. Monika loved cooking pirogues and, occasionally taking soaring glides around the mountain. Jack and Margo liked these family trips as well. Tourists lucky enough to capture video of the whole family were enriched by selling the images to FOX News.

The couple left Shovi when the sheer number of pilgrims and tourists that had come to glimpse them nearly overran village resources despite the capacity of the new Marriott-Shovi Hotel and Resort. Vlademar Katavili was sad to see them go. As the Marriot-Sochi manager he would be in charge of an almost empty hotel until the ski season started again in October.

"Oh, well." Vlademar said as the angel family soared toward Tbilisi, "All good things must end."

■■